Praise for Follow Me Home

'Bishop's novel, set in Helmand during the current Afghan conflict, is a compelling variant on a theme that has a long history – that of soldiers trapped in enemy territory and striving to get home . . . The stripped-down simplicity of Bishop's narrative is made even more effective by the detail he conjures up from his own experience as a foreign correspondent in war zones, including Afghanistan.'
The Sunday Times

'Impressively authentic. The author knows his subject, British infantry soldiers and their fight in Helmand, very well and his instinctive understanding of the military should satisfy even those harshest of critics, the very men and women who have served in Afghanistan.'
Patrick Hennessey, *Evening Standard*

'Read it and enjoy a novel of great subtlety and insight; one that explores the age-old themes of loyalty, humanity and forgiveness, and that you finish feeling strangely optimistic about the future.'
Saul David

'*Follow Me Home* does the details and the heroics well. It is a good, easy read and impressively authentic . . . Insofar as any book about a troubling, complex, bloody, contemporary conflict can be entertaining, this one is . . . It is a ripping yarn in which the swash and buckle of old has been replaced with the crack and thump of sniper rifle.'
Scotsman

'Veteran foreign correspondent and respected military historian Patrick Bishop brings all his experience to bear in this crisp, action-packed tale set in Afghanistan . . . a compelling novel.'
Mail on Sunday

'The first g
Sun

About the Author

Patrick Bishop has followed the British Army on all its major deployments since 1982, spending twenty-five years as a foreign correspondent covering conflicts around the world. He is the author of two best-selling non-fiction books on the current Afghan conflict, *Ground Truth* and *3 Para*, as well two hugely acclaimed books about the Royal Air Force during the Second World War, *Fighter Boys* and *Bomber Boys*, and a novel set in that period, *A Good War*.

Also by Patrick Bishop

A Good War
Ground Truth
3 Para
Bomber Boys: Fighting Back 1940–1945
Fighter Boys: Saving Britain 1940
The Provisional IRA (*with Eamonn Mallie*)
The Irish Empire (*with Thomas Keneally*)

PATRICK
BISHOP
FOLLOW ME HOME

HODDER

First published in Great Britain in 2011 by Hodder & Stoughton
An Hachette UK company

First published in paperback in 2011

2

A CIP catalogue record for this title is available from the British Library

Paperback ISBN 978 0 340 95175 0

Typeset in Caslon by Hewer Text UK Ltd, Edinburgh

Printed and bound by CPI Group (UK) Ltd, Croydon, CR0 4YY

Hodder & Stoughton policy is to use papers that are natural, renewable and recy-
clable products and made from wood grown in sustainable forests. The logging
and manufacturing processes are expected to conform to the environmental regu-
lations of the country of origin.

Hodder & Stoughton Ltd
338 Euston Road
London NW1 3BH

www.hodder.co.uk

Oh, hark to the big drum calling,
Follow me – follow me home!

Rudyard Kipling

Glossary of Military Terms

binos	binoculars
chaplis	cross-strap sandals as worn in the region
charpoy	wooden frame bed
CO	commanding officer
comms	communications
D and V	diarrhoea and vomiting
dicker	Taliban scout
dishdasha	Soldiers' term for long tunics such as are worn in Iraq and applied equally to Afghan shalwar kameez
FOB	Forward Operating Base
green zone	the fertile cultivated area along Afghanistan's river valleys
ICOM	Make of walkie-talkie favoured by insurgents
IED	Improvised Explosive Device
Jimpy	General-Purpose Machine Gun
kay	kilometre
LZ	Landing Zone
NAAFI	Navy, Army and Air Force Institutes which run base minimarkets and coffee shops

OP	Observational Post
PJHQ	Permanent Joint Headquarters at Northwood, north west London, where all overseas operations are planned and controlled
PRR	Personal Role Radio
RPG	Rocket-Propelled Grenade
shemagh	Arab-style scarf favoured by British troops in desert warfare
sangars	sandbagged defensive position
SF	Special Forces
squirter	escaping gunman
stag	sentry duty
tab, to	to march rapidly, usually carrying a heavy burden of kit
terp	interpreter
Thuraya	make of hand-held satellite phone
UAV	Unmanned Aerial Vehicles

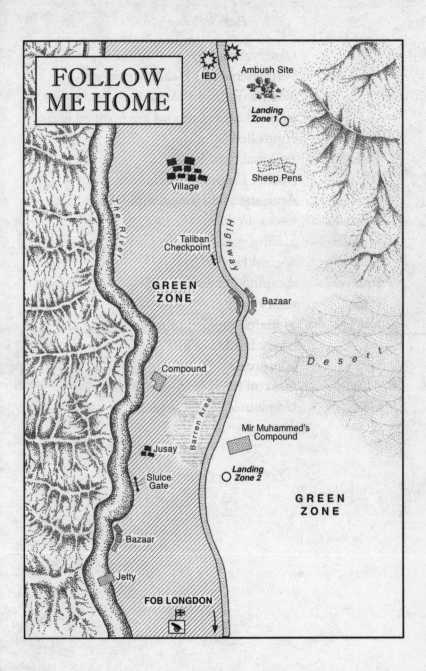

FOLLOW ME HOME

IED

Ambush Site

Landing Zone 1

The River

Village

Sheep Pens

Highway

Taliban Checkpoint

GREEN ZONE

Bazaar

Desert

Compound

Barren Area

Mir Muhammed's Compound

Jusay

Landing Zone 2

Sluice Gate

GREEN ZONE

Bazaar

Jetty

FOB LONGDON

For Henrietta and Honor, with love

I

'What's your idea of heaven?' asked Zac, as he handed me the night-vision binoculars. I studied the men, sprawled out under the almond trees, still fast asleep. The intensified light turned them into luminous green ghosts. I shook my head to shut him up. Zac had a habit of rabbiting on just before the shooting started.

'No, think about it . . .' He was off, floating away down a meandering stream of consciousness. 'These guys will soon be on their way to their . . . nirvana, paradise, whatever it is they call it. Seventy-two virgins, all the kebabs they can eat. Who came up with that one? Obviously it's just a crude projection of your average Muslim male's fantasies. Now my fantasies are a lot more sophisticated. In my heaven there would have to be women, of course. And good wine and food. But—'

'Shut up.'

'They can't hear us.'

'Please. Just shut it. Something's happening.' One of the prone figures had come to life. He got to his feet, yawned and stretched, collected his rifle and walked over to the nearest of the three pick-up trucks parked at the edge of the little orchard and started rooting around in the back. He returned with a portable gas stove, set it down on the ground and lit it. He fetched a pot, filled it with water from a jerrycan and squatted down to wait for it to boil.

I passed the binos back to Zac. He watched the innocent domestic ritual and grinned. 'First brew of the day,' he said. 'Can't be long now.' We had been watching them all night and I was stiff and nervous and anxious to get on with it. There were four of them down there in the orchard. They were Taliban, real Talibs, not the ten-dollar-a-day variety. They had arrived the evening before and settled down to wait for an important visitor. Mullah Zaifullah was what we called a high-value target. Normally he lived in Quetta, over the border in Pakistan, where he was something big in the Quetta *shura*, the war council that directed the insurgency in Helmand. He had survived several assassination attempts in Pakistan and was taking a big chance crossing the frontier. Why he had come was unclear – at least to us. Either the intelligence guys didn't know, or, possibly, they did and hadn't felt it necessary to share the information with us. Our job was to grab him. We had been inserted into the desert to the east by helicopter the evening before and had tabbed for five kilometres over the hills to get into position for the ambush.

Zaifullah was a major prize, a senior Talib commander who had been with Mullah Omar from the beginning.

His capture would be great propaganda, a much-needed sign that the war was heading somewhere. If we couldn't capture him, we were to kill him. It was quite an honour to have been given the task and easily the biggest thing I had done in my seven years in the army. At that moment, an hour before dawn, it was all looking good. Things were going according to plan. How often in the army could you say that?

The Talibs had no idea we were there. We had been waiting for them when they rocked up at about 2300 hours the night before and stopped, just as the intelligence brief said they would, at a compound at the side of a stony road that ran north to south along the river valley. There was a house inside the walls but instead of sleeping indoors they had chosen to kip outside – just as we would have done – to take advantage of the pre-dawn hours when the heat of the sun finally seeped out of the earth and the air freshened.

We were watching them from a hollow scraped in a bare hillside four hundred metres to the east. Beyond the compound was the road. Then, on the far side, fields, crisscrossed with dykes and ditches, ran away to the big river. Ten metres to the left of us, hidden among some rocks, were Robbie and Grant, our sniper pair. Scotty and Joe were lying up in a shallow fold in the hillside fifty metres beyond them, Jimpy at the ready, waiting for the signal to start. Jake and his boys were on the far side of the road, to the north of the compound, hidden in a maize field. Jake, Grant, Zac, Scotty.

Everyone in the army had blokey names these days. My father had lumbered me with Miles.

There were ten of us. With the mullah's bodyguards, there would be maybe ten of them, excluding Zaifullah. We'd kept the team small to reduce the risk of detection on the insertion. Anyway, the numbers didn't mean that much. We could call in any number of jets, attack helicopters, and long-range missiles if needed. It was hard at this point to see what could go wrong.

Down in the orchard there was plenty happening now. The Talibs were stirring from their pits. One wandered over to the gas stove and helped himself to a brew. Another was kneeling, head aimed at Mecca, getting in the first prayer of the day. The other was chatting on an ICOM walkie-talkie. Jake had an electronics warfare pair with him, one to monitor, and a terp to translate. They would be picking up every word of the conversation.

The plan was simple. Once Zaifullah arrived, Jake and his men would move out of the maize field and up to the compound to close off the Talibs' line of retreat. The terp would broadcast a warning that they were surrounded and order them to throw down their guns. Then it was up to them. They could surrender, or they could stand and fight. Capturing Zaifullah alive was the preferred option, but killing him would do. Either way, it seemed we were on a winner.

Zac's personal role radio buzzed. It was Jake calling

with the update from the ICOM chatter. He listened, smiled and nodded.

'He's on his way. Five kays.'

A few minutes later we heard the noise of revving engines coming from the south. Shortly after, a Ford pick-up appeared in the distance, swerving in and out of the potholes in the road. Four more vehicles trailed behind. That was unexpected. We had been told three. Zac and I exchanged looks of surprise. Jake, lying low in the maize field, would have seen nothing. Zac spoke briskly into the PRR net that connected us all up, warning him that the enemy numbers had risen.

The convoy was approaching the rendezvous. The front and rear trucks each had a pair of fighters in the back, armed with RPG launchers and rifles. The lead vehicle slowed, swung off the road and into the orchard and the others snaked in behind. They parked in a neat line and the gunmen jumped down and took up firing positions facing outwards. They looked rather more professional than your average Talib. I felt a prickle of concern.

The second vehicle in line was a four-by-four, a Land Cruiser or similar. The driver slipped out and hurried round to open the passenger door. A big, barrel-chested man in a white turban climbed out. He looked around and raised a hand in greeting to the welcoming party who were hanging back respectfully under the trees.

The two vehicles sandwiched in the middle were also four-by-fours. The doors stayed shut. The windows were tinted almost black. There was no way of knowing who or what was inside. The Talibs shuffled forward and embraced Zaifullah one by one, shyly, like polite nephews greeting an uncle. They chatted for a few minutes. Then Zaifullah moved in under the canopy of trees with one of the bodyguards and the others went over to the closed-up trucks.

The first vehicle looked almost new. There were stickers printed with some kind of logo taped along the side. A Talib tapped on the windscreen and waved at whoever was inside to come out. The doors opened and two men emerged. One was dark-skinned, Arab-looking. The other was fair, European or maybe Australian or South African. They were both wearing combat gear, but the sort you get in Gap, not the quartermaster's stores. The dark one opened the boot and pulled out a camera and a tripod.

Zac and I looked at each other again. No one had said anything about a media team. The dark one hoisted the camera on to his shoulder and they both turned towards the second four-by-four. Two Talibs walked over to it and opened the rear doors, gently, as if they were wary of what was inside. A small figure, wrapped loosely in light blue cloth, was perched on the back seat. Hesitantly, it descended.

'Jesus,' breathed Zac. 'A woman.'

She stood there for a moment or two by the side of the car, stock still with her head bowed, and her burqa

flapping in the early morning breeze. Then the cameraman was pointing his camera and one of the gunmen
jerked his rifle at her, propelling her towards the
orchard where Zaifullah was sitting cross-legged on a
carpet, holding a glass of tea.

Zac's earpiece started to buzz. It was Jake again. Zac
listened and shook his head. 'No, no, no,' he said. 'Stay
where you are until I work out what the fuck's going
on.'

Two guards led the woman over to a tree at the edge
of the orchard and pushed her to the ground where
she subsided in a small blue heap. They went over to
join the rest of the group who were squatting around
Zaifullah, like obedient children. The mullah was
talking, and smiling. I could get a good look at him
through the binos. His teeth looked white and healthy,
gleaming out from an iron-grey beard. The men were
laughing at whatever he was saying. All the while the
cameraman strode around, capturing the scene from
this angle and that while his buddy hung back, leaning
against a tree trunk and apparently trying to keep out
of the way.

The mullah was taking his time. As he chatted on, I
could feel alarm stirring in my guts. Over to the east,
light was streaking the tops of the mountains. Dawn
came up fast here. We were relying on the cover of
darkness. If Zaifullah went on much longer it would be
broad daylight. The others must have been starting to
worry too, for Zac's earpiece was buzzing again. 'No, I

said, no,' he hissed into the mike. 'I don't know where this going.'

But it seemed pretty obvious to me. They were going to kill her. She had been found guilty of adultery or spying or another of the many crimes that the Taliban punished with death. They had brought her here to kill her and taken a camera crew with them to record the event. In their book this was good propaganda. By nightfall the images would be on jihadi websites around the world.

Then Zaifullah stopped talking. He began to rearrange his robe. He said something and the cameraman put down the camera and fetched the tripod. He fixed the camera on top and made some adjustments while the mullah carried on with his preparations for his into-camera, patting his turban and running his fingers through his beard. At last he was ready. They exchanged nods. Zaifullah started talking again, staring into the lens and making slow, emphatic gestures with his big, bear-paw hands.

' Zac. They're going to kill her,' I said.

'I know,' he snapped.

'What are we going to do?'

'That's what I'm trying to work out.'

2

I could imagine the calculations that were racing through Zac's head. Everything was speeding up. I should have known. The foolproof plan was buckling under the weight of the unexpected. The arrival of the girl had changed everything. A few minutes before we had been looking at a perfect outcome. The likelihood was that the Talibs would accept that they were on a hiding to nothing, jack it in and come quietly. If we intervened to stop the execution, there was no chance that would happen now. Jake and his team were about three hundred metres from the compound. They wouldn't get there in time to cut off the line of retreat and with no blocking force in place, Zaifullah and his men would almost certainly escape. There was no guarantee that we would even save the girl's life. She would be lucky to survive the mayhem of the firefight.

Down below, the drama looked as if it had only a few minutes left to run. Zaifullah seemed to be winding up his speech. He gave a final flourish of his meaty hands, stopped talking and got clumsily to his feet. The cameraman dismounted the camera from the tripod and the two of them walked over to the orchard area.

Under the fruit trees they were pulling the girl upright. Four of them unshouldered their rifles and lined up in front of her. One moved over and stood in front of the camera. His mouth opened and shut as though he was making some sort of proclamation. The girl just stood there, motionless except for the breeze ruffling the startling blue of the burqa.

I looked at Zac. He was staring blankly down at the girl, the firing squad, the camera crew and the mullah, as if waiting for some signal that would tell him what to do. The seconds crawled by. The proclamation reader moved out of the way. The cameraman started to shift his tripod again, a real professional, anxious to get the best shot.

'Zac,' I pleaded. 'Do something.'

He glanced over. His eyes swam back into focus. 'OK, this is how it is,' he rapped. 'Robbie's going to take out Zaifullah. Then the others will start up with the Jimpy. You get on to Jake and tell him to move up immediately.'

He pressed the tit on his radio. I heard him telling Robbie to whack the mullah as soon as he could get a clear shot. Then he was talking to Joe and Scotty operating the Jimpy. They were to try not to hit the girl or the TV crew – a fairly forlorn hope, I thought, in the circumstances. I got on my PRR to Jake to tell him to move out of cover and close on the target area ready to cut off squirters.

It should have been a straightforward shot for a sniper. Zaifullah was hovering next to the firing squad, anxious, it seemed, to get a good view of the execution. Robbie needed only a few seconds to line up on him. But as we tensed for the big thump of the sniper rifle, the reporter suddenly appeared at Zaifullah's side. There was an electric lead dangling from his robes – the microphone cable, I guessed – and the reporter was trying to unclip it.

'OK, OK, Robbie, no dramas, take your time,' said Zac into the radio. A big clock was ticking in my head and still the bloody reporter was fussing about, fiddling with the mike. The mullah was getting impatient. He glanced around, and for a few seconds he seemed to be looking straight at our position. It was as if a warning instinct had kicked in, the one that had kept him alive when he should have been dead many times over.

He pushed the reporter aside and moved on. His bodyguards closed around him in a huddle. I could see him through the binos in the middle of the group. He was shouting and pointing to the girl, anxious now to get the business over with. He stomped towards her with his men surging around him.

'It's now or never, Zac,' I said.

'Shut up, Milo,' he growled. Zaifullah stopped and said something to the firing squad. 'Now Robbie,' breathed Zac.

There was an awesome crack and thump and the man next to Zaifullah flew backwards and flopped on to the ground. Then there was the crack-thump again and another man was flicked over and the dirt of the orchard floor was kicking up as if it was being pounded by a monster rainstorm, and leaves and twigs were showering down from the trees as Joe and Scotty came in with the Jimpy.

The Talibs panicked, running around firing in all directions, hosing tracer up into the dawn sky. They made a quick recovery, scrambling for the cover of a broken mud wall on the side of the orchard facing our hillside. They picked up the muzzle flash from our guns and for a few minutes we were all at it; rounds were cracking and buzzing over our heads, bouncing off boulders and gouging lumps out of the dirt.

It went on like that for two or three minutes, I suppose, though you could never really tell. Time became elastic in a firefight, expanding and contracting according to no discernible rules. Then, over the cracking and buzzing, I heard a different noise. There was a flat bang followed by a sound like a giant broom being swept across a cement floor and a puff of dirty-grey smoke blossomed on the hillside very close to Joe and Scotty's position. Then there was silence. We waited for the Jimpy to start chattering. When the shooting started up again, though, it was only the Talibs who were firing.

Zac shouted into the PRR, yelling at Joe and Scotty to talk to him. There was no answer. I lifted my head, cautiously, for a look at their position. Nothing was moving.

Someone had to go to them, to check whether anyone was alive. The sixty metres that separated us looked like a mile. I felt Zac's eyes on me. He didn't need to say anything. I nodded. It was, we both knew, a big ask. I popped my head up for another look. Smoke was drifting from their shallow trench where the grenade had hit. My mouth was suddenly dry and sour. I was just bracing myself to break cover when Grant's voice came from the boulders to the left of us. 'Give me cover will you guys?' he called. Then, before I could object, he was counting down 'three, two, one,' and his lanky body launched into the open, and he was loping up the hillside with rounds bouncing and sparking off the ground around him.

We tried to cover him but the Talibs had us pegged. Their fire was splintering the rocks behind us, forcing our heads down. I lay there, heart pounding, breathing hard. I tried to calm myself by staring at the patch of dirt in front of me. The small stones and lumps of dried earth seemed to glow like jewels.

Then, thank God, the shooting slackened. I heard Zac's PRR buzzing. 'Yes, Grant,' he said. He listened for a few seconds, his face hardening at whatever it was he was hearing. 'Right, that's it then,' he snapped. 'Get back now. I'm calling in an air strike.'

He turned to me. 'Did you get that?'

I nodded. 'Are they dead?' I heard myself asking, even though I already knew the answer.

'Yep,' he said briskly. 'Tell Jake to get into cover and wait out.' Once Zac put in the call, the jets would be overhead in a few minutes. By the time they had dropped their bombs, there wouldn't be much left of anyone down in the orchard, including the girl and the camera crew whose presence had messed everything up. At that moment it didn't seem to matter that much. All I was worried about right then was my own survival.

A burst of rifle fire stitching the ground beside me reminded me that it was still in question. I felt a spurt of panic, then remembered my orders. I pressed the tit on my PRR and got Jake. He took the bad news calmly. 'OK,' he said. 'No dramas. We're on the road now. There's a ditch on the left.' He gave me the grid reference. 'We'll wait up there.' The Taliban fire had stopped. Grant took his chance to scramble across and tumbled into our hollow behind the boulders, out of breath but unharmed. Robbie scuttled in behind him, lugging the big rifle. I risked sticking my head up to look down the slope. The dawn was well advanced now and I didn't need the binos to see what was going on.

The Talibs were moving out. The bodyguards were hustling Zaifullah towards his vehicle. The others were lugging the limp bodies of the casualties into the back of the pick-ups. Next to me I could hear Zac talking urgently into the big radio set that linked us to the base. 'This is Emerald Two Eight, Emerald Two Eight, are you receiving me?' He said it four or five times. I looked over. He was crouched over the canvas backpack we carried the radio in, flicking furiously at a switch.

'Bastard thing,' he hissed. He gave it a vicious thump. 'Here, Robbie, you have a go.' Robbie slid over and took one look at the apparatus.

'It's fucked,' he said authoritatively.

'What?' I said. I could hear the anxiety in my voice. The radio was our lifeline. It linked us to base where there were jets waiting to scream in to get us out of trouble and helicopters to whisk us home. 'What do you mean?' I croaked.

Robbie slid the radio out of its canvas holder. There, in the middle, was a bright gash of exposed metal where a round had gone straight through its electronic guts.

The sound of revving engines tore my eyes away from the awful sight. I peered over the edge of our shallow pit among the rocks. The last doors were slamming and bodyguards were hoisting themselves on to the back of the trucks. I couldn't see Zaifullah. Presumably he was safely inside the biggest of the four-by-fours, which was now following the lead pick-up out of the compound gate. There was no sign either of the girl, or the cameraman and the reporter. I got to my feet and watched the convoy move jerkily on to the road and head north in a cloud of dust and exhaust fumes.

We stood there, looking down the hillside at the cars dwindling into the distance. The others moved away to collect their gear, leaving Zac staring at the column of dust hanging in the air in the convoy's wake.

'What now?' I asked eventually.

'I'm thinking,' Zac said irritably. I knew how bad he must feel. This had been a big opportunity for him. In a few minutes it had slipped out of his hands. Instead of returning as the star of a brilliant success, he would now have to carry the can for yet another fuck-up.

When Zac was thinking hard he had an almost childish look of concentration on his face. He was wearing it now. After a second or two it cleared. 'OK,' he said decisively, and turned to me. 'Call up Jake,' he said. 'Tell him to wait for us on the road. Grant, go back to the OP and pick up the Jimpy and Joe and Scotty's day sacks. God knows when we'll be able to retrieve the bodies.'

Grant set off back up the hill. I got on the PRR and told Jake the news about the radio. He listened in silence and said he was on his way. He didn't sound quite so cool now.

While we waited for Grant to return, I tried a few consoling words on Zac. 'Don't worry,' I said. 'We'll be out of here soon.' I had a comforting picture of the big helicopter that was due to pick us up in an hour or so, looming out of the sky. 'Everyone will have forgotten about this in a week.' He grunted. 'Joe and Scotty's families won't,' he said.

I didn't bother to reply. A few minutes later, Grant

was back, carrying two day sacks. 'Where's the Jimpy?' asked Zac.

'It's useless,' Grant replied. 'They took a direct hit.' That was real bad luck. Rocket-propelled grenades were pretty inaccurate at any range.

'Right,' said Zac. 'Let's go.' Then he paused. 'No, wait a second. Get back everyone.' He raised his rifle and fired two or three shots through the radio. Then we set off down the steep hillside, slithering on the scree, and on to the dirt road.

The compound was about four hundred metres to the west; the landing zone, a flat field by the side of the road where we were due to be picked up, was a little way beyond it to the south. Jake and his three men were waiting for us, crouched out of sight in the shade of some tall crops that lined the left-hand side of the road. He got up and came towards us. He was a rubbery, athletic guy whose skin had tanned and hair lightened in the Helmand sun. I had only known him a few weeks. He seemed like a good bloke.

His face was clouded as he came towards us. 'What happened to Joe and Scotty?' he asked.

'I'll tell you later,' said Zac tersely. 'The important thing now is to get off the road and into cover. We're going to the compound. At least we can defend ourselves there. Lead on, will you Jake?'

Jake returned to his men. They got to their feet, loaded up, and trudged off down the rutted, potholed track that was the area's main north–south artery.

They were strung out in a line with five metres between them, moving methodically, swivelling their heads left and right in a synchronised security drill that had been worked out on the streets of Northern Ireland. We followed about twenty metres behind them.

We had been walking a minute when the first bomb went off. The blast rocked me back and I felt a searing heat like a furnace door opening. The road ahead was blotted out with thick black smoke. There was a brief silence then shouting and shrieks of pain.

Someone was yelling, 'Take cover! Take cover!' I obeyed without thinking, scurrying to the right side of the road and throwing myself full length into a shallow trench. As I stretched out, there was a second, shockingly loud bang ahead. I knew immediately what had happened. There had been one IED in the road. Another was waiting in the ditch for the survivors when they ran for the nearest cover. I lay face down, rigid with fear, terrified to move unless I touched off another explosion.

I stayed like that until I heard the sound of Grant's voice. I turned my head and he was looming over me, reaching down with an outstretched hand. 'Out you come mate,' he said gently. I took it and he hauled me up on to the road.

The smoke had cleared. Two bodies lay in the road in various states of dismemberment. Twenty metres ahead, Zac and Robbie were peering into a section of the ditch where flames still guttered. I went over to them, quickly, as if moving fast diminished the chances of tripping a bomb. The four of us stood there, staring into the ditch. There wasn't much left to see.

I glanced up the road. The compound gate was only fifty metres away. That was the one place we could be sure there were no IEDs. I said so to Zac. He nodded. 'Right,' he breathed. 'OK everybody. Follow me.' We trotted behind him, past the body parts and the patch of scorched earth where the first bomb had gone off, through the gates and into the compound. It seemed a haven of peace after the scene on the road – until you spotted the blood trails where the Talibs had hauled away their dead and the cartridge cases littering the ground.

We flopped down under the trees where Zaifullah and his men had been sitting. We all carried hydration packs of drinking water on our backs called Camelbaks. I pulled out the toggle and drank. A faint breeze stirred the leaves. It was still cool and I felt the sweat drying on my face. The adrenaline rush subsided and my head cleared. I started to think about what would happen next.

It was broad daylight now. I looked at my watch. 0800. That meant there was another ninety minutes before the chopper was due to arrive. Without the radio, there was no way we could raise the alarm and call in a rescue mission earlier. Our enemies didn't know that of course. They knew we were here, though. They would have heard the explosions. The assumption had to be that they would be back soon in the hope of finishing us off.

Zac was crouched down examining a map spread out on the floor. He looked up as I came over. 'We can't stay here,' he said. He was right. There were just the four of us now. We had only our rifles and a few grenades. Even if we managed to hang on until the helicopter came, there was no way it was going to land in the middle of a firefight.

'So what do you reckon?' I asked. He smoothed out the map, a satellite imagery patchwork of greens and browns. 'Move south,' he said. He traced a line through the fields running along the highway. 'Stay off the road to avoid IEDs and running into the enemy. Make our way here' – he pointed at a khaki square on the map, showing a patch of open ground where the hills on the east side of the road flattened out – 'then pop out when the chopper comes looking for us.'

It made sense. If we failed to show at the rendezvous landing zone, the helicopters would conduct a search. If we were out in the open ground they could hardly fail to miss us.

'Let's see.' He moved out of the way and I took a good look at the map. Each square represented one kilometre. There were five between us and the proposed landing site. We would be travelling parallel to the road, through fields and crops, which would make the going a bit slower. But if we got a move on we should be able to get there OK in the

– I checked my watch again – eighty minutes that remained.

I stood up. 'Sounds good,' I said.

'Great.' He looked relieved. He turned to the others, still stretched out under the trees. 'Grant, Robbie,' he called. 'We're moving out.' They stood up, snapping on their webbing while Zac told them the plan. Neither said anything.

We picked up our weapons and filed towards the gate. Grant was in the lead. He paused and looked up and down the road then waved us on. I was last in line. It was just as I reached the compound gate that I noticed a flutter of movement out of the corner of my eye. There was a patch of light blue in among the bushes at the edge of the orchard. Then I heard a low noise, like the whimper of a wounded animal. The others heard it too and swung round. We crept forward, rifles raised, towards the source of the sound. She was crouched in a bundle, behind a bush, trying to make herself small. When we were a few feet away she raised her head and I glimpsed frightened eyes glowing from the narrow window in her veil.

A young man was stretched out beside her. He had on a long brown shift and baggy pants like the Taliban wore. His eyes were closed and he didn't seem to be breathing.

'Is he dead?' I asked.

'I don't know,' said Zac. He gave the body a sharp

tap in the ribs with his boot. I saw something flicker across the man's blank features.

'He's faking,' I said.

Zac tapped him again, except this time it was more of a kick. The man's eyes opened. Slowly, he sat up.

3

It was Robbie who broke the silence. 'Do you want me to whack him, boss?' he asked. He sounded quite keen on the idea. The barrel of his big sniper rifle was about two feet away from the Talib's head. I had a brief, nasty vision of what would happen if he pulled the trigger.

Zac didn't answer. His eyes were cold. He started to press the safety catch of his rifle, left and right, on and off. The Talib must have understood what was at stake but whatever it was he was feeling didn't show on his thin, downy face. He just kept staring at us blankly, like he was resigned to whatever came next. The seconds dragged by – treacle time, we called it, when a lot was going on in a very short space and everything felt as though it was happening under water. The sniper rifle weighed a ton. The barrel started to wave about as Robbie tried to keep it straight.

Zac stopped clicking. A big, pulsing silence filled the air. Robbie shifted his grip on the rifle. Sweat was pouring down his face. Grant stared anxiously at Zac, shifting his big frame nervously from one leg to the other.

And then Zac shook his head. 'No,' he said, firmly. Robbie, a bit reluctantly it seemed, lowered the barrel.

For a second, the Talib's face seemed to sag with relief. Then it went blank again.

The tension evaporated. Everyone relaxed a little. But now one dilemma had passed, another popped up to replace it. If we weren't going to kill him, what were we going to do with him? And her. The girl was still curled up in a foetal ball, though the whimpering had stopped. We couldn't leave her behind. Christ knows what would happen to her when the Talibs got their hands on her again. As for the man, my first thought was that we should turn him loose. When I said so to Zac, though, he had other ideas.

'No,' he said. 'He's coming with us.'

'Why?' asked Robbie. A frown creased his forehead. He didn't often speak up. He sounded pissed off.

Zac ignored him. 'We haven't got time to stand here yakking,' he snapped. 'Get moving.' He turned to Grant. 'You can speak a bit of Pashto, can't you?' Grant Gibbs was a serious guy underneath the tattoos.

'A bit.'

'Well tell him to get up. He's under arrest.'

Grant said something. The Talib's expression didn't change but he got to his feet.

Zac grinned at me. 'You're good with women, Milo.' He nodded to the sky-blue heap on the ground. 'You can take care of her.'

I levered her to her feet. She was as light as a bundle of twigs and stood there, meekly, head lowered, which seemed to be her default position. Most of the women wore all-enveloping veils with a sort of lattice-work panel so they could just avoid bumping into things. This veil had a clear opening like a letterbox. I could see her eyes as I lifted her up. They were big and brown. I was surprised to see that they were circled with eyeliner and the lashes were caked with mascara.

'Everyone ready?' Zac looked round. 'Let's go.'

We crossed the road, gingerly, all too aware of the horrible surprises that might be buried under the gravel, then thankfully entered the fields on the far side. The road ran north to south. To the east lay a line of barren hills. The land on the west of the road formed a lush band of fields and orchards, irrigated by the big river which lay about three or four kays away. This was the green zone. The people who farmed it lived among their crops, in mud-brick houses enclosed by compound walls.

The route Zac planned took us south through the green zone, parallel with the highway, for about five kilometres. Then we would emerge to cross the road, take up position in the area of flat desert on the far side, and make ourselves as obvious as possible to the pick-up helicopters which, according to the drills, having failed to find us at the rendezvous should then have begun a search.

The ground would provide us with shelter and cover, but it was also full of people, and among the people were the Taliban. Even over the short distance we were travelling it would be difficult to pass through unnoticed. Out on patrol, I sometimes got this idea in my head that the green zone was the sea and we were in a boat and as we cut through the waters we were leaving behind a bow wave that rippled outwards until it washed up against our enemies.

We walked strung out in a line, with a few metres between us; Grant in the lead where he usually was, the point man who ran the greatest risk from IEDs. Then came the Talib and Robbie, then Zac and, behind him, me and the girl.

The first field was full of withered poppy stalks. The opium harvest was in now and the farmers were busy replanting the land with wheat. We stuck to a line of trees that ran along an irrigation ditch on the far side. In the distance, towards the river, I could see splashes of mustard yellow and bright blue – the burqas of the women starting their day's work. At the edge of the field a wooden bridge led on to a path that ran through a plantation of green maize, already grown above head height. It was a relief to be out of sight. For a while we followed a muddy track that passed in and out of maize fields and small vegetable patches.

The path was slippery. The Talib had *chaplis* on his feet, the cross-strap sandals worn by all the locals, regardless of the weather. The girl was wearing flip-flops. We tried to maintain a steady pace but they both had trouble keeping up. He was thin, like most of them were, and as always it was hard to tell his age – anything between twenty and thirty, I would say. His head was bare – no turban or *pakol* cap like the fighters usually wore and hair was coarse and dark and matted with dust, like the hide of one of the small donkeys you saw around the place.

Despite his size, he didn't seem very nimble. The paths by the ditches were slippery; every now and then he stumbled and Robbie had to catch him, which slowed us down considerably. As we were crossing a narrow dyke between two ditches, he lost his footing and fell in. The water was only a few feet deep and he lay there on his back with his dishdasha floating around him, glaring up at us, utterly helpless. Despite myself, I felt a little twinge of sympathy at his humiliation.

I scrambled down the bank and held out a hand. He took it. He had long, slender fingers like a girl. His hand felt as fragile as a bag of chicken bones as I hauled him upright. I half expected him to show some gratitude but he just stood there, arms by his side, with his empty expression back in place, and we set off again down the track.

You could sense the presence of other humans, tending their crops, just a few dozen metres away, but for a while we didn't actually see anyone. I hoped that meant that they couldn't see us. We seemed to be hidden, even from the compound roofs, which was where the dickers often operated from. The dickers were the Taliban scouts. Out on patrol we'd see them appear in the middle distance, cutting about on the humpbacked rooftops of the houses, walkie-talkie in hand, following our movements and reporting them back to the bad guys. We'd fire a few warning rounds to force them down, but sometimes they didn't budge. If that happened, we'd shoot them for real.

We were safe for the moment. It felt creepy, though, hemmed in by all this fertile greenery, breathing the hothouse air and knowing there were unseen people all about.

And then we saw some. The track we were following took a sharp turn and in front of us a little crowd of children were playing in the dirt outside a compound gate. They jumped when they saw us, and stared at us with wide, scared eyes. We stopped. We smiled and waved, acting friendly and unthreatening as per standard operating procedure when encountering civilians. Then Grant went forward slowly and crouched down next to a little girl. She was too young to be veiled and peered up at him from under a thick brown fringe. He pulled out a sparkly plastic hair slide from his webbing and held it out to her. She looked bewildered. He unstrapped his helmet and took it off and stuck the slide in his own tawny hair. Then he handed it back to her. Her eyes lit up. She pushed the slide under her fringe and smiled. The others all laughed, then crowded around Grant as he pulled more plastic goodies from his pouches; hair slides for the girls and biros for the little boys.

We stood back and watched. Grant's face was glowing with pleasure. It was part of the job to interact with the locals – or to try to, but for me, at least, it always felt like a duty. Grant really enjoyed it though.

Grant believed. He had volunteered to go on a Pashto course and came out top of his class. Just before we deployed he'd given the battalion a talk on Afghan culture and customs. He ran marathons to raise funds for Afghan charities and tried to persuade the guys to contribute to some scheme for adopting refugee children. The kids always seemed to sense his good nature – but then kids were always willing to let their curiosity overcome their caution and the warnings of their parents. It was the adults who shied away from us, as we were just about to see again.

A grating noise cut through the chatter and the metal door in the compound wall scraped open. A woman's head showed in the gap. She shouted something and the children broke away and darted through the door. It slammed shut behind them.

You didn't need much imagination to put yourself in her shoes. We had loomed up out of nowhere, four pale men in helmets, carrying guns, with two Afghans in tow. Wherever we went we trailed a banner of fear in our wake. As we walked on, the feeling came back to me that behind the mud walls and the ramparts of maize there were people lurking, watching, praying that we would move on quickly, taking our infectious danger with us. Out on patrol I'd seen the same thing happen, many times. You'd stumble on some innocent scene, men laughing and smoking, women sitting around chatting while they were doing the washing or making dinner, and then we'd come round the corner and they would freeze, like a herd of deer catching sight of a prowling lion. It was as if the green zone was the plains of Africa and the farmers and their families were the zebras and gazelles, constantly watching for lurking predators; and the predators – the lions and the jackals – were us. Us and the Taliban.

The path ahead was empty again. We hurried on, past the cluster of compounds and back into the fields. No one talked; we marched along, sunk in our own thoughts. It was only now that I started to think back over what had happened. Everything had been going right, then it had all turned to rat shit in the space of a few minutes. There was no one to blame particularly. It wasn't anyone's fault. Well, maybe it was. Surely the intelligence guys should have known about the media crew? But then again, we should all have got used by now to the possibility – no, the *likelihood* – that the intelligence picture could change in an instant. It happened all the time.

Nonetheless, there would be a lot of questions asked and a lot of explaining to do once we were home. As fuck-ups go, this one was museum quality. Six men were dead. I had never known anything like it before. None of us had. We died in ones and twos in Afghanistan. I can't pretend I felt real grief as I remembered the smoking pit by the side of the road and the scattered arms and legs. I hardly knew the dead men. They belonged to a different unit from Zac, Robbie, Grant and me.

The team had been put together only a few days before. We were all guinea pigs, taking part in an experiment to test the feasibility of using small groups of regular troops on strike operations against high-value targets. If things had worked out, Zac, me and poor old Jake would all have got command of our own specialist units. That wasn't going to happen now. It was easy to imagine the finger-pointing and blame-dodging waiting for us when we got back.

The sound of Zac's voice calling a halt stopped me going any further down that line of thought. He pulled out the map and compass and studied them. When I went over he was frowning.

'Shit,' he said.

'What's up?'

'As far as I can see we've only made it to here.' He tapped at the map, three squares away from where we had started off.

He glanced at his watch. 'We've got thirty minutes before the choppers are due. We're going to have to get a move on.'

He turned to the others. 'Let's pick up the pace, guys.' He pointed to the Talib.

'He's going to have to move faster. Grant, tell him to stop messing about, will you?'

Grant said something to the Talib but he gave no sign of whether or not he had understood.

We set off again at a faster pace. The girl lifted her burqa. Underneath it she was wearing tight white leggings. She skipped along, her flip-flops pattering on the mud path. The Talib, though, was still floundering. After a hundred metres or so he fell over again.

'What's the matter with him?' demanded Zac. 'You'd think he'd never worn sandals before. Robbie, give him a hand.'

Robbie sighed and reached down. The Talib pulled himself upright. As soon as he let go of Robbie's hand he gave a yelp of pain and toppled over again. He lay there groaning, gripping his ankle with both hands.

'He's done his foot in,' said Robbie. 'Let's leave him.'

'No,' said Zac sharply. 'Get him up and keep him up.'

Robbie grunted and frowned. He shook his head and muttered something but he did what he was told. He pulled the Talib upright and hooked a short, tattooed arm under his armpit. Then he set off waddling down the track with the Talib clamped to his side.

For a while the pace improved. We were used to carrying huge loads and the Talib didn't look as if he weighed much. I was nervous though. I couldn't stop glancing at my watch. Stuck inside the high crops, which blotted out everything, it was impossible to tell what progress we were making.

We hustled along the track, Grant in the lead. Every few minutes we had to slow down for the girl and Robbie and the Talib to catch up. Then Grant held up his hand and we came to a complete stop.

'Listen,' he said.

He pointed northwards, back from where we had come. I strained my ears but couldn't hear anything. Then I picked up a faint hum, fading and swelling, coming from the east. I glanced at my watch. It was 0920 hours, ten minutes to the rendezvous hour.

'It's them!' shouted Robbie.

I couldn't see anything. The greenery swamped out everything except the sky directly above.

'How much further? I asked Zac.

'We've still got a kilometre to go,' he said grimly. 'We've got to move faster.' He glanced around. 'Right everybody,' he said, 'follow me .'

He hurried to the front of the column, past Grant, and set off at a jog. Grant stepped back to let us pass. The girl knew what was expected and gamely picked up the hem of her burqa and scurried along as fast as she could, but I could see that she was never going to be able to keep up.

After a few dozen yards I stopped her. She looked up at me, confusion in her black-rimmed eyes. I pulled off my day sack and Camelbak and slung them over my chest. Then I scooped her up and hoisted her on to my back. She weighed nothing. It was like giving a piggy back to a five year old. As I trotted along she wrapped her arms and legs tightly around me. I could feel the heat of her breath on the back of my neck.

After a few minutes more I twisted round to check on progress behind. Grant had stopped, waiting for Robbie and the Talib, who were hobbling, fifty metres adrift, like contestants in a three-legged race. I stopped now. So did Zac.

'What the fuck is going on?' he shouted angrily. He turned and jogged back. 'This is hopeless,' he said. 'Oy Robbie!' Robbie looked up, his face red and shining with sweat. 'We're going ahead. Just crack on as best you can, will you? Don't worry: we won't go without you.' Robbie nodded and resumed hobbling.

I set off behind Zac at a fast jog, the girl bouncing on my back like a jockey. My watch showed 0925. We were cutting it pretty bloody fine if we were going to catch the helicopters. That, of course, depended on them hanging about to conduct a search. In a few minutes they would be hovering over the compound. The Taliban had learned by now how we did things. If this lot were smart they would have worked out that choppers would be coming to pick us up and would be waiting for them. If that was the case, there would be no search and rescue mission. The helicopters were sure to bug out as soon as the first shot was fired.

But if there was no ambush and the choppers did come looking for us, there was not much chance of them finding us, stuck where we still were in the middle of the green zone. We had to get into open ground in order to be spotted.

I shouted to Zac. 'How much further to the LZ for Christ's sake?'

'Shit, I don't know. Just keep moving.' He sounded as puffed as I was.

I slowed down. 'Fuck this. We're going to have to find somewhere nearer.'

He glanced around. 'OK, smartarse,' he panted. 'Where?'

I glanced rapidly around. It seemed to me that the crops and trees thinned out a bit over to the left.

'There's some open ground over there,' I yelled. Now that I looked again I wasn't so sure.

But Zac was shouting back, telling me to lead on.

I swung off the track and crashed through a small orchard and halted at the far side. The field beyond was full of weeds and bushes but in the middle was a ruined compound, and poking above the compound walls was a building with a flat roof. Zac and Grant panted up behind me. 'See that?' I asked, pointing to the roof. 'If we can get up there . . .'

'Go on then,' urged Zac.

I shook the girl off my back and struggled over a low wall and into the field. I moved cautiously up to the compound door. Inside, there was no sign of life, just a few plastic cooking oil containers littered about, and a dried-up melon patch. The house looked uninhabited. It was two storeys high – a perfect platform on which to attract the helicopter crew's attention – if only we could get on to the roof. Some of these places had external staircases built on to the gable end. This one didn't. Then, lying in amongst the weeds lapping round the house, I saw a rough wooden ladder.

Grant gave me a hand dragging it out and we propped it against the wall. I scrambled up without bothering to test my weight on the rickety rungs and Grant followed me.

Zac stayed below. 'Good,' he said as we clambered on to the roof. 'Keep your eyes peeled for the helicopter. I'm going back for the others.'

We looked around. To the north, there was nothing visible in the cloudless sky. There was no sound either. Maybe they had landed and were searching for us on the ground. The silence was reassuring. It meant they hadn't been ambushed. Things were looking good. Any minute now they would take off again and start looking for us. Here, up on the roof, we would stick out – as my old instructor at Sandhurst would say – as plain as the balls on a dog.

I heard voices drifting over from the fields behind. I went to the parapet that ran around the edge of the roof and saw Zac leading Robbie and the Talib into the compound. They moved into the shade of the wall. Robbie let go of the Talib, who slid to the ground, and Zac climbed up the ladder to join us.

'See anything?' he asked.

We shook our heads. 'I reckon they must have landed,' I said.

He unfolded the map and compared it to the landscape in front of us. 'That's where we've come from.' He pointed at an indeterminate spot in the middle distance to the northeast, where the sun was now climbing up the sky. In between lay a sea of grey-green foliage. I looked to the right. The road was clearly visible, only about 500 metres away and, on the far side, where the ridge fell away, I could see the stretch of open desert we had been heading for. Zac had been right. It would have made an ideal LZ. It was too late to worry about that now.

'Boss.' Grant's sharp eyes had seen something. Zac raised his binoculars.

'Yep,' he murmured. 'They're in the air.'

A few seconds later I saw them. At first they were no more than black specks. There was one large one – the Chinook. Above it were two smaller dots – the Apache escorts. They seemed to be moving in a pattern, quartering the ground below. The dots grew bigger. They were definitely coming in our direction. I was standing on tiptoe, straining towards the shapes in the sky, silently urging them on towards us.

4

I glanced over at Zac and Grant. Zac caught my eye and grinned. He flashed a thumbs-up sign. The helicopters were heading straight towards us now. In a few minutes they would be overhead. Grant started to unbutton his shirt. I realised what he was doing and did the same. We climbed up on to the parapet at the edge of the roof and flapped our shirts over our heads, like shipwrecked sailors frantically signalling to a passing vessel. I could see the Chinook clearly, and hear the whop-whop-whop of the twin rotors. It was flying high, at a thousand feet at least, keeping out of range of Taliban rockets, and the Apaches were higher still. If they kept on the way they were coming, even at that altitude, surely they were bound to see us?

Zac climbed up beside me and the three of us madly waved our shirts.

'They've spotted us!' shouted Grant.

The rotors of the Chinook were tilting, shifting west from the line of road, on to a bearing that would take them straight to us. We were all shouting now: 'Here! Here! Over here!' The Chinook seemed to be dipping down now, starting its descent. Zac and Grant were jumping up and down, waving and cheering.

Then something awful happened. The rotors tilted again and the Chinook swung back towards the road.

'No!' I yelled. 'You fucking idiots! Come back!' But the Chinook was facing away from us now. I could see the lowered ramp clearly and, on it, the outline of the loadmaster framed in the doorway.

Our shouts turned to roars of frustration. The helicopter kept whop-whop-whopping along on its new path. We kept it up, until we were hoarse, while the choppers dwindled to little black specks then disappeared altogether. At last the engine note faded away completely.

We stood there, looking at the empty sky. No one spoke. Then Zac put a hand on my shoulder. 'Don't worry,' he said. 'They'll be back.'

'Sure,' I said. I felt a stab of embarrassment that my dismay had been so obvious.

We descended the ladder, reluctantly this time. Robbie was standing in the shade of the wall, with the Talib and the girl squatting beside him.

'What happened?' Robbie demanded. His glum Midlands accent made it sound like an accusation.

'I don't know,' said Zac. 'Maybe they were low on fuel. Or maybe their monitors picked up a threat from the ground.' He put on a positive face. 'Anyway, they'll be back again soon and the next time we'll be ready for them.'

'How?' asked Grant. 'We don't have any flares with us. Or fluorescent strips, anything like that.'

Zac didn't reply.

Robbie muttered something.

'What's that?' asked Zac sharply.

'It's his fault,' he said, jerking his thumb at the Talib, who was resting against the wall with his head on his knees and his eyes closed. 'If I hadn't had to carry him, we'd have got to the LZ on time.'

He walked over and kicked him in the leg – the good one or the bad one, I couldn't say. 'Fucking sprained ankle.' The Talib didn't flinch. Robbie stood looking down at him for a moment. Then he looked round. He had a harsh grin on his face. 'Hang on a second,' he said. 'Maybe he was putting it on. Maybe there's nothing wrong with him at all.' He bent down and dragged the Talib upright and gave him a vicious shove. The Talib stumbled, then regained his balance. He stood there, steady as a rock, and looked at each of us in turn. He smiled.

'You little cunt,' shouted Robbie, lunging at him. The Talib dodged nimbly out of range.

'That's enough,' said Zac sharply. 'Leave him alone.'

I was quite looking forward to seeing Robbie's beefy fist wipe the smile off the Talib's face. I was starting to think that it might have been better if we had shot him straight away. I looked at him, lolling against the wall now, his face unreadable again, acting as if he was disconnected from all that was going on.

Robbie was still hovering over him, fists clenched. Then Grant stepped forward. 'OK, calm down, Robbie,' he said soothingly. 'The important thing is, what are we going to do now?'

Zac looked at him gratefully. 'Grant's right,' he said. 'Now everybody just cool down and give me a few minutes to work on plan B. Miles, come with me, will you?'

He led me over to a stunted tree that provided a scrap of shade. It was not yet ten o'clock but the land was already starting to throb with heat. He spread the map out on the dirt and knelt down to study it for a minute or two. I watched as he traced a line southwards.

'Right,' he said eventually. 'Here's what I reckon we should do.'

He stood up and looked straight at me. It was one of his most effective tricks. It made you feel as if you were as responsible for whatever happened next as he was – even though he hadn't asked for my opinion about how we were going to get ourselves out of the shit we were so obviously now in.

He acted relaxed. When he spoke, though, it was in a low voice, as if he didn't want the others to hear. 'Whatever I said just then, we can't rely on a chopper to get us out of here,' he said. 'They're bound to keep on looking for us. Without a radio, though, there's no way we can signal our location and it's pretty unlikely they'll be able to find us just flying about.'

He paused and looked straight at me again. 'As far as I can see, Milo, we're going to have to find our own way home.'

Well, I'd already come to that conclusion myself, but him spelling it out made it sound worse. There wasn't much to say. I just nodded and let him carry on.

Getting that out of the way seemed to give him confidence. He squatted down again and addressed the map. 'Now, we're here,' he said, tapping a square at the top. I hunkered down beside him. 'The nearest base is here.' He pointed to a red circle at the bottom edge of the chart. It was FOB Longdon, the Forward operating base that sat on the east bank of the river way off to the south. In between, the satellite imagery showed a vast expanse of brown and yellow wasteland with a grey-green strip running down the middle.

'How far?' I asked.

'Fifty kilometres as the crow flies.' But a crow, of course, would fly across the broad stretches of desert that lay between us and our destination. There was no way we would be able to march across all that rock and grit. There was no water there and no cover. If the heat didn't get us, the Taliban would.

I told him what I thought. 'That's right,' he said. 'So we're going to have to stick to the green zone all the way. That will mean detours, lots of stopping and starting. It's going to take us two days at least.' He paused. 'That's how I see it. If you've got any alternative suggestions, I want to hear them.'

I couldn't think of any. 'Nope,' I said.

He smiled. 'Good,' he said. 'Well. We'd better get a move on. Let's tell the others.'

I watched as Zac outlined the plan to Grant and Robbie. He gave good brief. He was clear and concise and didn't play down the difficulties, but made you feel that if everyone followed the drills, everything would be OK. They listened closely, but I noticed that only Grant was nodding in agreement. 'Any questions, any thoughts?' he asked at the end.

Grant shook his head.

'Move out then,' said Zac briskly. But then Robbie broke in.

'What about them?' He jerked his head towards the girl and the Talib, lounging against the wall.

'What do you mean?' asked Zac coldly.

'Are they coming too?'

'Sure.'

'But why?' It came out as a growl. There was a dull fire behind his eyes. I had never seen him like this before. 'He's trouble,' he said, glaring at the Talib. 'As for her, she can fend for herself now.'

Zac stiffened. For a moment it seemed he was going to go for him. Then, to my relief, I saw him relax and he held up his hands in an appeal for reason. 'Robbie, Robbie, think about it,' he said gently. 'We can't just leave her here. She'd be dead before sundown. Forget the Taliban. Her family will probably top her first, once they know she's been hanging out with us.'

Robbie frowned. 'What about him?' he persisted.

'He won't cause any more trouble, believe me,' said Zac. 'And he'll earn his keep. He'll know the lie of the land – valuable local intelligence. Grant will get it out of him, won't you?' Grant gave a neutral grunt. I could see that Robbie was still simmering, but he seemed to think he had said enough. He hefted his rifle and stared sullenly at the Talib.

'That's settled then,' said Zac cheerfully. 'Let's get going.'

5

We traipsed back through the orchard and on to the track and set off southwards. There was no need to hurry now. We moved cautiously, taking the narrow paths where we were less likely to run into workers coming and going from the fields. It turned out to be an unnecessary precaution. The farmers tended to move around according to some agricultural logic that escaped me. One day they would be in one place. The next day they had all shifted somewhere else. Today, there was no one about. I could see some workers in the distance, though. A few kilometres away in the fields over by the river, men, women and children were toiling away, chopping and hacking while the donkeys stood by, waiting to be loaded up.

We moved strung out in a column, with Zac at the head. Then came the Talib, with Robbie hot on his heels, then Grant, then the girl, then me. We made steady progress. The Talib was keeping up without any trouble now, his *chaplis* slapping steadily along the mud paths. At this pace the girl's burqa wasn't so much of a hindrance. Underneath it, she didn't walk so much as glide, as if she was trundling along on castors.

It was bloody hot and I took frequent slugs from the Camelbak. Every now and then, Zac would lift his hand to signal a halt while he took a look at the map and compass. The first time he did it I went up to join him, assuming he would want to consult with me. He ignored me for a minute or two before he gave me his attention. After that I left him to navigate alone.

It was more than a bit annoying, but not unexpected. He was nominally in charge of the op but strictly we were equals with the same rank and the same seniority. The difference was in our attitudes.

Zac was a convert to army life and was dead keen to make a success of it. He came from the Surrey suburbs – Croydon, Epsom, somewhere like that, where his father had a car dealership which, from what I could gather, had made him quite rich. The way Zac told it he was halfway through university and heading for a career in finance when he happened to see a documentary about the SAS. After that he didn't want to be a City boy any more. He wanted to be a soldier.

Like many converts, he liked all the trappings and traditions, more so than those who had been born into the faith. That was the category I fell into. My father, grandfather, great grandfather, had all been military men. I had been brought up in barracks and bases and schools where everyone's dad was a soldier. Zac often seemed slightly annoyed that I wasn't as keen on it all as he was. The truth was that I hadn't really chosen the life. It had chosen me, and it's hard to feel much enthusiasm for the inevitable.

We'd met up at Sandhurst. He was one of the stars of the year. I was a bit of a plodder by comparison. We both made it into the same regiment, which was one of the newest in the army but already convinced it was by far the best. I had got to know him in Iraq where we went late in the day when the heavy fighting was over. He got one mention in dispatches for quelling a riot in Basra and another on our first Afghan tour. We were now starting our second.

It had been Zac who suggested we sign up for the new unit. The outfit had been dreamed up by our commanding officer. He wanted to show that his men could be as effective as the Special Forces teams. His motives weren't entirely selfless. He'd been passed over for some SF command and this was his way of showing those who had made the decision how wrong they had been. I hadn't needed much persuasion to volunteer. It seemed better than spending six months stuck in a fort, dodging IEDs every time you set foot outside.

Zac saw it as a chance for more glory. He'd spelled it out to me during the course of a long drunken night just before we left. It had started off as a quiet drink in a riverside pub. I was staying in a flat in a mews in Kensington which belonged to my father. He and my mother had separated a few years before and he spent most of his time in Northern Cyprus, dabbling in the property business. I was close to mum but I didn't see dad that often. He'd happened to be passing through London at the end of my pre-deployment leave and we'd spent two nights under the same roof, the first time we'd done so in years. It had worked out fine, somewhat to my surprise. I still felt resentful at his treatment of mum and didn't want anything that was going to upset my emotional equilibrium.

The last few days before you set off are tricky. You're under a lot of pressure from family and friends to meet up to say goodbye. I often used to think that with friends it was more for their benefit than mine – so that if I didn't come back they could congratulate themselves on what good mates they'd been. Frankly, though, I preferred to be on my own, filling up the final hours with chores to take my mind off things.

Even so I was feeling a bit lonely that Saturday morning. Dad had left the night before. I had nothing planned that evening. I'd thought for a bit about calling my ex-girlfriend, Alix, to ask her out for supper. I soon realised that it was not a good idea. She had a new boyfriend, for one thing – although that would not necessarily mean she would say no. After all, I was off to Afghanistan. It might be the last time she ever saw me. She'd feel guilty if she turned me down. I decided to spare her the dilemma. How much fun would it have been anyway, listening to a progress report on the new relationship?

I was quite pleased then when my mobile rang and Zac was on, asking if I fancied a few beers to talk about the coming tour. People always assumed we were better friends than we actually were. I liked his company. He was always at the forefront of the after-dinner *craic* in the mess and most of the guys regarded him as good bloke – if a bit pushy at times. After a while, though, he could become a bit overpowering. I preferred to take Zac in small doses.

Zac didn't seem to mind that I turned down half his invitations to go out on the lash. I was never sure why he was so keen to pal up with me – maybe it had something to do with my military pedigree. Anyway, it was good to hear from him and we agreed that he would pick me up at the mews and we'd go down to one of the pubs near Hammersmith Bridge.

When you're out on patrol you're not supposed to daydream. You're meant to have your tactical awareness finely tuned, watching for the slightest sign of danger. The danger was real enough, but it was still bloody boring trudging along. I often found myself tuning out, only snapping out of the daydream when someone spoke or something happened.

Padding along the pathways with only the occasional insect sting to distract me, I found myself doing it now. Our big night out had been only, what, ten days ago? It felt like aeons. Once you got on that plane at Brize Norton, home became another planet.

It had been a nice summer evening, I remembered, warm in a gentle, English sort of way. Zac turned up on time at six o'clock in a borrowed black BMW. We rippled over the cobbles in the mews then turned into Ken High Street and headed west towards Hammersmith. I was lying back in the passenger seat, letting the warm air wash over my face when we ran into a traffic jam. A bus was trying to turn left into North End Road and the driver was having trouble getting round the bend. She was a big black woman and I could see the sweat glistening on her face as she wrestled with the wheel. There were roadworks in the far lane, leaving only a narrow gap to squeeze through. The driver of a white van ahead of us was leaning on his horn with one hand. The other was poking out of the window, a cigarette clamped between the fingers, making wanking gestures. The door opened and he climbed down. He was wearing shorts and a vest and had tattoos down to his wrist on both arms. He stomped over to the cab of the bus and began shouting at the driver. His face was red and distorted and I heard 'cunt' and 'bitch'.

The black woman seemed terrified. She just stared ahead and kept on struggling with the wheel. Then the bus moved forward and got round the corner, knocking over a load of traffic cones as it went. It was a nasty little slice of urban aggro and I was surprised when Zac called out 'well done, mate' to the van guy as he waddled back to his vehicle. He looked over and smiled. Then Zac asked him if he had a light. That was also a surprise as Zac didn't smoke.

The van driver walked over and stood by Zac's door, fishing in his shorts for his lighter, ignoring the honking coming from the queue of cars behind us. Suddenly Zac slipped the clutch and our car shot forward and I felt the bumps as the rear driver's side wheel crunched over the van guy's feet. We zoomed away and when I looked back he was rolling on his back like an upturned tortoise, yelling with pain. Zac was laughing his head off. 'Good one, eh?' he said. 'Teach that fat twat a lesson.'

I smiled at the memory. I had liked Zac for doing that. In fact, that evening I liked him more than I ever had done before. We started off in The Ship. It was rammed with all-day drinkers and there was lots of loud chat and jackass laughter.

Zac had dived through the crowd and emerged a while later with a couple of pints. I watched him struggling back through. He grinned, his teeth showing healthy and white. Someone once said he could have made a living as a cosmetic dentistry model. He was good-looking all round, in what I thought of as a modern way: narrow head, high cheekbones, black hair that swept back in a widow's peak.

He seemed determined that we were going to enjoy ourselves that evening. Everyone was in a good mood. The crowd was mostly made up of men and women in their twenties and thirties, many of them Aussies and Kiwis, all dressed for the beach. There were a few barbies set up on the patch of grass beyond the pub and the summery tang of charcoal smoke and hot meat mingled with the wet clay smell of the river.

That evening Afghanistan felt like something I had dreamed. I knew that none of the drinkers ever gave it a thought. Maybe Tommies going back to London after a spell in the trenches had the same experience. Zac seemed to sense what I was thinking. He looked around at the flushed, laughing faces. 'Don't they know there's a war on?' he demanded, faking outrage. I laughed. They didn't but it hardly bothered us. The war was our business and the knowledge of that drew us together.

We kept getting jostled so we moved to a quiet spot by the river wall. It was then that I'd asked him who he'd seen during our week of pre-deployment leave. I hadn't expected a proper answer and I didn't get one. 'No one in particular,' was all he'd say. For all his bonhomie, Zac was mysterious about his private life. I've never seen Zac's Facebook profile, but if he was honest he would have to select 'it's complicated' from the drop-down options on the 'relationship' box. On second thoughts, he'd be more likely to choose 'single' to make sure he didn't deter any new potential girl-friends. There had been several girls around in the time I had known him, but it was rare to actually meet them. I dredged up a name from the memory bank.

'What about Rachel?'

He looked startled. 'Yes, I did see Rachel as a matter of fact,' he said cautiously.

'And?'

He shook his head. 'You don't want to know. Really.'

'That bad huh?'

'Worse.'

'Don't tell me. She's up the duff.'

'Can we change the subject please?'

There was a hint of bad temper there so I had left it alone and he had suggested that we 'talk about something more important, like what we were going to be doing next week.'

It was then that he'd taken me by surprise. He took a swig of lager and cleared his throat. 'I reckon this is going to be the grand finale for me,' he said solemnly. 'If you must know, I spent the last day or two thinking about my future. I don't want to hang around for another six years waiting until I get command of a company. And once you've done what we've done, non-operational stuff just seems like a waste of time. I've more or less made up my mind to jack it in when this tour's over. So I'm going to make sure I go out with a bang.'

I really had not expected this. With all his relish for the military life, I assumed he was in at least for the medium haul. It was almost more or less taken for granted that at some stage he would want to live the dream, as we said, and try for the SAS.

'What about selection?' I asked. He shook his head. 'I dunno. It would mean signing away another five years of my life. Anyway, there's no guarantee I'd get in.' He smiled. 'I want to do something big while I'm still young. I need to make some money too.'

'What, get a job in the City?' Plenty of officers did.

He wrinkled his nose. 'Nah. Too boring. Maybe set up a security outfit. Like old Gus.' That was something else that ex-officers went in for. Angus Fraser had resigned his commission to set up a private military contracting business just after we had arrived. He was now a rich man and attracted an admiring crowd when he turned up at regimental functions.

Then Zac had grasped my shoulder and looked at me hard. 'There will always be a job for you at Zac Global Security Solutions,' he said in the sort of American military accent we loved to mock. 'Friend, you have my word on that.'

I'd laughed and shaken my head. 'Outstanding, sir,' I said. 'But honestly, I'm OK where I am.' I meant it at the time. It wasn't that I loved the army. I just couldn't really imagine a life outside it. It would take powerful events or the irresistible pull of a vocation to wrench me away from it.

I'd felt the urge to press him on the change of heart and wind him up a bit in the process. 'I thought you weren't interested in money,' I said. 'This hasn't got anything to do with Rachel, has it?'

'Stop talking about bloody Rachel, will you?' he laughed. 'Drink that up and get them in. I feel like getting pissed.'

And for the rest of the night that is what we did. After a few more at The Ship we went into town to a club called Fitzrovia House, where Zac was meeting a journalist mate called Max. We dumped the BMW and took the Tube. I remember looking at the cargo of chattering and laughing girls and boys being swept up the Piccadilly line towards a night of fun, and feeling somehow sad and proud at the same time, at how remote they felt from us and our world. After that things got a bit hazy.

Now, as I marched along in the gathering heat, with only the tramp of boots and the jingle of weapons and webbing disturbing the silence, I remembered the chill air of the club as we walked up the stairs from the hot, crowded pavement and the prickly taste of the champagne that Max had waiting for his hero Zac. I remembered the two girls, Caz and Gemma, who appeared at some point, again courtesy of Max, who helped us drink the next bottle and the ones after that. I remember a taxi ride back to the flat they shared in Clapham and some sweaty wrestling on a too-small bed. And I remember the morning and the four of us around a pine table in the kitchen, drinking coffee and calculating how long we would have to go on talking to each other before it would be OK to say goodbye with a modicum of grace and courtesy.

'Milo!' Zac's voice jerked me out of the daydream. He had stopped and was waving me forward. I jogged up to him. 'Look.' He pointed over to the high ground to the east. Two helicopters were hovering at about a thousand feet, making small movements backwards and forwards, then shifting southwards a little and repeating the process.

'Reckon they're looking for us?' he asked.

'They could be.'

They were at least five kilometres away. The sight of them only emphasised how unlikely it was that a random search such as the one they were conducting would ever find us. We watched them for a while, then they gave up and headed off south.

Everyone's shoulders seemed to sag as we set off again. Normally, when you were out on patrol, there was a bit of banter going back and forth along the column. There was none now. Zac obviously felt our dejection. He had taken the lead but he stood back to let Grant and Robbie pass, saying something to them as they went by. I didn't hear what it was but it raised a dutiful laugh.

Then he fell into step with me. We walked for a bit in silence. He nodded at the girl, gliding along a few feet in front.

'What do you think?'

'What do I think of what?'

'The burqa. Do anything for you, does it?' It was good of him to try and raise my spirits, but I wasn't in the mood. It didn't matter because Zac was already sweeping on.

'There's a school of thought that says what you don't see is a turn-on. The lure of the unknown, sort of thing. I've never been convinced. Until now, that is. Look at her.' He gazed admiringly at the girl, who somehow seemed to have sensed what we were talking about. I

56

had the impression that she was swinging her hips under the burqa, which swayed slightly like a curtain in a gentle breeze.

'She's got real grace.' We watched her shimmering along in a cloud of blue. 'What do you think they wanted to kill her for?'

'I don't know. Painting her toenails? Why don't you ask him?' I pointed to the Talib.

'I will, when I get the chance,' he said. 'Anyway, she's safe now. We've rescued her. Our good deed for the day.'

A satisfied smile flickered across his face. I felt an unreasonable urge to wipe it off.

'Maybe,' I said. 'But we don't owe the Talib anything. I sort of think Robbie's right. We should turn him loose. He ought to be thankful we haven't shot him. After all, he's already fucked us over once.'

Zac's complacent look vanished. He shook his head. 'No, he's coming all the way. Don't you see? He's a prize.'

'Not much of one. He's just a foot soldier.'

'But he's all we've got,' said Zac grimly. 'We must have something to show for all this.'

The decision hadn't made much sense to me before, but now I could see Zac's logic. In his mind he had just lost big. He had told me when we were standing with our pints by the river that he that wanted to 'go out with a bang'. Well, he'd had his chance and missed it. The little guy flip-flopping along in his sandals represented a sort of result – a very insignificant one if you asked me. I didn't want to have an argument.

'OK,' I said. 'It's your call.'

'That's right.' He smiled again, confidence restored. 'And it's a good one.' He slapped me on the shoulder and strode off back to the head of the column.

6

By the early afternoon I was licked out. I was knackered and thirsty and starting to feel really hungry. We rounded a bend and I saw an abandoned compound lying off to the left. It looked like a good place to get out of the sun for a while, so I shouted to Zac to stop. He did so rather reluctantly and I went over and checked it out. It was basically four walls enclosing a few stunted trees, but inside it we would be invisible from the path. When I got back I proposed that we lie up for an hour or two in a tone that made it clear that this was more than just a suggestion. Zac seemed about to overrule me but the warning looks on the faces of the others persuaded him. He agreed and we walked over to the crumbling mud walls. Robbie took the first watch and the rest of us tried to find some shade to stretch out in.

I parked myself under a fruit tree. The girl settled down a few feet away from me next to a wall. I unstrapped my helmet. It caught on the wire of my PRR rig. I unplugged it and stowed it in my day sack. We wouldn't be needing those any more. I leaned back, pulled out the rubber nozzle of the Camelbak and drank. The water was warm now and there wasn't much left. As I sucked, I felt the girl's eyes on me.

It hadn't occurred to me that she must be parched. I told myself it was the burqa. It stopped you from thinking of the women here as human beings with ordinary human needs. I took off the Camelbak and offered it to her but she shook her head. I shrugged and resumed drinking. I looked over and saw the girl staring at me again. Her eye-liner had run in the heat. It made it look as if she had been crying. I offered her the water again.

This time she took it. A small hand emerged from the sleeve of her robe. For a second I glimpsed a stripe of white skin, like scar tissue, on the inside of her wrist, before it disappeared again. She flipped up her veil, lowered her eyes and began sucking away happily.

I took a good look at her. She hadn't said a single word to me so far, intelligible or otherwise, and all I could see of her face was her sad, panda eyes. Despite that, I felt that I knew something about her. I could sense a streak of independence under the subservience. Maybe that was why the Taliban had wanted to kill her. I found myself wondering what was under the sky-blue tent. Perhaps Zac was right and the burqa did have something going for it.

When she handed the water back, her eyes lit up briefly in a thank you. Then she looked away and moved off to lie down in the furthest corner of the compound.

Zac came over. 'That was a good idea of yours,' he said graciously. 'We'll lie up here until 1500 hours and then getting moving again when it's a bit cooler. Before we get our heads down, though, we should do a quick inventory.'

He called to the others and we totted up what we were carrying amongst us. It was obvious straight away that we were short of everything, starting with water. I had ten litres in the Camelbak when we set out. Now I had maybe two left. There was water all around us, of course, and we had Puritab sterilising tablets, but we had only been expecting to be away for a few hours and had only brought ten each. That was enough for forty litres, which would not go far in this heat.

We had the minimum amount of food for a short op – four one-day ration packs between us – and we had already made inroads into them during the night. As for ammunition, we could muster three hundred rounds for our three rifles and two 9mm SIG Sauer pistols. We would get through that in a few minutes if we got into a firefight. We had six grenades. They were only for use at close quarters, though. I had never thrown one in anger in my life. Robbie's sniper rifle had the opposite problem. It was a long-distance weapon and not much use if we were ambushed. The truth was, if we got into a scrap, we were in big trouble. We were used to fighting with machine guns, grenade launchers, mortars, Javelin missiles that could destroy a tank. If all that failed do the trick, we could call in jets and helicopters. That option had disappeared with the radio. We were on our own, in a way none of us ever had been before.

We sat there, letting the facts sink in. For a while, no one said anything.

Once again, Zac tried to lift our spirits. He stood up and held out his arms, appealing to us. 'Come on guys. *Nil* fucking *desperandum*. We've been through worse than this in training, for Christ's sake.' It wasn't true and there was no change in our glum expressions.

The silence started to feel sinister. All of a sudden I was anxious to shore him up. 'He's right,' I said in what I hoped was a confident tone. 'We can screw the nut on this one easy.' Screw the nut was a handy army expression. It meant 'do the job', 'get it sorted'. It seemed to have a magical effect on the mood.

Grant chuckled. Robbie was smiling too. 'That's right boss,' he said. 'Every man an emperor, right?' We all nodded at this reference to a hallowed compliment that had been paid to the regiment.

'Right!' said Zac. He was almost exuberant now. 'Let's crack on then.' He clapped his hands together. 'We need to eat,' he said. 'Keep our strength up. There's no point in hoarding what we've got. We should be able to scrounge something from the locals later on. So eat now, then grab some rest. We'll lie up here until mid-afternoon and see how far we can get before dark.'

I felt much more hopeful about things after that, though nothing had changed except our mood. The others had also cheered up. Robbie was whistling as he went back to his post and rested the SA80 he had swapped for his sniper rifle on the wall facing towards the road. I returned to my little tree and pulled a ration pack from my day sack. I saw Grant go over to the girl, lying in the corner. He squatted down next to her and started to talk. After a while he held out a sachet from his rations but she didn't take it. He stood up again and came and sat down next to me.

'She's not hungry?'

'So she says. Must be bloody weird for her, trailing along with us.'

'Did you manage to get anything out of her? Where she's from? What she's called?'

'Her name's Ghazala,' he said. 'That's all she would tell me. It means gazelle. They all have these poetic names.' He smiled.

He looked at the plastic sachet in my hand. 'What have you got there?'

'Vegetable lasagne.'

He grinned. 'Wanna swap?'

'What've you got?'

'Chilli con carne.'

'That'll do.'

In fact chilli con carne was my least favourite of the ration pack offerings, but there was something touching about Grant's attempts to keep faith with his vegetarianism. I felt a ripple of affection for him as I handed it over.

'Thanks mate.' He ripped open the top and dug in a plastic spoon. We sat chomping for a few minutes.

'Did you know Scotty at all?' said Grant eventually.

It took me a second to realise what he was talking about. I thought back to the morning's events.

'Yeah, sure,' I said.

'I mean really know him?'

'No, I can't say that.' Scotty had joined the special unit from another battalion. I'd first met him only a few days before and had trouble now remembering what he looked like.

'Well I did.' Grant frowned. 'We went through training together. He was a good bloke.' He scooped out some vegetable lasagne and chewed for a while in silence.

'I knew his girlfriend,' he went on. 'They were planning on getting married when he got back. I was going to be best man.'

I felt a bit uncomfortable with all this. What was the point of harping on all this now? 'Best not to think about it,' I murmured.

Grant nodded as if I had said something meaningful. He spooned out the last corner of lasagne, then carefully folded up the sachet and stowed it in a pocket.

'Anyway,' he said brightly. 'There'll be no more fuck-ups. What happened this morning was bad luck, that's all. We'll be all right. I've got faith in him.' He nodded across the compound towards Zac. He laughed. 'And you, of course.'

I forced down the last of the chilli and buried the packet. I was about to chuck the junk that came in every ration pack – the chewing gum, pepper and salt and miniature bottle of Tabasco sauce – but something made me stop. It seemed foolish to throw anything edible away.

Zac took over from Robbie on watch – 'stag' we called it – and the rest of us lay down and tried to make ourselves comfortable. I stretched out under my tree and looked up through the thin branches. It was dead quiet apart from the occasional buzzing of a fly. There was a nice smell of baked earth.

Way up, at thirty or forty thousand feet, a white condensation trail crawled across the sky. It was moving from east to west, one of the airliners that ploughed the stratosphere above us day and night, carrying passengers from Mumbai or Singapore to Frankfurt or Paris or London. It would be lunchtime now and the flight attendants would be wheeling the trolleys down the aisles, offering them the chicken or the beef. I often wondered whether they knew it was Helmand they were flying over and if they sometimes looked down and saw the glitter of tracer and the smoke from one of the firefights that were always going on somewhere and realised what was happening. All of a sudden I wanted to be up there with them, settling down to watch a good movie, on my way back to civilisation.

I began to wonder whether what I had said to Zac back in London was true. Did I really want to carry on doing what I was doing? This war could go on for ever, though if I was smart I could probably avoid being at the sharp end of it in future. But what would be the point of that? I would only be marking time. Up until now I had had plenty of adventures, seen far more action than my father and his generation, who had spent their careers in Northern Ireland or dreary German bases. It was not, I realised now, real life. Real life was what the people up there in the airliner lived. One day I would have to join them.

The thought excited me in a way but it also made me feel uncomfortable. For a moment, I saw myself as the outsider in this company. I looked at the others – Grant and Robbie stretched out in the shade and Zac hunkered down, rifle at the ready, against the wall.

They were all believers in their way. Zac's affair with the army might turn out to be brief but there was no doubt it was passionate. I could imagine him back in civvy street, regaling business associates as the wine went round with accounts of his glory days in Helmand. Grant would stay faithful to the end. Even if he left to become an aid worker, which always seemed a possibility with him, he would remain a soldier at heart. Robbie was a proper soldier too. He was proud of what he did. He was gruff and he was cynical but that was the face the Toms put on for the outside world. Dig down and you found a decency and a loyalty that I suspected you hardly ever encountered in civilian life.

I had seen it once at a battalion boxing night a few months after we got back from our first tour. One of the guests was a sergeant who had been shot in the spine and was now looking at spending the rest of his life in a wheelchair. I knew him and liked him well enough, but when I went up to talk to him I found I had nothing to say. I just stood there, struck dumb with embarrassment and awkwardness. I could feel his relief when I left. Robbie, though, was a star. He spent the evening bringing him drinks, making him laugh, treating him like he was still a fully paid-up member of the human race.

It was me that was the agnostic. I realised now that long familiarity with the army had steered me close to contempt for its ways. It wasn't a good thought and I wanted it to go away. I closed my eyes and tried to sleep.

7

I was woken up by Zac's voice giving orders. We were moving on. I checked my watch. It was already mid-afternoon. As I hauled myself up and strapped on my helmet and webbing, he came up and gave my shoulder a quick squeeze. 'All right, Milo?'

'I'm fine.'

'Miserable twat. Say it like you mean it. We'll be out of here soon. When have I ever let you down?'

I pretended to think for a few seconds. 'Where do I begin?'

He grinned and there was a glint in his eyes and you could be forgiven for thinking that he was actually enjoying himself. His smile seemed to say that, though there might be a bit of trouble along the way, it was nothing we couldn't handle; we would have a great story to tell when it was all over. I felt myself grinning too. The truth was that Zac had never let me down exactly. What he did do, though, was to persuade you to do things that your own instincts told you were rash, dangerous or just daft. These schemes were always his initiatives. But when they went wrong, as they often did, they became collective enterprises. I remembered the time when he led us all in a raid on a nightclub, which had refused entry to a bunch of the boys when they turned up drunk. The idea came to him at the end of a dining-in night. It was, in the cold light of day, obviously an incredibly stupid one, but we went along with it nonetheless. Somehow, with Zac, you didn't want to be the one to spoil the fun. We piled into a few cars, all of us about five times over the limit, raced down to town and told the bouncers we were taking over the club. There was some pushing and shoving and the police were called. When we were all hauled before the CO, we kept waiting for Zac to take the rap, but he just kept his head down and looked embarrassed like the rest of us. Well, no harm had come out of that in the end.

Anyway, Grant was right. We had no choice but to put our faith in Zac. He was in charge and the fewer arguments we had the better. Pretty soon we would be home, safe and sound, and all this would be just memories, to be laughed about at reunion piss-ups.

We stepped out of the compound and returned to the track. We stuck to the back paths to try to keep out of sight, but as the shadows lengthened we began to run into little groups of farmers and their families as they headed home from the fields. They stopped when they saw us and stood back meekly to let us pass. Each time, Grant called out a greeting to the men. Sometimes he got a response, a word or a smile. More often it was a sullen look. It didn't mean anything necessarily – just the natural caution of people who had the bad luck to live in a war zone – and it didn't worry me too much. These people didn't want trouble.

Then, something alarming happened. We were walking along a path between two open fields when two men on a motorbike pulled out from a side track about forty or fifty metres ahead. They stopped when they saw us and stared at us hard for a few seconds before turning round and driving back along the road they had just come down.

'See that?' called Robbie. We had, and we all knew what it meant. You saw them, all the time, pairs of young men, perched on crappy little 125cc bikes. Nine times out of ten they were dickers, scouts who were spying for the Taliban.

'Everyone off the road,' ordered Zac. There was a gap in the wall just ahead and we trotted through it over open ground towards a field of maize on the far side. Once inside, we were hidden from the road. Zac ordered a halt and called us to gather round. 'It had to happen sometime, I suppose,' he said. 'How do you reckon we should play it, Milo?'

I would have given my opinion anyway, but nonetheless I felt pleased that he was asking for it. We had to assume that the guys on the bike had gone straight off to tip off the local Taliban that there was a patrol in the area. Sooner or later they would want to take a look at us. When they saw there were only four of us, they would be pretty well sure to attack. Our best chance of evading them was to do something unpredictable. It would be dark soon. They would be expecting us to bed down in the green zone, in the reasonable comfort of a compound. The desert, though, was only a few kilometres to the east and was full of dips and folds where we could literally lie low.

'I think our best bet is to head out into the desert and stop there for the night,' I said. 'If they do find us they're not likely to attack over open ground. And they won't know that we don't have comms. They'll be reluctant to start anything if they think we can call in air support.'

Zac thought for a few seconds then nodded. 'All right,' he said. 'That sounds reasonable.' He looked around. 'Anyone got any better ideas?'

No one had. We tunnelled further into the cover of the crops then paused to consult the map and compass.

The map showed a cluster of compounds between us and the desert. We would have to skirt round them, which meant a three- or four-kilometre detour. By the time we reached the desert, night would have fallen and, barring mishaps, all we had to do then was find the nearest bit of dead ground, hidden from the green zone, and bed down.

The light was dimming as we set off. When we emerged on the far side of the maize field we could see the edge of the desert, off to the east, a band of khaki shimmering in the heat haze. Beyond it rose a jagged range. The peaks were starting to glow red as the sun sank towards the horizon. At this time of day, in this part of the world, I sometimes remembered what it was like to be a child again, as the dark descended, masking what was familiar and making everything mysterious and threatening.

Grant was leading and we turned this way and that, working our way around compounds and waterways, but the progress was steady and we only stopped once or twice to check our bearings. After an hour we had reached the edge of the fields. In front lay the road, the same stony track we had crossed at the start of the day. Beyond stretched a sea of grey clinker.

We stood for a few minutes, scoping out the desert. It ran flat for a bit then rose and fell in a series of loose folds scratched with goat tracks. Behind us, in the green zone, there were lights burning, and I heard the faint screech of Pakistani pop coming from a radio. Nothing seemed to be moving, though, and no one seemed to be watching. Zac waved Grant on and we crunched out into the desert and over the brow of the first low hill.

The desert swallowed us up. There were miles of nothing ahead of us and the lee of the hill behind, and we were safely out of sight in dead ground. The moon was rising and the desert glowed silver like the surface of a lake. Off to the left some low stone walls formed a rough enclosure. Zac led us over and we peered in. It was divided into two pens. One was empty. The other was dotted with low, hump-backed shapes. At first I thought they were mounds of earth. Then one of the shapes moved and made a snuffling noise. Sheep.

We climbed into the empty compound. I looked at my watch. It was nearly 2000 hours. I was exhausted. We would have to keep one man on stag throughout the night and I knew that if Zac asked me to take the first watch I would never be able to stay awake. It was Robbie, thank God, who drew the short straw. Grant was next and I would take the last watch, lasting through until dawn. That gave me eight hours of wonderful sleep. I lay down in the dirt, barely registering the stones digging into my cheek and toppled into unconsciousness.

I had nice dreams for a change. In the best one I was on a boat in a turquoise sea with my girlfriend, Alix. The boat was flying along without oars or sails, skimming over the waves towards an emerald-green island. On and on it went, with us never quite arriving, but we didn't mind, soaking up the warmth of the sun, feeling the wind and the spray on our tanned faces. It ended when Grant shook me awake. It took me a few seconds to remember that I was hundreds of miles from the nearest coastline and that my girlfriend was now my ex-girlfriend.

I picked up my rifle and moved to the lee of the stone wall. The moon was up, covering everything in a pearly light. The others lay sunk in sleep, still as corpses. They looked serene, as if they felt that no harm could come to them now. The Talib had a faint smile on his face. What was he dreaming that made him so peaceful and happy? The air was cool at last. The sky was dusted with millions of stars.

One of the corpses was stirring. The smallest one. Slowly, the bundle of blue cloth came to life. The girl got to her feet and glanced around. I moved tighter into the wall. She didn't seem to have seen me. I watched as she slipped over the sheep-pen wall and disappeared from sight. Where the hell was she going? Then it dawned on me. Sure enough, five minutes later she slid silently back into the pen and sank down on the ground. The poor thing. She must have been desperate.

An hour went past. Every now and again I would move around the four corners of the pen, systematically scanning the landscape through the night-vision binoculars. The light gain from the infrared illuminator made everything cold and unreal. There was nothing to see. My attention started to wander.

Then a sound cut through the silence. Somewhere out there a creature was howling. It was joined by another, then another, until there was a full chorus of Transylvanian wailing and yelping. It scared some people shitless the first time they heard it, but I knew what it was by now, just the warning the stray dogs gave each other when there was a jackal about, and every time I heard it I found it strangely comforting.

It stopped as quickly as it started and the landscape was still and peaceful again. I was just beginning to feel drowsy when I thought I heard another noise. It sounded like an engine. I listened hard but the noise had gone. Then there was no doubt about it. A car or a truck was approaching coming from the direction of the green zone. I trained the binoculars on the low ridge that shielded us from the village and the road. The noise got louder. The engine was roaring now, as if the driver was gunning it to get it up the slope. I turned round and shouted to the others to wake up.

I turned the binos back to see the square silhouette of a pick-up truck appear on the crest of the ridge. It sat there for a few seconds then started to bump down the slope towards us. I heard a metallic *thock* and glanced round to see Robbie cocking his rifle. Everyone was awake now and on their feet.

'Get down!' ordered Zac, and we sank into the cover of the wall and watched the truck move slowly towards us, steering carefully around boulders and potholes.

'What's he fucking doing?' hissed Robbie.

I thought I knew the answer to that.

'These must be his sheep,' I said. 'He's coming to check on them.'

I turned to Zac. 'What are we going to do?'

'Just let him keep coming,' he said. 'The last thing we want is for him to piss off and tell everyone we're here.'

Robbie was tensing behind his sniper rifle. Zac pushed the barrel gently downwards 'You won't need that,' he said. 'Keep calm, everybody, and leave this to me.'

The truck reached the bottom of the slope and speeded up. It stopped in a cloud of dust and grit ten metres from where we hunkered down. A guy wearing a dishdasha and baggy pants, a *pakul* cap and a waist-coat got out, went round the back and let down the tailgate. As he did so, Zac got to his feet, with his rifle held casually across his chest.

'*Salaam aleikum,*' he called.

The man froze. He turned towards Zac.

'*Aleikum es salaam,*' he said, carefully.

'Right Grant,' said Zac. 'Tell him to come over here. Tell him we don't mean him any harm. We just want to talk to him.'

Grant got to his feet and began speaking in a friendly, reassuring voice. He sounded at ease in Pashto. Useless at languages myself, I was always impressed.

The man relaxed. He started to walk slowly towards us. I could see now that he was youngish, in his twenties, I guessed. He had a pockmarked face and a wispy beard. He was wearing that inscrutable expression all the Afghans had, evolved from centuries of having to cope with the unpredictable demands of foreign invaders and local tyrants.

Grant helped him over the wall. Zac greeted him respectfully. He held his gun in one hand now and pressed the other to his heart to emphasise his sincerity.

'Sit down, sit down,' he said. 'We can't offer you a brew I'm afraid.' He turned to Grant. 'Translate, will you?' he whispered.

Grant translated. The man smiled obligingly.

'Good, good,' said Zac, encouraged. 'Just keep him chatting for a while, will you? I need to talk to Miles.'

Grant sat down next to the man who pulled out a pack of cigarettes and lit up. Zac took me by the arm and led me out of earshot of the others. He was grinning when he spoke.

'This could be a godsend,' he said eagerly.

'I don't follow.'

'Don't you see? His truck. If we grab that we could be in Longdon in time for breakfast.'

I did see. My spirits rose. It was very risky, of course. We would have to travel along the main highway and the Taliban controlled the road. They operated checkpoints along its length to levy 'taxes' on the long-suffering locals who were obliged to use it to get their goods to market or their children to the clinic. On the other hand, the insurgents were lazy bastards in some respects. There was little or no traffic on the roads at night, so no need to man the checkpoints. If we set off now and moved quickly we might be well on our way to Longdon before they turned up to work.

If we did run into trouble, we at least had the advantage of surprise. The last thing they would expect if they flagged down the pick-up would be to find a bunch of desperate Brits on board. I had a brief fantasy of us barrelling through a flock of astonished Talibs, blasting away merrily with our SA80s. It was swiftly overtaken by another vision – of the truck's bullet-riddled carcase lying smoking at the side of the road, with our dead bodies scattered around it.

I pushed the image from my mind. Zac was babbling on excitedly. 'What a result, eh?' he said. 'What a tale to tell! A fifty-kay journey through hostile territory. Sort of a modern Xenophon.' He paused. I could sense what he was thinking: *And what a great way of burying the unfortunate story of how we landed in the shit in the first place.*

I didn't care about that. The important thing was that – despite the risks – it was the best chance we were likely to get of putting a swift end to the ordeal. Now that I had made up my mind, I was anxious that we should act fast.

'Right, I said, 'but we have to move right now before it gets light and the Talibs wake up.'

I jerked my head at the truck's owner. 'Better tell him the good news.'

'He won't mind. I'll be generous.' He patted a pouch on his webbing. We always carried a bundle of money with us to sweeten the locals when we needed to borrow their homes or to pay for collateral damage.

We walked back to where Grant and the man sat chatting. The Talib was squatting nearby. He seemed to be taking a keen interest in what was being said. Zac told Grant the plan. Grant listened, nodded and translated. The man didn't seem surprised at what he was being told. But when Grant had finished he held his arms wide, palms outward and said something. You didn't need to know Pashto to understand. There was a problem. The Talib's face broke into a smile.

Grant turned to Zac.

'Bit of a hitch,' he said. 'Apparently he's almost out of diesel.'

'Fuck.' Zac frowned. His faced cleared again. 'Maybe he's lying. Robbie, go and check.'

'Yes, boss,' said Robbie. He turned to the man and held out his hand. 'The keys,' he said.

The man twigged what was happening. He pulled them from his waistcoat and handed them over. Robbie hopped over the wall, walked over to the truck and ducked into the cab. After a few seconds his head reappeared. He looked towards us and nodded. 'It's on empty,' he called over.

'That's the end of that then,' I said. The vision of breakfast in Longdon vanished as quickly as it had appeared.

'No it isn't,' said Zac fiercely. 'He'll have some diesel somewhere. Ask him to take us to it.' His eyes were blazing. 'No, *tell* him.'

Grant began speaking again. The man listened, then started to reply. He seemed to be agreeing to the demand, when the Talib leaned forward and grabbed his hand. He spoke to him in a sharp, urgent voice. The man looked at him in bewilderment, then back at us, unsure as to which of us he should obey.

'Shut the fuck up,' shouted Zac, but the Talib gabbled on. Grant reached out as if to clamp a hand over the Talib's mouth, but he dodged out of the way.

'Grant,' Zac demanded, 'what's he saying?'

'He's telling him that if he helps us he'll be killed,' he said.

'Stop him,' Zac ordered. Grant darted forward and pulled the Talib and the man apart.

As he did, the Talib spoke again. This time we understood him fine. 'Take your fucking hands off me, will you?' he snapped. And in those eight short words, the Brummie accent rang out as clear as a bell.

8

There was a chorus of astonished swearing.

'Who the fuck *are* you?' demanded Zac.

The Talib lowered his head and shook it emphatically, angry at having given himself away.

'Nothing to say.'

'What are you doing here?'

'No comment.'

'What's your name?'

His face was blank again. Zac stood back and looked him up and down. 'Don't worry. There'll be plenty of time to find out.'

He got down to business. 'Got your cuffs Robbie?' Robbie produced from his webbing a pair of the rings of tough plastic we used to bind the hands of suspects.

'Put 'em on him.'

'Pleasure,' said Robbie. He moved behind the Talib and grabbed his arms. The Talib struggled but his wiry frame was no match for Robbie's gym-pumped muscles. 'Don't make me have to hurt you,' he breathed. He pulled the cuffs tight on the narrow brown wrists with a satisfied grunt.

Zac shoved his face into the Talib's. 'If you threaten him again,' he jerked a thumb at the truck owner – 'you're dead. Got it?' He mimed a pistol shot to the Talib's head.

The Talib gave a superior smile, as if it no longer mattered. The damage was already done.

Zac seemed elated again. 'What a turn-up, hey?' he said. 'Looks like we've got ourselves a real-live, home-grown jihadi!'

He looked round triumphantly.

'Now we really have got a result. I mean, we've all heard about these guys but this is the first time anyone has actually seen one.'

It was true. There were frequent reports that Brits were serving in the ranks of the insurgents, guys from the Midlands and the North who had been fired up by the local preacher and headed off to Pakistan for training. No one had ever produced one, though. I tended to regard them as another Afghan myth – like the story of how, when the Mujahideen took the Kajaki Dam, they fed the Russians guarding it into the turbines of the generator, one by one. Now, it appeared we had captured a genuine specimen.

'He's going to be trouble, though,' I said. 'He's obviously sussed that we're in the shit. We're going to have to watch him like a hawk.'

Zac looked irritated. 'Good old Milo. Always look on the bright side, eh? Robbie will keep an eye on him all right, and anyway, he's not going to try any more tricks. He knows what will happen to him if he does.'

It seemed to me that the Talib, whatever his name was, had worked out by now that he was not in any danger of being whacked and had a free pass to carry on causing us grief. I kept it to myself, though. Zac had a point. The capture of a British Talib would be a bit of a coup for us. I resolved to be more upbeat.

He looked across the compound. The sky was already starting to lighten in the east.

'Come on,' he said. 'Let's get a move on. We need to pick up that fuel and be on our way before the Taliban wake up.'

We rejoined the others. Grant was deep in conversation with the driver. Eliciting the information about where he kept his fuel seemed to be taking a long time. Why did that surprise me? Even the simplest transaction involving the locals took an eternity. It was no wonder they were stuck in the Stone Age. I was on the point of telling Grant to get him to hurry up, but I stopped myself. Any attempt to speed things along invariably had the opposite result.

Finally the talking stopped.

'Well?' Zac asked impatiently.

'He says he's got some diesel in his compound. It's near here. Just next to the village.'

'He took all that time to tell you that?'

Grant shrugged. Unlike some of us, he tried hard to fit in with the Afghan way of doing things. When we called a *shura* to discuss something with the locals, he would sit around for hours drinking tea and shooting the shit with the village elders, apparently enjoying himself while the rest of us were yearning to wind things up. It sometimes made me feel a little unworthy, but not now. I could sense the first, treacherous rays of sunshine peeping over the mountains.

'Right, let's get going then,' I said impatiently, and hopped into the back of the truck. It was a Toyota Hilux, the pick-up of choice around here for Talib and farmer alike. Grant got in with the driver. The others climbed up beside me. The girl was the last to get aboard. There wasn't much room. She wedged herself against the tailgate next to Robbie. The truck jolted its way up the hillside. I looked at the heads jerking and lolling opposite me. The Talib had closed his eyes. It gave me the chance to inspect him properly.

It was the first time I had really looked at him as a fully-fledged human being. The truth was, I never took much notice of the people we lived amongst. The natives were a mystery to me. We were supposed to win their trust. 'The people are the prize' – that's what we were told. But to me 'the people' weren't a collection of individuals, each with their own hopes and fears. They were an anonymous mass, whose hopes and fears didn't particularly interest me. Nor could I fathom the motivations of the insurgents – not that I spent much time trying to work them out. Given that our entire existence was devoted to defeating them, they were strangely remote from the proceedings. They were figures in the distance, dodging out from an alleyway or scuttling over a rooftop. Sometimes, waiting for a helicopter, you ran into some captives, on their way back to the base prison, bound hand and foot, their eyes blanked out behind taped-up goggles. They scarcely looked as if they belonged to this earth. It was embarrassing to admit it, but this guy had changed that. He was, to all appearances, the enemy. But he was also an Englishman. Maybe one day he could explain it all to me.

We reached the top of the ridge and Zac banged on the roof of the cab and shouted to Grant to tell the driver to stop. At the bottom of the slope, the low walls of the village houses stood out in the pre-dawn light. Plumes of smoke were rising from breakfast cooking fires. The village was waking up.

Zac hopped out and went to the passenger's side.

'Get him to point out his place,' he said.

There was a muttered conversation.

The driver poked an arm out of the window. He was pointing straight at a distant jumble of mud bricks on the far side of the village.

'Jesus,' said Zac. 'It's miles away.'

He jumped back in and banged on the truck and we jerked forward and on to a track that led down to the highway. The direct route to his compound led straight through the village. If we'd had time, we would have skirted round it to avoid advertising our presence. It was too late for that now.

As we entered the broad path that led through the houses, I could smell the smoke from the fires and hear the clash of cooking pots behind the compound walls. Ahead, four or five men were loading tools into panniers slung across their donkeys. They glanced up when they heard the engine and froze. They turned away as we passed, all except one man with an ink-black beard who looked straight at me with a stare of pure hatred. As we drove through the compound, doors clanged shut behind us. When we exited on the far side, I turned back. It was empty. It looked as though a plague had struck the place.

The driver made laborious progress up the rutted and rock-strewn track that led to his home. Behind us, a sliver of red was showing above the jagged eastern mountains. In twenty minutes, it would be daylight.

'Get a fucking move on,' I muttered to myself as the Hilux roared and whined its way in and out of the ditches that cut across the path. And then we were over the worst and on to a flat stretch that ended at the entrance to the compound. The gates were open. We drove through and into a scrubby enclosure. A goat was tethered in the corner and a few chickens fluttered around in the dirt. There was animal shit everywhere.

The driver parked up and got out. He walked towards his living quarters, a one-storey mud hut with a veranda running round it and sacking hung over the windows. We climbed down and watched him disappear inside.

'Where's he gone?' demanded Zac.

'He's waiting for you in there,' said Grant. 'He wants to talk about money.'

'Oh for fuck's sake,' snarled Zac.

Grant held his hands out appeasingly. 'We can't go anywhere without him,' he said.

'OK, OK,' said Zac wearily, and led the way.

The driver reappeared at the door. As Zac was about to cross the threshold, he pointed at his feet. We all got fed up with the palaver of taking off your boots when you entered an Afghan's home. Most had mud floors and the carpets were cheap and garish, mass-produced in Pakistan, yet the owners behaved as if you were walking into a palace.

We unlaced our boots and stepped inside, leaving the girl squatting by the door. The room smelt like a rabbit hutch. There was nothing inside except some ancient bedding stacked against the wall, and the only decoration was a plastic clock and a few painted tin plates propped up along a shelf. The driver sat down on a pile of rugs with his legs crossed. We made a semi-circle around him on the floor. The Talib settled down in the shadows against the wall.

'Let's get on with it then,' said Zac sharply.

The driver started talking in a low, reasonable voice. It sounded like the preamble to a hefty opening bid. Sure enough, Grant's translation confirmed that the Hilux and fuel weren't going to come cheap.

'He's saying that you're asking a lot. The truck is a good truck. It's also his livelihood. He can't look after his sheep without it. If he were to sell it to you, he'd have to buy another one and they're expensive, especially now the war is stopping people driving them in from Pakistan.'

'Yes,' said Zac. A phoney smile was glued on his face. 'Tell him we understand his predicament. And that we will of course pay a good price so he can buy an even better truck to replace it.'

Grant translated. The driver looked pleased. Zac seized the moment and interrupted.

'So just ask him how much he wants.'

Grant did so.

The driver's smile expanded. My spirits rose. But then he started shaking his head ruefully. I knew what that meant. *Oh no, my friend. Not so fast. These things take time.*

Zac could see where this was going, too. His voice was hard now. 'Tell him we're in a hurry and if he doesn't want to do business, we're off.' The driver caught the tone and stopped smiling.

Grant translated. The man nodded and slapped his hands on his knees. He rapped out a few words – his price, I presumed.

Grant chuckled. 'Worth a try, I suppose,' he said. 'He wants twenty thousand US.'

'Tell him to fuck off,' said Zac. 'Politely, of course. I've got five thousand. He can have the lot for the truck and a full tank. But make sure he knows that's the final offer.'

Grant did so. The driver looked grave and nodded. He started talking back and his reply went on and on. It clearly wasn't yes and it wasn't no. It was somewhere in between. Maybe the words yes and no didn't exist in Pashto.

I was squirming with impatience now. A golden shaft broke through a gap in the sacking curtain. Specks of dust bobbed in the rays. It was daylight again. The room seemed hot all of a sudden and the smell too much to bear. I wanted to get out of there, out of the compound and on our way, with or without the truck.

Now Zac was interrupting the driver's monologue.

'Five thousand, take it or leave it.'

Grant translated. The driver shook his head and resumed talking.

Suddenly, Zac was on his feet. 'Tell him thanks for his time. We're taking the truck anyway.'

'You can't do that,' said Grant.

'Oh yes I can,' said Zac. 'He had his chance. Tell him we'll get his truck back to him once we get to Longdon.'

Grant's blue eyes blazed with anger. I'd never seen him like this before.

'I'm not doing your dirty work. You fucking tell him.'

'Remember who you're talking to.' Zac's voice was ugly.

Grant gave a contemptuous laugh. 'What's that? A threat?'

I'd had enough. 'Shut up, the pair of you,' I said. They both looked round. 'We're wasting our time here. The sun's up. It's too risky to drive now anyway. Let's start walking.'

Zac shook his head vigorously. 'No way,' he said. 'I'm in charge here and you'll all do what I say.'

I'm sure that as soon as he said it he regretted it. If there is one sure way of undermining your authority it is to remind everybody that you are the boss. There was a moment when it seemed he might do the intelligent thing and back off, apologise, and let everyone take a deep emotional breath. He didn't though.

'We're taking the truck,' he said looking hard at each of us in turn. 'Understood?'

We nodded. Short of a mutiny there was nothing else to do. As we headed for the door I made one last intervention.

'At least leave him some money,' I pleaded.

But Zac wasn't going to show any weakness now.

'I said I'd get his truck back to him,' he replied stiffly. 'And I will.'

After the dim room, the morning light was blinding. The truck stood glinting in the sunshine.

'Where do you think he keeps the diesel?' asked Zac. No one answered.

He glanced around the compound. 'Over there.' He pointed at a shed in a corner. 'Robbie. Check it out.' Robbie obeyed.

The driver had appeared in the doorway now and was shouting.

'Tell him to shut it, Grant,' said Zac.

Grant shook his head firmly.

'OK, I will then.' Zac strode past him and took the driver by the shoulders. He pushed him through the doorway and shut the door.

The Talib was standing on the veranda watching everything closely. He was clearly enjoying the proceedings, and that irritating smirk of his was working overtime. There was a flurry of wings and some outraged squawking from the far corner of the compound and the shed door opened. Robbie emerged carrying a solitary plastic jerrycan.

'That's all there was,' he said apologetically. He went over to the truck where Zac was unscrewing the fuel cap.

'It'll just have to do,' he said. 'Pour away.'

Robbie lifted the can and the diesel gulped into the tank. Some of it splashed down the side of the truck.

'Careful!' snapped Zac.

Robbie upended the container and shook out the dregs.

'Get the others,' commanded Zac.

I went over to the veranda and placed a hand on the Talib's arm. He shook it off and made his way over to the truck. He climbed in, hauling himself up awkwardly by his cuffed hands, and slid to the floor with his back to the tailgate. The girl was still crouched by the door. She looked up at me, questioningly. I remembered her name. Ghazala. Gazelle. I smiled and nodded and she got to her feet and walked over. Grant held out his hand and she hoisted herself aboard.

Just as I turned to join them, I saw the driver looking at us through the gap in the sacking curtain. His face was clenched with anger. Another victory in the battle for hearts and minds, I thought as I walked away.

Robbie and Grant were standing by the truck.

'Who's going to drive?' demanded Zac.

' You can,' I said. 'It's your idea.'

'OK, I will,' he said defiantly.

He handed his rifle to Robbie.

'Take this. Use it if you have to.'

Robbie and Grant got in the back and stood up, leaning against the back of the cab with their rifles propped on the roof. Zac opened the driver's door. I went round and got in beside him. The ignition key was dangling in the lock.

'Thank God for that,' he said. He turned the key and the engine started up. We nosed out of the compound gate and bumped down the track towards the village.

The villagers must have been watching our progress. Nothing that they had seen had changed their first, instinctive judgement that we were trouble, for the doors stayed shut as we drove through and the only sign of life was a tethered goat that looked up at us with satanic yellow eyes when we passed.

9

We hit the highway and turned right, heading southwards.

'The map's in my day sack,' shouted Zac over the whine of the engine. 'Get it out.'

I obeyed. The village showed up as a scattering of rectangles on the satellite imagery.

'How far?' he asked.

I counted the squares.

'Thirty-three kays.'

I squeezed the grip of my rifle and flicked the trigger nervously.

Zac picked up speed. Soon we were moving fast – too fast for the road. The highway was pitted with potholes. There were trenches where culverts had collapsed. We slalomed from one crater to another. There was a loud banging on the cab roof.

'Slow down, for Christ's sake,' Grant shouted.

Zac slackened off for a bit but soon we were jolting along at the same mad rate. I feared that we would break an axle or blow a tyre. I put a restraining hand on Zac's arm. He turned to me. He was sweating and there was a look of wild determination in his eyes.

'Ease up,' I said. 'You're going to roll it at this rate.'

'OK, OK,' he said and decelerated again. This time he kept to a reasonable speed, but you could see it was a struggle for him.

We bounced along. The road ran straight at first, through open fields, and there was no traffic, just a pick-up truck, loaded with goats, coming the other way, and a couple of old men on a moped.

We passed a tiny mosque on the right of the road, just a mud-brick cube with a tin crescent and a loud-speaker on the roof. It featured on the map. We had come five kays already. My hopes began to rise but I quickly damped them down again. This was the easy bit. The real danger lay in front of us. The map showed the road veering to the left three kilometres ahead. Just beyond that lay a bazaar. It sounds exotic, doesn't it, 'bazaar'? It makes you think of beaded curtains and carpet sellers and men hawking coffee from big brass pots. In this part of the world, though, it just meant a row of stalls strung along the roadside selling food, electrical goods, cheap clothes and suchlike.

It was there that the Taliban were most likely to set up their checkpoints, so as to sting the locals as they came to buy or sell. I looked closely at the map, searching for any tracks across the fields that we might be able to take to skirt round the bazaar. There were a few trails showing, but whether they were driveable or not wasn't clear. We could waste a lot of time finding out. And diesel. I looked at the fuel gauge. The contents of the jerrycan had raised the needle to just above red.

I glanced at Zac, wondering whether it was worth asking him to stop for a consultation. One look told me not to waste my breath. He was hunched over the wheel, face clenched in concentration. We were just going to have to risk it. I checked my watch. It was only just after seven o'clock. With any luck it was still too early for the Taliban to have arrived at their posts.

The bend in the road was in sight now. It was marked by a clump of tall, dusty-green eucalyptus trees. The surface of the road improved as we approached it. Someone had taken the trouble to fill in the potholes with gravel. Zac speeded up again. When we hit the bend we must have been doing forty kilometres an hour.

As we swung into the turn I heard the crack of a rifle directly over my head, then another. Grant and Robbie were shooting – but I had no idea what they were aiming at. Then I saw the target. A hundred metres ahead there were men at the right side of the road. There were four of them and they were sitting on chairs, next to a trestle table, with rifles propped up by their sides.

As I watched they jumped to their feet and raised their guns. I saw some spurts of yellow muzzle flash and a blur of green tracer whipped past the windscreen. Above my head, Grant and Robbie's guns were cracking in unison. One of the Talibs was taking careful aim. His gun was pointing directly at me. I braced for the bullet. Then suddenly his body slackened and he dropped gracefully to the ground.

Inside the jolting cab it was impossible to hold my rifle steady enough to take proper aim. I unsnapped my pistol, reached through the window and started firing towards the three left standing. Zac had his foot to the floor. We were charging towards them and bullets sparked and clanged off the bonnet. There was a hammer thud on the windscreen and it exploded inwards, showering us with shattered glass.

The faces ahead showed clearly now. A fat man in a black turban was standing in the middle of the road with the barrel of his AK-47 jerking wildly. As we closed on him he jumped off to the side. I shot him just as we went past. He reeled back, clutching his throat, and bright blood bubbled through his fingers.

Then they were behind us. The remaining two kept shooting. Robbie and Grant fired back.

After a few hundred metres the noise stopped. We slowed down. Zac, though, was struggling with the wheel. The truck was lurching to the left. It was all he could do to keep it going in a straight line.

'The front tyre's shot out!' he called. As he spoke there was a loud hissing noise and a geyser of steam and water sprayed from the bonnet. You could feel the power ebbing from the engine. We staggered on for another hundred metres. Then the Hilux groaned to a halt.

I holstered my pistol, shoved the map in my day sack and got out. Robbie and Grant were already climbing down from the back, clutching their rifles. Ghazala scampered after them and darted into the cover of the bushes at the right-hand side of the road. The Talib was rolled up in a ball in the corner by the tailgate making himself as small as possible. For a second I thought he must have been hit. I tapped him on the shoulder. He lifted his head. He looked frightened. After his perform-ance with the owner of the car, I felt rather pleased about that. Maybe he was beginning to realise that his fate was entirely bound up with ours now.

'Come on,' I said.

He nodded obediently and struggled to his knees, holding his bound wrists awkwardly in front of him. I reached up, hoisted him over the back and lowered him down. I pulled out my knife and cut off the handcuffs.

'Thanks,' he said. He sounded almost polite. I hustled him into the bushes where the others were waiting.

'Looks like it's back to plan A,' said Zac. He seemed a lot calmer now. The dramas of the last few minutes had sobered him up, thank God.

'Everyone OK?' We all nodded.

'Let's get out of sight then. They'll be looking for us.' A field of tall maize lay just beyond the bushes. We tunnelled inside it until all we could see was a few feet in front of our faces. It felt like sanctuary. My adrena-line buzz finally subsided.

After a few minutes, Zac stopped and we drew up behind him.

'Got the map, Milo?' He sounded subdued, maybe even a bit embarrassed.

I handed it over. He looked at it and pulled out a compass.

'Well, we're quite a bit further on,' he said. He tapped the map.

I did a quick calculation.

'Seven or eight kays, that's all. With the detours we'll have to make, that still leaves twenty-five or so.'

'I know,' he said wearily.

He stared at the map again, as if it might suddenly reveal a quicker way home.

'All we can do is keep heading south. Stay between the highway and the river. Avoid the locals wherever possible. Just put one foot in front of the other.'

That seemed to be about right. We set off, shifting southwards. The maize was planted in rows about a metre apart. The going was fairly easy for us but Ghazala's burqa snagged in the stalks and we kept having to wait while she unhooked herself.

As usual, once the adrenaline had ebbed, a grey tide of depression seeped in to replace it. It wasn't just the thought of the danger and misery of the trek ahead. We could make it home, I was still sure of that, if only we kept our heads and took the right decisions. But the man who was responsible for taking them was Zac. I no longer knew if I trusted him to take the right ones.

No, that wasn't true. After the events of the last few hours, I was pretty sure I didn't. I knew Zac could be impetuous. He'd got me into scrapes at home, but they had been nothing compared to this - just domestic escapades where the worst that could happen to us was a bit of a telling off.

Whenever I had been with him in real danger, in Iraq and Afghanistan, he had always struck me as essentially pretty cool and professional. His instincts had often seemed uncannily sound.

Now I was wondering whether he had lost his touch. Or maybe he had just been unlucky. Bad luck, though, had been stalking us at every stage of the trip. I was beginning to think that it was Zac who had brought it along.

We cleared the maize and entered a string of orchards. Now that we were out in the open, Ghazala was moving quite easily. The name suited her. I could imagine her skinny legs skipping along under her robe. I had been sweating buckets in the steamy heat of the plantation. I sucked at my Camelbak and raised a tepid mouthful. I sucked again and got only a gurgling noise. I cursed myself for not thinking of filling up when we had the chance at the truck owner's compound.

My mouth felt shrivelled and sour. I licked my cracked lips with a tongue like sandpaper. There was water all around, of course, in the channels and ditches that fed the fields; full of shit and dead animals, no doubt, but I didn't care too much about that. It was water and we had the Puritabs.

I caught up with Zac.

'Hi,' he said. I caught a gust of rank breath.

'I'm out of water,' I said. 'I need to fill up from somewhere.'

'Me too. We'll stop when we find one.'

The sun was beating down now. The Afghan equivalent of midges had materialised and a cloud of them had formed an escort around my head. My tongue felt as though it was filling up the whole of my mouth. Everyone seemed to be feeling the heat now. We marched in silence, broken by the jingle of webbing, the padding of boots and the patter of flip-flops and *chaplis*.

At last we came to a wide irrigation channel. The flow was sluggish and the water was fudge-brown. Grant had a greenie mug, cut from a plastic mortar-bomb carrier case, and we took turns to fill our Camelbaks, drop in the Puritabs, give it a good shake, and drink. It tasted of mud but it was the wetness that counted.

I had gulped down about half the contents of the Camelbak before I remembered my manners. Ghazala was looking at me with big thirsty eyes. I noticed she had wiped off the make-up. She looked very young. I handed her the tube. She took it, lifted her veil and drank. Her neck bobbed gently as she swallowed. She finished the lot and passed the tube back. For a moment our eyes locked. She stared back confidently and smiled. *Tashakkur*, she said. Even I knew that one. It was Afghan for thank you. I felt absurdly pleased.

I looked around. Zac had moved away and was studying the map again, as if the answer to all our problems was encoded in it somewhere if only he could find the key. Robbie and Grant were sitting on the bank, talking in low, confidential voices. I guessed they were discussing Zac. I went over and joined them. They stopped talking and looked up, somewhat guiltily I thought.

'Hi,' said Grant.

'Hi,' said Robbie.

'Can't hang around,' I said. 'Let's fill up again and move on.'

'OK boss,' said Robbie. He got to his feet. A look of alarm flickered on his face. 'Where's he gone?' We looked around. The Talib was nowhere to be seen. Then I saw a patch of brown cloth showing from the foliage, about ten metres away. The Talib was kneeling, head down and hands outstretched, pointing in the approximate direction of Mecca.

'Wanker,' growled Robbie, and strode towards him. He grabbed him under one of his outstretched arms and hauled him to his feet.

'Let him be.' Zac's voice stopped Robbie dead and he pushed the Talib away.

'Come here. Both of you.'

They shuffled over.

'Don't do anything like that again, Robbie. Understand?' Robbie nodded. 'He's our prisoner. He gets treated properly.'

'And you.' He looked at the Talib. 'I'm getting fucking fed up with you. You'd better start to behave yourself. You can start by telling us your name.'

The Talib stared at him. He was looking defiant again and for a moment I thought he was going to refuse to answer. Then he spoke.

'Majid,' he said.

'Just Majid?'

'That's all you need to know,' he said haughtily.

'So be it. Well, Majid. I'm not going to stop you praying. But the next time you want to do it, tell someone. OK?'

He nodded.

'Show's over,' said Zac. 'Let's get going.'

10

For the next few hours we made good progress. Much of the area we passed through was planted with maize. It would be while before the crop was harvested, so there were no workers around and we plodded along the paths that ran through the fields unnoticed.

By the early afternoon we were about eight kays nearer home. We were close to the river now and could see the shingle shoals and banks through the gaps in the crops. I was feeling licked out and very hungry. I was grateful when we came to an abandoned compound and Zac called a halt.

It looked as if someone had been living there until fairly recently. A clay oven stood in one corner, with a wooden shovel propped against it. A few metres away there was a large hole in the ground with a pole slung across it and a bucket dangling from a rope underneath. A few stunted trees gave a little shade. A faint breeze from the direction of the river stirred the branches. In the state I was in, it seemed a pretty nice place.

I slipped off my day sack, unsnapped my webbing, took off my helmet and sank down against a wall. My hair was plastered to my scalp with sweat. I looked around. I saw that Majid had grabbed the best spot, under the biggest tree. Grant had noticed too. He walked over. 'I think this is reserved for the lady,' he said. Majid sighed theatrically. He got up and walked away to stretch out next to the clay oven. Ghazala watched the performance from a few paces away. Grant waved her over. She gave a little bow and settled under the tree.

I volunteered to take first turn on stag. After the others had settled down, I took a tour round the perimeter. The nearest houses were two or three kilometres away and the compound was hemmed in by crops on three sides so we could only be seen from the river. I went over to the well and peered in. The water shimmered in the sunlight, a few feet below. I lowered the bucket and filled my Camelbak. I settled down by the western wall, facing the river. Off to the north, a queue of women and children and men on motorbikes were waiting on the bank to board a chain ferry. I watched for a while but the ferry appeared to be stuck on the other side. The line of people became part of the landscape. I could imagine the scene. There would be no pushing and shoving, no raised voices, no efforts to get the ferrymen to hurry up. It was just something else to be endured.

Inside the compound, everyone was stretched out except Zac. He was propped against a tree trunk, knees drawn up, with his eyes half shut. The sight of him sitting there, sunk in his thoughts, disturbed me. Zac liked to talk. Sometimes he talked too much. Now, though, he seemed separate from the rest of us. I half hoped he would look up and see me and make some bantering remark. I looked away. Next time I glanced over he was lying down on his side, facing away from me. I couldn't tell whether or not he was asleep. I hoped for his sake he was.

After two hours, Grant relieved me. Nothing at all had happened during my watch and the main event as far as I was concerned was the growing feeling of emptiness in my stomach. I found a spot in the lee of a crumbling wall and tried to sleep. As soon as I closed my eyes, the events of the morning began to play themselves back in vivid detail. I relived the fight at the checkpoint; saw the green streaks of tracer and the blood pulsing through the fingers of the man I had killed. It was like watching a movie in which one was playing a part – intense and yet remote at the same time.

When I woke up it was already dark. I got up, stretched, and looked around. Zac was standing by the wall. I went over and he looked up and grinned. He seemed in good spirits and I felt grateful for that. He handed me the night-vision binoculars.

'Have a look,' he said. Normally they bathed the scene in front of you in a luminous green glow, but all I could see was blackness.

'The batteries are dead,' he said blandly. 'They're supposed to last ten hours at least.' I'd forgotten about batteries.

'Oh well,' I said casually. 'Doesn't make that much difference, I suppose.' And it didn't, given the scale of all our other problems. There was an awkward silence.

'Bit of a fuck-up this morning,' he said, eventually. 'Taking the truck I mean.'

I didn't reply. Zac persisted.

'It was worth a try though? Don't you think?'

He was looking at me closely, willing me to say yes. I felt almost embarrassed for him.

I didn't want to challenge him. He had taken a gamble – a stupid one if you asked me – and it hadn't come off. But, no one was dead. The important thing now was to stop him doing the same thing again. I felt I had to humour him.

'Sure,' I said neutrally. It seemed to satisfy him.

'So, got any bright ideas then?' He sounded almost pathetically hopeful.

I thought for a moment.

'Not really, mate,' I said. 'I can't see what we can do except crack on.'

'Right,' said Zac forlornly. He was back inside his shell again.

Gazing out into the velvety darkness, I felt the first stirring of hopelessness. I had put off analysing our situation too closely. Instead, I'd been concentrating on the little achievements – like the fact that we had managed to walk eight kays today. That still left seventeen to go, by the map, which meant nearer twenty five with the inevitable detours. We had been travelling for two days now and we were only halfway to Longdon. At this rate it would be two more before we got there – barring further mishaps, which now seemed all too likely. We had no food, and the water we were drinking would make us sick before long. The longer we were out here on the ground, the more our chances of survival dwindled. We were going to have to move faster.

'Zac?'

He was looking gloomily out into the blackness. 'Yeah?'

'Let's not hang around here tonight. Why don't we rest up for a few more hours and then get on our way?'

He didn't reply, so I persisted. 'I know everyone's knackered, but that's tough. We'll cover more ground by night. It's cooler and there's less chance of us running into anyone. At dawn we can find somewhere safe to rest up.'

If he was hearing what I said he didn't show it. The silence started to be bother me.

'Listen,' I said fiercely. 'If we don't speed things up we're all fucking dead. You do realise that, don't you?'

At last I had his attention. His head turned towards me. His eyes were bright and he was nodding emphatically. '*Yes*,' he said, as if the idea had just come to him independently. 'Just go for it. Straight home. Pedal to the metal.' His despondency had evaporated. 'We're going to need all our strength, though.' He patted his stomach.

'I'm fucking ravenous. You must be too. We can't go anywhere until we've had something to eat.'

He clapped his hands together, his old decisive self. 'Someone's going to have to find supper.'

11

The 'someone' turned out to be Robbie.

'Go off and see what you can find,' Zac instructed him breezily. 'Eggs. A chicken. Anything you can lay your hands on.'

Robbie was reluctant. 'Why me boss?' he asked plaintively.

'You're good at that sort of thing,' Zac replied.

It seemed unlikely to me that Robbie's upbringing in the backstreets of Birmingham had equipped him for life as a hunter-gatherer. He knew better than to argue, though.

'All right,' he said sulkily. 'But who's coming with me? There's no way I'm wandering around on me own.'

'Of course,' said Zac reasonably. He looked around. I felt his eyes fall on me and began to feel a bit shifty. I was on the point of reluctantly volunteering when help came from an unexpected quarter.

'I'll do it.' It was Majid.

Robbie voiced what we were all thinking.

'Why?' he asked.

'Why do you think?' said Majid. 'Because I'm fucking starving.'

Robbie seemed amused. 'Right,' he smiled. 'A bit of local knowledge might come in handy.'

Zac looked at me. 'Any objections?'

I shook my head.

'OK,' said Zac. 'Off you go.' He handed Robbie his SIG Sauer pistol. 'If he tries anything, use this.'

We watched them climb over the wall and disappear into the darkness.

'The media ops guys will have a lot of fun with him when we get him back,' said Zac.

'What do you mean?' asked Grant. He sounded sceptical.

'Well, he proves a point, doesn't he?' said Zac. 'I mean, the line is that we're fighting this war here so we don't have to fight it back home. Majid's the link between the poppy fields of Helmand and the mean streets of Britain. That's how they'll present it, anyway.'

'What, you think Majid's a player?' Grant chuckled. 'Mr Big?'

'Well, we don't know, do we?' Zac sounded huffy. 'He could be.'

'I don't think so,' said Grant. 'He seems like a bit of a knob to me.'

He raised his arms, stretching his lean body to its full six foot plus.

'Well, I'm going to try and get a bit of kip,' he said, and loped off to a corner of the compound.

The exchange seemed to have put Zac into a bad mood. Without saying anything, he moved away and sat down against a tree. It was the same one he had propped himself against earlier, and he took up the same position, with his knees drawn up and his eyes apparently shut. He hadn't said anything about whose turn it was on stag. It looked as if it was mine. I went over to the wall and stared out into the empty blackness.

It was two hours before Robbie and Majid returned. I heard them before I saw them. They sounded as if they were having trouble. Robbie's voice drifted over on the night air. It sounded as if he was alternately laughing and swearing. When they came into view I saw that they were carrying something between them. It was wriggling and jerking and it was all they could do to hang on to it.

Just as they reached the compound, their burden broke free. I saw now it was a small goat. Bleating with terror it skittered away, zigzagging towards the river. It was moving fast, but not fast enough to escape Majid who sprinted after it, his knees pistoning away beneath his dishdasha. When he was a few feet behind it, he launched a rugby tackle, catching a hind leg as it scampered up a bank.

I couldn't help laughing. Zac and Grant were doing the same.

'Well done mate,' said Grant, slapping Majid on the shoulder as he carried the goat into the compound.

Robbie took it from him, pinned it to the ground, pulled out a knife and deftly cut its throat. Blood pumped into the dirt.

'Now we just need to cook it,' said Zac. 'Any volunteers?' He looked at Grant.

'I'm a vegetarian.'

Zac grunted. 'Well you'll have to forget your principles tonight if you want to eat. What about you, Robbie?'

'Haven't I done enough?' he said. 'It's thanks to me – ' he glanced at Majid '– and him, that we've got anything to eat at all.'

I'd noticed that Ghazala was following closely what was going on. Surely she must know how to cook a goat.

'What about her?' I said.

'Perfect,' said Zac. 'Tell her we've got a job for her, will you, Grant.'

Grant translated. She seemed happy to oblige. She picked up the small carcase by the tail and walked over to the clay oven in the corner, holding it away in an outstretched hand to keep the blood from dripping on her burqa. Grant went with her. A few minutes later a fire was crackling and the air filled with the smell of wood smoke. Then I remembered something. I went over to the oven. Grant was feeding the fire while Ghazala was busy skinning the goat with Grant's knife. They looked at ease with one another, like a contented married couple. I showed her the pepper, salt and Tabasco I had saved from the ration pack. 'Thought you might be able to use these,' I said. She took them and smiled. She stripped the last skin from the carcase and started cutting the meat into cubes.

Grant threw a branch on the fire and joined me. It was the first time we had been together and out of earshot of Zac and Robbie. I sensed he had something to say and there was a short, uncomfortable silence while he steeled himself to say it. I knew what the subject would be – Zac. The other ranks often bitched about their superiors behind their backs. It was quite a big deal, though, for an NCO like Grant to make his feelings known to an officer like me.

He seemed to be having trouble getting the words out. I helped him.

'You want to talk about Zac, right?'

'Yeah.' He gave an awkward smile. 'I feel a bit disloyal speaking to you like this. I've always had a lot of time for him, you know that. I think he's a good leader and a good bloke. But I'm worried about what went on today.'

I nodded, saying nothing but encouraging him to carry on.

'Do you think he's losing it?' he asked.

'Do you?' It was a bit cowardly of me to turn the question back on him, but I wanted to know what was going on in his mind before I revealed what was going on in mine. I had a lot of time for Grant. He had emotional intelligence and a natural decency that made me value his judgement. More importantly, he was smart.

'I'm beginning to wonder,' he said. 'Up until this morning you could say we'd just been unlucky. But travelling on the road in daylight.' He shook his head. 'That was a bad call.'

'We got away with it.'

'Just.'

I dropped my caution. 'You're right,' I said. 'I agree with you. That was a pretty silly thing to do. What's worse is he wouldn't listen to anyone. We can't afford to let that happen again.'

'I'm glad you feel the same way,' he said. 'It's a relief. I wondered whether it was just me.'

I thought for a moment. 'Have you spoken to Robbie?'

'Yeah.'

'And?'

'You know Robbie. He whinges a bit but he does what he's told.'

The fact was I didn't really know Robbie. He hadn't been in my platoon. I'd noticed him that night at the boxing match but, until this business, I hadn't had any reason to think about him. He was just another private soldier, and as far as I knew conformed to type. He liked football, lager and girls. Out of uniform he would have looked to the world like any other tattooed chav. I knew better than to underestimate him, though. He was, I was sure, a real professional – all the guys in the regiment were. That was what the army did. It took rough diamonds and polished them up. I would instinctively have trusted Robbie with my life and indeed might well have to. One thing I did know about him was that he was a fully trained medic, a bloody good one by all accounts. Once again I felt the stirrings of inadequacy. Grant and Robbie knew what they were doing. I wasn't so sure I did. And now I had serious doubts about whether Zac did either.

'We've just got to hope this morning was a one-off,' I said. 'He seems to be back to normal now. Let's keep a close watch on him anyway. If you have any worries, tell me. Agreed?'

'Agreed.'

I turned to go. 'Best to keep this between ourselves, though. Yeah?'

Grant nodded.

I walked back to the clump of trees where the others were sitting. Robbie and Majid were chatting to each other. Zac looked up, amused, as I arrived. 'Sit down,' he said. 'This is amazing. It turns out these two practically lived next door to each other.'

'Not really,' corrected Majid. 'I was in Balsall Heath. He was in Highgate. There's a big difference. Ain't that right, Robbie?'

'Yeah,' said Robbie. 'We don't have any Pakis in Highgate.'

'Just blacks,' said Majid.

Robbie laughed. 'Right enough. Anyway, in Birmingham you can live half a mile from somewhere and it might as well be on Mars for all you know about it.'

The hostility between the two of them seemed to have melted, at least for the time being. They were sitting side by side. They were almost exact physical opposites. Robbie was short, his pale skin packed with muscle that would turn to flab if he didn't take care of himself. Majid was a shade taller, skinny and delicate-looking. Robbie's three-day stubble was coarse and gingerish. Majid's whiskers were fine and downy. It must have been a bit of a handicap in a world where bushy beards were *de rigueur*.

Now that he had opened up a little, I took the chance to find out more. 'How old are you?' I asked Majid.

'Twenty-five.'

'Same age as you then, Robbie.'

'I'm twenty-three.' Robbie didn't seem to like the assumption that the two of them had anything more than geography in common. I turned to Majid. 'How long did you live in Birmingham?'

' Not long.'

'Really. You seem to have picked up the accent pretty well.'

'Yeah,' he said cautiously. He seemed to want to drop the subject as well.

A gust of wood smoke drifted over, mingled now with the scent of roasting meat. We might have been on a camping trip.

I changed tack. 'That smells good,' I said.

Zac, though, seemed reluctant to let it go. He looked at Majid. 'So what are you then: an Afghan or a Pakistani?'

Majid said nothing.

Zac laughed softly. 'Come on,' he said. 'It's hardly classified, is it? I'm just curious.'

Majid thought for a bit. Then he smiled. 'A Pashtun is what I am.' He said it with pride. 'My name. Majid. It means "glorious".'

'Does it now?' said Zac. 'Well, it's a long way from Birmingham to here. I'd be interested to hear the story some time.' He left it at that.

I waited to see whether Majid would take the bait. I suspected a streak of vanity in him. He had an eager audience in front of him. The fact that they were his enemies made the attention all the more flattering. I was pretty sure he would find it hard to resist the temptation to climb on to the platform.

'You're right,' said Majid. 'It is a long way.' He looked at the ground as if he was searching for the opening line of his story. I really think that he had made up his mind to tell it, but just then we heard Grant approaching. He was coming towards us holding the wooden shovel that had been lying by the oven. He placed it on the ground in front of us. Ghazala came up behind him and stood by his side.

It was piled with cubes of goat meat, gleaming with hot fat. The smell wakened a hunger in me that was almost painful. I was about to grab a chunk without waiting to be asked when Grant intervened.

'Ladies first,' he said. Ghazala didn't need any encouragement. She crouched down and took a kebab from the shovel. She lifted her veil and popped it in her mouth. I glimpsed a delicately pointed chin, no more. I'd seen her eyes and her chin now. I wondered if I'd ever see her whole face.

And then we all piled in, including Grant the vegetarian. I'd never had goat meat before. It was a bit chewy but it tasted as good as anything I had ever eaten. Everyone was grabbing and chomping away, and in a few minutes the meat was all gone.

'Any more for any more?' asked Grant.

'Bring it on,' said Robbie. Grant went away and returned with another shovel of glistening cubes. This time we took it more slowly. So we sat there, peaceably, savouring the meat, and for a while the only sound was the noise of chewing. The moon was up, huge and mysterious, ringed with a misty halo, hanging in a night sky that was dusted with stars like an advent calendar.

12

'You were telling us about your adventures,' said Zac eventually. 'How you came to be here.'

'I wasn't actually,' said Majid. The last word came out *ackcherly*. It was a strange combination, the Jasper Carrott whine and the jihadi get-up. He carried on chewing, slowly. He seemed to be regretting his earlier informality.

I thought that was the end of that. Then Robbie intervened.

'Suit yourself,' he said. 'But I want to hear what was going on back there.' He nodded in the direction of Ghazala. 'What were you planning to do with her?'

Majid gave a superior smile and shook his head as if Robbie was too ignorant to merit an answer.

'Don't fuck me about,' said Robbie warningly. 'I want to know.'

'Really?' Majid looked up. 'All right, I'll tell you. You might learn something.' He said it in the tone of a schoolteacher imparting wisdom to the class thickos.

'I know how you all see it. She's some poor down-trodden bitch and we're a bunch of murdering women-haters. You lot, of course, are the knights in shining armour.'

That, I thought to myself, just about summed it up, but I kept my mouth shut.

He carried on. 'Well you're wrong. She's not some little innocent. She deserved to die.'

'How's that?' asked Grant calmly.

'She's from a village in Panjwai. You must know it.'

'Yeah,' said Robbie. 'We did a couple of ops there on the last tour.'

Majid looked round. There was no doubt now that he was enjoying the attention. 'Well, a while ago the Canadians started to build a base there, next to her village. They brought in a load of troops to provide security while the contractors started work. Every day they went out on patrol. People noticed that soldiers were always going into the compound where she was living.'

He paused and looked at Ghazala. She seemed to know what he was talking about. She got up and moved away from us, settling down by the wall.

Majid nodded approvingly and resumed. 'Anyway, the neighbours wondered what was going on. They told me – well, not me, I wasn't there at the time, but the local commander – what was happening and our friends started to keep a watch on the place.' He glanced round at his rapt audience. 'In one week the Canadian soldiers went there three times. And each time they had a female with them. An interpreter. Why would they do that?'

We could all, I'm sure, think of perfectly reasonable explanations, but no one offered one.

He carried on. 'Well, after a while, things became clearer. We had someone who knew what was going on in the house. An old woman lived there – a widow.' He nodded in Ghazala's direction. 'Her grandmother. She wasn't from around there – she came from some-where up north. The local people didn't trust her. They thought she was kind of . . . a witch, I suppose. Anyway, our guy told us what was going on. Why the soldiers were going there and what they were after.'

I leaned forward. We all did.

'Which was?' I said.

'The contractors building the fort were foreigners – Indians from the south, nonbelievers. A lot of them were Christians. They weren't happy with the work. They weren't getting paid what they had been told they would and they couldn't get any alcohol or women.'

Majid stopped. He raised his hands and clapped them down on his skinny thighs as if further explana-tion was unnecessary.

'So?' said Robbie. 'Keep going.'

Majid shook his head at Robbie's obtuseness. 'It's obvious, isn't it? The old woman offered the girl to the Canadians for the contractors. In return for money, of course.'

There was a long, uncomfortable silence. Then Grant spoke.

'She told you this, did she?' he asked, reasonably. 'Ghazala did, or her grandmother?'

'Not them,' said Majid irritably, 'of course not.'

'Then who did?'

'Someone who knew.'

'Who?'

Majid shook his head. 'It doesn't matter,' he said.

Grant continued. 'So on the strength of this rumour you were going to take her off and kill her. In public. In front of a camera. Is that it?'

'We're fighting a war,' said Majid reasonably. 'She was a collaborator. She was betraying her people and her religion.' His face lit up as a thought struck him. 'That's what you do to collaborators, isn't it? What's the difference between that and what the French Resistance did to women traitors?'

I was about to object to this comparison, but Grant was already talking.

'What happened to the grandmother, by the way? Why wasn't she there when we ambushed you?'

Majid looked uneasy now. 'She died,' he said quietly.

'You killed her, you mean.'

'No,' said Majid hastily. 'She had some kind of seizure. A heart attack. When they went to arrest her.'

'I see,' said Grant. 'Well,' he continued, mildly. 'It would be interesting to know the full story. Why don't we ask Ghazala?'

'She won't want to talk to you,' said Majid abruptly.

Zac had been keeping quiet, but now he intervened. 'That's for her to decide,' he said firmly. 'Grant. Ask her to come over here, please.'

Majid rolled his eyes at the silliness of this idea. Despite the show of unconcern, though, he seemed uncomfortable with the way things were heading.

Grant walked over to where Ghazala sat propped against the wall. I sensed she had been listening intently to everything, even if she didn't understand what was being said.

There was a brief conversation. She seemed reluctant at first. Then she got to her feet and walked over and sat down. Grant settled protectively next to her. He said something to her in a gentle voice, encouraging her to tell her story, I guess.

She collected her thoughts for a minute or two. Then she started to speak in a low, hesitant voice. She stopped frequently. Grant had to keep prodding her gently with questions to get her to carry on. Even so, the story was thin and full of gaps. She was nineteen years old. She had been married since she was seventeen. After a time she had gone to live with her grandmother in the neighbouring village – why, she didn't say. Her grandmother was ill. She was too sick to leave the house to shop at the market. Ghazala was too afraid to go out often. Whatever had forced her to flee her home made her frightened of the world outside the compound walls. The neighbours weren't any help. They hated the old woman and shunned Ghazala. The pair lived inside their compound like pariahs. When the Canadians came the first time, they told them their story. The soldiers offered to return with food. And so the visits began. Every other day they would bring bread and fruit and sometimes a chicken. That was all there was to it.

Ghazala stopped talking. Majid looked around at us with an apologetic smile as if to say he was sorry she had wasted our time with this nonsense.

Zac took over. 'I just want to clear a few things up,' he said. 'Why did she move in with her grandmother?'

Grant translated. She answered hesitantly.

'She says her husband mistreated her,' he said.

'In what way?' Majid shifted uncomfortably as Grant repeated the question.

'She says he beat her,' relayed Grant.

'They all say that,' said Majid dismissively.

'Because it's true,' said Robbie.

We were all staring at Ghazala now. She looked straight back. Her shyness had gone and her voice was harder now and more defiant. I had a sudden vision of the narrow brown wrists I'd glimpsed when I offered her that first drink, and the pale flash of white.

'Just a minute,' I said. 'Ask her how she got the marks on her wrists.' I held out my hands towards her, palms open to demonstrate. She didn't need Grant's translation for this one. Slowly, her hands emerged from the folds of her burqa. She turned them upwards. Both wrists were striped with scar tissue. She spoke and this time her words sounded fierce and angry.

'She says it's her bastard husband's fault. He made her life such hell that she had no choice but to kill herself.'

'Well, she doesn't seem to have succeeded,' said Zac drily. Grant ignored him. Ghazala was rattling on.

'Anyway, she ran away to her grandmother's but the husband came after her. This time he was going to kill her. He tried to get into the compound a few times but the old woman kept him out. He turned the neighbours against her. In their eyes she had disgraced herself by running away. That's why she was afraid to go out.'

'And how did the Taliban get involved?' I asked.

Grant put the question to her. Ghazala replied, calm again now.

'The husband,' he said. 'After the Canadians turned up, he went off and told the boys that she was a whore,' said Grant.

There was a silence while we digested the story.

'So there you are then,' said Grant. Now that he had stopped translating he seemed to be the one who was most affected by the recital. He turned on Majid.

'You try and make out you're bringing justice to the people. Didn't it occur to you to check anything? It was obviously all bollocks. What Afghan village woman is going to sell herself to foreigners? You must have known her arsehole husband was just out for revenge.'

Majid squirmed. 'I never met him,' he said.

'What?'

'I only heard the story for the first time in the car,' he said. 'I was just along for the ride – with Mullah Zaifullah. They needed someone to translate for the camera crew. It was meant to be a propaganda thing – Zaifullah going back to preach jihad in the heart of Helmand. We picked the girl up on the way. That was the first I heard about an execution.' His voice dropped. 'I just do what I'm told,' he said. 'Like you.' He sounded deflated now, as if he had been fooling himself and Ghazala's testimony had confirmed what he had suspected all along. He got to his feet and, without saying anything, walked away.

'Hey, where are you going?' shouted Robbie, but Majid didn't look back.

'Let him be,' said Zac quietly. He got to his feet. It was clear the evening was over. He looked at his watch. 'It's just gone eleven. We're going to move out at three. I'll take first stag. Robbie, you relieve me at one, will you?' He picked up his rifle and left us.

Ghazala started to clear away the remains of the meal. Grant fussed around beside her. They seemed even more like a couple now.

I took myself off to my tree. Sleep wouldn't come. My head was too full of thoughts. I went over what Majid had said. He didn't seem a very convincing jihadi. He hardly seemed able to convince himself. He had appeared pretty self-assured at the beginning, but he hadn't been able to keep up the front for long. He was more like a student politician than a warrior. The most impressive thing about him was that he was here. He didn't seem to belong. But then neither, of course, did we. I pushed away the thought and tried to get comfortable.

It was no good. I sat up and looked around the compound. Zac was propped up against the west wall, as still as a statue. I wandered over. He glanced up and smiled. I crouched down next to him and looked out over the dark plain, streaked with the mercury glint of the narrow waterways reflecting the light of the moon.

'Hallo Milo.' He pointed at the glittering sky. 'What's that one then?' It was a game we started playing when we were together in Iraq, manning a border post that was supposed to deter Iranian smugglers. We whiled away the long nights trying to outdo each other identifying constellations, but somehow we never got beyond picking out Orion and the Plough with any certainty.

'Easy. The Big Dipper.'

'Bollocks. It's Ursa Major.'

'Don't talk crap. Ursa Major is over there.'

'You are so totally wrong. Thank Christ we've got the compass.' And so it went on for a while, the trading of bullshit back and forth that was our way of showing affection.

Eventually we stopped and just looked at the stars.

'Feels a bloody long way from home, doesn't it?' he said eventually. He sounded wistful. I hadn't heard that note in his voice before.

'It sure does,' I said gently. 'Normally I don't miss it that much. I do now, though.'

'Me too.' He flicked at the trigger.

I yawned.

'Time to get my head down,' I said.

He smiled. 'You do that.' As I moved he laid a hand on my arm. 'I'm glad you're with me, Milo,' he said. 'I'm not going to be able to get through this without you.'

He's the leader. Would he admit this, even to a friend?

I felt touched. Moved even. It was the closest I had ever seen Zac come to admitting that he needed someone. It was only when I shut my eyes that I began to wonder whether that was good or bad.

13

We left the compound at two. The landscape glowed in the light of an enormous yellow moon, bright enough to cast shadows. Dawn came up at six. Travelling at a reasonable pace and taking account of detours, we should be about ten kays closer to safety by daylight. Tomorrow night, if all went well, we could be home. I was in fairly good spirits as we set off.

We marched for an hour in silence, following the line of the river, trying to keep on the straightest trajectory that the paths would allow. We stopped once to fill up with water, then again to watch the pyrotechnics from a distant firefight taking place beyond some hills to the southwest on the far side of the river. Fountains of green and red tracer climbed into the sky and fell away, aimed at nobody, it seemed, followed a few seconds later by the faint popping of rifles and machine guns. Somewhere men like us were fighting men like Majid – or like Majid wanted to be. Whatever was happening seemed unconnected to our fate, as ephemeral and inconsequential as a fire-work display.

The going was easy at first. After two hours, I began

to feel thirsty. I sucked on the Camelbak but the water was warm and rank. We were rationing the Puritabs, using one for every two litres, which increased the chances of a dose of diarrhoea and vomiting – D and V as we called it. D and V was part of the Helmand experience. It sounded innocuous. I was halfway through my first tour before I went down. I hadn't felt too bothered when the first twinges came on. An hour later I was bent double, twisting in agony. It was what I imagined it felt like to be drawn and quartered – as if your nuts were gripped in a slowly tightening vice while your stomach tried to exit your body through your anus.

Zac was leading. Whenever we passed through a straggle of compounds he picked up the pace. Inside my body armour, sweat coursed between my shoulder blades and my pulse was fast and feverish. The dawn seemed premature today. The hills to the east already looked flushed with red. I felt a twinge of fear at the thought of the harsh, exposing daylight. The others seemed to feel it too. I looked at them, heads down, pounding along. We were like a bunch of vampires trying to reach the castle gates before the sun came up.

My body wasn't working properly today. I was already out of breath and overheating. As we arrived at a stretch of open ground at a bend in the path, I pleaded for a breather. Zac agreed reluctantly. As we sank down I noticed a cluster of tall, thin poles, standing out against the sky. Faded flags hung droopily from them, like giant bats' wings. A long-handled spade lay next to a mound of freshly turned earth. We were resting up in a graveyard.

The place gave me the creeps. Despite my grogginess I was not sorry when Zac got us on our feet again. We walked on for another hour through fields and compounds. The people inside the walls must have heard us in the almost perfect stillness. In this part of the world, though, they knew better than to come out and investigate strange noises.

The sun was glowing behind the mountains to the east when Zac called another halt. 'It's getting too risky to stay in the open,' he said. 'Let's get off the path.'

He led us into a maize field and turned down one of the rows in the rough direction we were heading. He was setting a cracking pace. Sure enough, Ghazala was soon in trouble. Her burqa seemed designed to catch on the branches. I felt her frustration as she kept having to stop to disentangle it. I was feeling increasingly frustrated myself. The gap between her and Robbie got wider and wider. There was nothing I could do to help – carrying her wasn't going to make any difference. Zac appeared not to have noticed. He ploughed on at the head of the column without a backward glance.

I was going to have to intervene. Reluctantly, I shouted for him to slow down.

'What is it?' His voice was loaded with exasperation.

'Ease up, will you? Ghazala can't keep up.'

'Jesus. OK, halt everybody.'

We rejoined the back of the column but as soon as we reached it, Zac set off again. Five minutes later I was shouting at him to stop. When we caught up he was glaring at us. 'What's going on?' he said.

'She's doing her best, but it's that bloody burqa. It's like trying to . . .' I couldn't think of a simile. 'Swim in an overcoat,' I finished lamely.

He looked at her coldly. 'She'll have to take it off, then.'

'You can't ask her to do that, Zac.'

'Why not?' he demanded. 'We're saving her fucking life, aren't we?'

I couldn't really argue with that. Fortunately I didn't have to. Zac had turned to Grant.

'Tell her to lose the burqa,' he said.

Grant sighed. 'If you insist. But I know what she'll say. You might as well ask her to strip naked.'

'Just do it, will you?'

Grant obeyed. Ghazala listened, shook her head and said something in reply.

'She won't do it. She says it's best if we just leave her here.'

Majid was watching the exchange with sly enjoyment.

'What's so funny?' I asked.

'Nothing,' he smirked.

I caught Grant's eye. He seemed to be silently urging me to intervene.

I turned to Zac. 'This is getting us nowhere,' I said. 'We're just wasting more time. We can't leave her here and you know it, so let's just get a fucking move on.'

Grant gave me a discreet nod of thanks. Not discreet enough, though, to get past Zac.

'What was that?'

'What was what?' I said, straining to sound innocent.

'What are you two up to?'

'Nothing, Zac. We're not up to anything. Now can we just get on?'

He glared at us. 'You'd better not be. OK. Let's get going. And you – ' he pointed at Ghazala '– had better keep up.'

He stomped off again, but at a slower pace this time. I hoped that meant he had decided against extending the confrontation. Anyway, I was relieved to see bright daylight showing through the green rows of maize, and a few minutes later we had reached the other side of the field.

My relief did not last long. As we emerged from the foliage we were confronted with a broad stretch of flat, open ground. The area seemed to have suffered a mini-drought. There were abandoned compounds scattered across the landscape, but they had sunk to little more than mounds of parched earth. There was no cover at all to speak of. The next stretch of cultivated land looked to be about two or three kilometres away. It was broad daylight now. The next stage of the march would be like walking across a khaki-coloured pool table.

'We're just going to have to go for it,' said Zac. 'We've no other choice.' No one could argue with that. Nonetheless we still hung back, reluctant to leave the protection of the maize.

'Come on,' said Zac. His voice was softer now. 'The quicker we're across the better.' He moved out of cover and set off steadily, cutting diagonally across the dusty field in front of us, heading towards the belt of greenery beckoning to us in the distance. There was a wall running along the far edge of the field with a gateway cut into it. Through it I could see a path, which seemed to run in the direction of the green zone. That made things easier. Once we were on that we could, if we moved fast, be back inside cover in twenty minutes.

We crunched across the baked earth, strung out in a line. I glanced anxiously around. We were the only things moving in the landscape. We must have been visible for miles. Then Zac led us through the gate and we were standing looking down a wide dirt and gravel track. It looked very much as if we were back on the main north–south road.

'You know where we are ?' I said.

'Sure,' said Zac. 'The highway. And the sooner we get off it the better.'

To the right, the road led straight to the cultivated area. We had no choice but to get down it and into cover as fast as we could. Zac led us off at a brisk jog.

I stayed at the back, behind Ghazala, hoping to Christ that she'd be able to keep up. I needn't have worried. She picked up the hem of her burqa and skipped along like the gazelle she was named after.

The sun was already hot and soon I had to wipe the sweat from my eyes to see where I was going. The road ahead was deserted. So were the fields, and seemed likely to stay that way. It didn't look as if anything had grown in them for years. The band of green ahead was getting closer. It stretched into the distance, lush and concealing.

I suppose, as back marker, I should have been more alert. I should have looked behind me more frequently. But I didn't. I was too intent on getting down that road and into cover and out of sight. I can't be blamed for not hearing anything. The noise of pounding feet, the jingle of rifle and webbing and the thumping of my blood in my ears drowned out everything – until it was too late, that is.

The Jeeps were only about two hundred metres behind when I finally heard them. I spun round and there they were, bouncing down the track towards us. I yelled a warning to the others. They turned, slowed down, saw what I had seen and then kept on running.

Zac shouted for everyone to stop. The others halted, reluctantly it seemed. He jogged back to me. The others moved to the side of the road. There was nowhere for us to hide. I stood looking as the vehicles drew nearer, trailing a banner of dust, and tried to control the anxiety tingling inside me.

'Maybe they're harmless,' Zac said. I saw now there were three of them. In the lead was a pick-up and behind it a big SUV. Another pick-up brought up the rear. Then we saw the silhouettes of men with guns standing up in the backs of the trucks.

It was the standard mode of transport for anybody who was anybody around here. They could be Taliban. Or it could be the entourage of some local landlord. There was no way of knowing until they arrived.

They were fifty metres away now. 'Be ready to shoot,' ordered Zac. 'But don't do anything until I tell you to.'

The lead pick-up was slowing down. There were three guys in the back and their rifles were all pointing straight at us. Even if Zac had ordered us to open fire that second, we still wouldn't have had a chance.

The first truck passed us and stopped. The gunmen in the back swivelled round to cover us with their Kalashnikovs. The SUV pulled up neatly alongside us. It was big, shiny and new, a rich man's car. The harsh sunlight bounced off the tinted windows. It was impossible to see who was inside. We stood looking at our reflections in the glass for a second or two. Then, with an electric hum, the passenger window scrolled down, revealing a large man with a glossy, blue-black beard. He smiled, exposing large white teeth.

'Good morning,' he said.

'Good morning,' we chorused back.

'Americans?' he asked politely.

'British,' we said.

'Ah, British. Welcome British! British are my friends!'

Relief flooded through me. I looked around. Everyone was grinning.

The big man seemed to have exhausted his supply of English. He turned away and had a murmured conversation with the driver. The driver listened, nodded, then leaned across to the window to speak.

'Mir Muhammad would like to invite you to his home,' he said. 'It's not far from here.' He was young and clean-shaven and his English sounded excellent.

I looked at Zac. He paused for a moment and glanced at me. I couldn't read his expression. 'Very kind of you,' he said to the big man, carefully. 'Thank you very much.'

Mir Muhammad smiled and settled back in his seat.

The young man took over. He pointed at Zac and me. 'You two can come with us,' he said. 'The others can go in the trucks.'

There seemed to be no room for disagreement. We climbed obediently into the frigid interior of the Jeep and sank into the leather seats. The front pick-up moved off, with Majid and Robbie in the back. Through the windscreen I could see Majid talking to one of the bodyguards.

The young man pushed the automatic shift forward and the SUV surged away. He glanced back at us. His eyes were bright and appraising.

'Sorry, I should have introduced myself,' he said. 'My name is Omar. I am assistant to Mir Muhammad.'

'I'm Miles,' I said. 'And he's Zac.'

'Pleased to meet you,' he said.

He slowed down to negotiate a pothole.

'So what brings you to these parts?'

Zac flashed me a warning look, as if to say, *Leave the talking to me*.

'We're on patrol,' he said.

'Really?' Omar sounded sceptical. 'There don't seem to be very many of you. And who's the woman?'

Zac ignored the question. 'How far is Mir Muhammad's house? I'm saying it right, aren't I? Mir Muhammad?'

'Yes, that's right,' said Omar. 'Mir Muhammad.' He pronounced it reverently. 'He is the biggest landowner in the district. He owns everything that you can see around us.'

We had left the barren area and were among the fields now. They made a startling contrast. It was the most fertile land I would remember seeing in Afghanistan. On either side of the track were vineyards, watermelon patches and orchards. In between were large open fields, with the green shoots of a new crop poking out of the clods and furrows.

'And that – ' Omar pointed ahead where to the left of the road the ochre walls of a large compound showed through the greenery ' – is his home.'

14

The lead pick-up swung left and on to a long, straight drive. At the end was a large gate, flanked by two sentry posts. We crossed a bridge over a fast-flowing river that curved away and disappeared under the compound walls. The big double doors were freshly painted, a cheerful shade of blue. They opened inwards with a squeal as we arrived, pulled back by armed guards.

Behind the high walls, Mir Muhammad had created his own lush domain. We parked beside a broad stretch of bright green lawn and beds of startling red and yellow flowers. Almond and pomegranate trees provided shade and a fountain played underneath a rose-covered pergola. A low flight of marble steps led to a veranda that ran the length of the front of the house.

The guards moved forward to open the doors of the SUV. Mir Muhammad climbed down and walked towards the house.

Omar motioned us to follow.

We climbed the steps and crossed the veranda into the cool interior of the house. A corridor stretched ahead with doors to either side. There were marble slabs on the floor and tiles covered with elaborate calligraphy hung in frames on the wall.

I saw Mir Muhammad's broad back disappearing round a corner. I went to follow him but Omar stopped me. 'No,' he said, 'he'll join you later. In the meantime, you must wait in here.' He opened a door on the left. I walked through, followed by Zac, Grant and Robbie. There was no sign, though, of Majid or Ghazala.

'Where are the others?' I asked.

'Don't worry about them,' said Omar easily. 'They're being well taken care of. Now, how about some drinks?'

We thanked him and he left. As soon as the door shut behind him we all began to talk at once, but Zac shouted us down.

'Shut up everyone,' he ordered. 'Listen to me. This is very important. Don't say anything out of turn. You're to leave me to do all the talking. Understand?'

We nodded obediently. He was charged with confidence now, elated almost. 'If I handle this right,' he said, 'this could be our ticket home.'

I saw Grant looking meaningfully at me. *Here we go again*, I could hear him thinking.

'How are you going to play it, then?' I asked mildly, anxious to avoid any suggestion of a challenge.

'It's simple.' He opened his hands wide, like a politician miming sincerity. 'I'm just going to ask him to do us a favour. Lend us a vehicle to take us to Longdon. His men can provide an escort.'

'What's in it for him?' asked Grant.

Zac smiled at the simplicity of the question. 'Enough to make it worth his while. If he helps us out, the allies will owe him a major favour. And anyway, if that doesn't work, he'll do it for money. I've still got that five thousand. Mind you, it doesn't look as if he's short of a bob or two. Where do you think he gets the cash for all this?' He gestured round the high ceilings and smoothly plastered walls. It was classy by any standards.

'I could have a pretty good guess,' said Grant. 'Did you see all those wheat fields?' I remembered the fresh green crops growing in the fields between the orchards we had passed on the way in. 'I bet they were all under poppy until a few weeks ago.'

Zac turned to me. 'So, sounds all right to you?' He seemed to have sensed our unease and was eager to get my backing.

'Yes.'

'Grant? Robbie?'

They nodded.

And, I must admit, it did sound good. Longdon couldn't be more than twenty kilometres away from here. Mir Muhammad could whisk us there in no time. He seemed friendly enough, and Omar appeared to be a sophisticated guy who would see where advantage lay. I felt a faint tremor of hope. I tried to suppress it telling myself that after all the disappointments I would be a fool to think a light had just appeared at the end of our tunnel. The feeling was too strong though. For the first time since the rescue helicopter had appeared in the sky, God knows how many days ago, I allowed myself to admit the possibility that the ordeal might really be almost over.

Zac was whistling as he unhooked his webbing and sat down at a chair at the rectangular table that stretched almost the full length of the room. It looked as if it was used for *shura*s or banquets. It had small windows set high in the wall, which let in a dim light. He tilted his chair back and closed his eyes. I could imagine what was going on in his head. If things worked out, we could be safe and sound by lunch-time – not exactly conquering heroes, but survivors with a great story to tell. We had a Brummie jihadi as a prize and a young Afghan woman we had snatched from the clutches of the baddies. The media ops would love it. The initial fuck-up would be obscured by a blaze of newspaper and telly publicity, bathing Zac in its golden rays. In the old days it was considered bad form to get yourself in the news. It could set back a promising career. Not any more. Nowadays, a jolt of exposure eased you into the fast lane. It was not surprising that a faint smile had formed on his stubble-flecked face.

I glanced at the others. We were all sunburned, dirty and unshaven. Our uniforms were caked in mud and crusted with dried sweat. There was no way that Mir Muhammad would have been fooled by our nonchalant manner. We looked like the desperate men we were.

The door opened and a team of servants entered. One was carrying a tray loaded with cans of Coke and Sprite. The others laid out plates and glasses. I grabbed a Sprite. The tin was beaded with cold moisture. I popped the tab and gulped. The liquid trickled icily through my guts. It felt incredibly good.

The servants left and returned a few minutes later with trays of food. We were being served a feast. There were steel dishes brimming with chicken livers and lumps of lamb floating in gravy, plates of sliced tomato and okra, bowls heaped with rice studded with raisins, and stacks of flatbread. We looked at it longingly. It seemed impolite, though, to start without our host. And then he was coming through the door, white teeth flashing through his dyed black beard, with his assistant Omar behind him.

'Eat! Eat!' he commanded, and took his place at the head of the table. We shuffled towards his end of the table and obeyed. He chuckled as we wolfed down the food. It would have tasted fantastic, even if I hadn't been starving.

Mir Muhammad took nothing himself. He watched us eating, his brown eyes twinkling. Between mouthfuls we made appreciative noises and waited for the conversation to begin. It was Omar who started it.

'So, gentlemen. You like the food?'

Zac chewed, swallowed and took a swig of Coke. 'It's brilliant. The best I've eaten in Afghanistan.'

Omar looked pleased. 'You look as if you needed it. Have you been out on patrol for long?'

'Long enough,' said Zac casually. 'And that's where I thought you – or rather Mir Muhammad – might be able to help us.'

He looked directly at Mir Muhammad, who was still smiling beatifically at the top of the table like some fraudulent Sixties guru. I noted that his eyes gleamed shrewdly above the mystic grin.

Zac looked hesitant. He held his hands wide in appeal. 'I won't pretend to you. The truth is we've got a problem. The helicopter that was supposed to pick us up has been delayed. It will be a while before it can get here. I wondered whether it would be possible for you to drive us to the base at Longdon. It's not far, as you know. And I'm sure the governor – ' he mentioned the official on whose behalf we were technically serving '– would be extremely grateful.' He smiled. 'We're needed back for a big operation that's going off soon.'

I was impressed. Zac's speech had hit exactly the right note. He'd flattered his host with an appeal to his hospitality and waved a carrot with the mention of the governor. He'd also hinted very delicately at the stick that might be brought into play if the request was not met.

Omar started to answer but Mir Muhammad shut him up with a wave of the hand. I suspected he could understood all that was being said. Local leaders often liked to start off pretending ignorance of English, speaking through interpreters, until they got the measure of their visitors. Now he revealed he not only understood it – he could speak it too.

'Of course,' he said. 'That's easy. No problem at all. Omar, go and find out who is free to take my friends to their home.' Omar pushed back his chair. 'And send Ali to me please.'

'Yes, *malik*,' said Omar and left the room. A moment later a slight figure appeared in the doorway. Mir Muhammad's face lit up in a genuine smile of pleasure. He murmured something in Pashto and a young boy, maybe nine or ten years old, came over and stood behind him. Mir Muhammad took his hand and placed it on his shoulder.

'My nephew, Ali,' he said. The boy looked haughtily at us with his gleaming black eyes and said nothing. Mir Muhammad started to caress the boy's hand and continued talking.

'Don't worry about your friends. They are being well looked after. Who are they, by the way?'

Zac hesitated. I could see he was uncertain about how much information he needed to impart. He plumped for full disclosure. As Zac talked, I watched Mir Muhammad's reactions closely.

'The man is a Talib,' said Zac. 'He's our prisoner. We captured him in an operation not far from here.'

'He must be important,' said Mir Muhammad, sounding impressed.

'*Quite*,' said Zac guardedly.

'So only *quite* important.' Mir Muhammad nodded. 'I see.' And of course he did see. It was obvious. A powerful man like him would have heard about everything that had happened in the area in the last few days – the failed ambush, Zaifullah's getaway, the casualties, the fight at the checkpoint. I tried to work out whether the fact that he already knew the whole story made us more or less vulnerable.

'And the girl?' I could see now that Zac had also caught on to the fact that Mir Muhammad knew perfectly well who she was. He carried on, though, dutifully playing his part.

'We came across her by accident. The Taliban were going to execute her. We stopped them.'

'Good, good,' said Mir Muhammad approvingly. 'And what will you do with her now?'

'I don't know,' said Zac lamely.

Mir Muhammad sighed. 'Trouble, endless trouble,' he said. 'What has my poor country done to deserve this fate? At least here in my home we have some peace.' He glanced at our empty plates.

'But you're not eating.' He mimed dismay. 'Ali?' He issued a command in Pashto. The boy withdrew his hand from Mir Muhammad's caressing paw and left, looking back sulkily at us.

A few minutes later the door opened again and the servants were back with another delivery of steaming plates. My appetite had been well and truly blunted, but I knew we would have to make an attempt to eat.

It was a local torture. Ordeal by hospitality. Custom demanded you to keep on eating as long as the host wanted you to. Mir Muhammad, however, still hadn't touched a thing.

He seemed to be enjoying our discomfort. 'Eat,' he kept urging as we chewed manfully. 'You are soldiers. You must keep up your strength.'

I took the opportunity to divert him.

'Did you do any fighting yourself?' I asked.

'Of course,' he said, chuckling. 'Which Afghani hasn't? I spent my youth fighting the Russians. Then, after they went, fighting my neighbours.'

'And after that the Taliban?' asked Zac.

'No, no.' Mir Muhammad shook his head. 'I had no quarrel with the Taliban. They were our saviours, in the beginning at least. If they hadn't picked a fight with America they would still be in Kabul and this place would be at peace.'

Robbie was starting to look worried. Mir Muhammad must have noticed it too, for he moved quickly to reassure.

'I understand why you have to fight them, of course. You are waging a war against terror and to you they are terrorists. But I must say I find it hard to look at them that way. You see, I know them. I grew up with their fathers and their uncles. To me they are just the young men of the district, who are doing what young men always do. They like to fight - look at yourselves! It doesn't really matter very much to them what they are fighting for.'

His obvious belief that it didn't matter very much to us either hung unspoken in the air.

The smell of the uneaten food congealing in the plates was suddenly nauseating. I glanced at my watch. It was ten o'clock. We had been here more than an hour. Where was Omar? How long could it take to arrange a Jeep and some bodyguards? It was then that I noticed the antenna. Mir Muhammad had on one of those long, camel-coloured waistcoats that Afghan men wear over their shalwar kameez. A black plastic wand was sticking out of one of the pockets. I knew instantly what it was. It was the aerial of a mobile satellite phone. They were called Thurayas and anyone of any importance had one. The mobile phone masts around here were always being blown up by the insurgents, and satphones and radios were the only reliable comms. The Thuraya was a godsend. If we could get our hands on it, in a few seconds we could be speaking to the base. One short call and a helicopter would be in the air and we would be counting the minutes until we were on our way home.

All it needed was Mir Muhammad to hand it over. I looked at it gleaming dully in the half-light. I was just about to ask him for it when I hesitated. Zac had ordered us to leave the negotiating to him. For all I knew the Jeeps might now be waiting for us outside.

I was still agonising when the door opened. Omar came in with a couple of armed men. He said something to Mir Muhammad who rose from the table and went over to them. There was a short, urgent conversation, as if some important news was being delivered. Mir Muhammad listened, concentrating hard on whatever was being said. Then he swept out of the room without a farewell or a backward glance, with the guards following.

We stood up. There was alarm on every face.

'What's happening?' asked Zac anxiously.

'Nothing, nothing,' said Omar, 'sit down, please. Finish your meal.'

'We've had enough, thank you,' said Zac. He was struggling to remain polite. 'We would like to know what's going on. Is the transport ready?'

'Not yet,' said Omar. 'There's a bit of a problem. The men we were going to send with you are working in the fields some way away from here and we can't seem to raise them on the radio.'

'What about the guards outside?' said Zac. 'Can't they go with us?' This time he failed to keep the desperation out of his voice.

Omar shook his head. 'They're needed for other duties. They have to escort Mir Muhammad to a meeting.' He smiled. 'Be patient, please. Your escort will be here soon, I promise. But if you've finished here, I'm going to take you somewhere else where you'll be more comfortable while you wait.'

He motioned us towards the door. We picked up our kit and weapons and filed out. Four armed men were waiting outside. Omar gave an order and two of them led off down the corridor. 'Come with me,' he said. As we set off, the other two guards closed in behind us. We walked back to the front door and then left along the veranda towards the corner of the house. The two guards in front stopped by an open door.

Omar pointed inside. 'You'll be comfortable in there,' he said. 'There are beds. You could probably do with a rest.'

'But how long is this going to take?' protested Zac. 'I thought you said we would be leaving soon.'

'And you will be,' he said. 'Trust me.'

Zac seemed to be bracing himself to argue. Then his shoulders sagged and he stepped over the threshold.

15

We followed him in. The room was lined with wooden *charpoy*s. It looked like a servants' dormitory. The door shut behind us. Then came the ominous click of a key turning in the lock.

'Shit,' I said.

'What do we do now?' said Grant.

'Please,' said Zac wearily. 'Let me think, will you?'

I had a vision of the Thuraya aerial sticking out of Mir Muhammad's waistcoat. 'I should have got the fucking satphone off him when I had the chance,' I said, more to myself than the others.

'What satphone?' Zac was staring at me.

'He's got a Thuraya. Mir Muhammad. Didn't you see it?'

'You twat!' Zac's face was bulging with anger. 'Why didn't you ask for it?'

'Because, *if you remember*, you told us to leave all the talking to you.' I was yelling myself now.

'Calm down.' Grant, the peacemaker, stepped between us. 'The question is, what do you think they're playing at?'

Zac's anger evaporated as fast as it had blown up. 'I don't know,' he said dully. 'Maybe they're telling the truth. Maybe they really are just waiting for the men to arrive.'

'Well, we've still got our weapons,' said Robbie. 'If the worst comes to the worst, we could fight our way out of here.'

'Don't talk bollocks,' said Zac. 'We'd be dead in a minute.' He walked over to one of the *charpoy*s and stretched out.

There was a window next to the door with shutters on the inside to keep out the harsh light. I went over and carefully pulled it open half an inch. I could see a pair of legs sticking out from a chair and a rifle propped next to it. They were obviously taking no chances. I had a good view of the compound. The sun sparkled on the water playing in the fountain. The lawn glowed an unnatural, emerald green. As I watched, the guards by the front gate got to their feet. One of them went over to the big SUV and got in. He started the engine and turned the vehicle round.

'Come and have a look at this,' I said softly.

The others joined me. Zac peered out.

'What's going on?' he asked.

'Wait a minute,' I said. 'I think he's leaving.' Sure enough, a few seconds later, Mir Muhammad trotted down the steps, with Omar a few paces behind him. They walked over to the SUV and climbed in the back. Two pick-up trucks took up station in front and behind. The gates screeched open and the convoy drove through, on to the drive, heading westwards. It seemed likely he was heading for the highway, which ran north to south, a couple of kilometres away.

'Well, that part seems to be true,' said Zac. 'It does look as if he's gone off to a meeting.'

He turned away and went back to his *charpoy*. He lay down on his back with his hands behind his head. 'All we can do now is wait,' he said. A few minutes later he was snoring.

I went to another bed and stretched out. Overhead a fan slowly churned the air. Grant and Robbie were holding a murmured conversation in a corner, out of earshot of the officers. The sight of them triggered a flutter of guilt. I supposed that by now they must both be losing faith in us. So far, Zac had led us from one crisis to another. I had stood passively by and let it happen. Oh well. There was no point in worrying about that now. I started to wander about Majid and Ghazala. I wanted to believe that she, at least, was being well looked after. A big place like this would have separate quarters for the women. Maybe now she was benefiting from some sisterly TLC from the ladies of the house.

The fact was we were completely in the dark. I tried to put myself in Mir Muhammad's place. He owed us nothing. But, like Zac said, self-interest might tell him that his wisest course would be to help us. Our logic was not necessarily his, though. In Afghanistan, you simply never knew which way someone would jump.

I fell off to sleep. When I woke, the light slanting

through the shutters had softened. I glanced at my watch. It was 1600 hours already. I sat up and looked around. The others were still asleep. I lay there for a few minutes, gazing at the patterns the fractured light made on the ceiling. All seemed calm and peaceful. Mir Muhammad was right. He had created a little haven for himself here in the midst of the all the cruelty and madness. Then, faintly in the distance, the sound of engines intruded. The noise got steadily louder and I got up from the *charpoy* and went over to the window. On the far side of the compound the guards were unlatching the gates. They pulled them back and a pick-up drove slowly through, followed by a shiny SUV. Mir Muhammad had returned.

'Wake up!' I shouted to the others. 'He's back.'

In a few seconds they were awake and on their feet. Zac reached the window first in time to see Mir Muhammad's bulky figure climbing down from the passenger seat of the SUV, followed by Omar. We stood back from the window. Then there were foot-steps on the veranda and the sound of the key turning in the lock.

The door opened and a shaft of afternoon sun lit up the room. There were two figures silhouetted against the glare. I couldn't make out who they were. They stepped inside. It was Omar. Standing next to Omar was Majid. They were both smiling.

'I am so sorry,' said Omar. 'Please forgive me. I'm afraid things have not worked out the way we would have hoped. It turns out we will not be able to take you to the base after all.' He shrugged and threw up his hands. 'The men we were going to send with you have disappeared. Typical, if I may say so. Anyway, Mir Muhammad sends his apologies, but you are going to have to get home on your own. We will of course do what we can to help you. You'll need water. We'll bring some right away.'

He paused. 'I'm sure you will want to get on your way as quickly as possible,' he said. There was no mistaking the meaning. He wanted us out of there right away.

'Sure,' said Zac quickly. 'The sooner the better.' He smiled ingratiatingly. 'Before we do, though, I wondered whether I could just ask for one small favour?'

Omar's face clouded. 'Go ahead,' he said cautiously.

'Well,' said Zac, 'I notice that Mir Muhammad has a satphone. A Thuraya. We should have thought of this before, but if we could just have the use of it for a minute we could call for a helicopter to pick us up.'

'Yes,' said Omar. He was smiling again. 'You could, couldn't you? Well, I'll go and put the request to him. In the meantime you should get your things together.'

He turned and left.

'Do you think he'll do it?' I asked Zac.

'How do I know?' he snapped. Then he softened. 'I really hope he does, though,' he said wearily. 'I don't know how much more of this I can take.'

We gathered up our kit and weapons and walked

out on to the veranda. Above the compound walls the sun was sinking in the west. Majid was chatting to one of the guards. They seemed to be getting on well. He glanced round when we came out, and shut up abruptly.

We set our kit down and waited. Above the compound wall the sun was sinking. In half an hour it would be dark. I had been asleep for five hours but I still felt weary. I shuddered at the thought of another night march. Then a man emerged from the house carrying a case of water. Behind him came Ghazala, her sandals slapping on the wooden boards. And behind her was Omar. To my joy I saw he was carrying the Thuraya.

He held it out to Zac. 'Go ahead,' he said.

I saw that Zac's hands were trembling as he took it from him. 'Thank you,' he said, numbly.

There was a white plastic table on the veranda. It looked out of place in the surroundings, the sort of thing you'd get in a UK garden centre.

Zac gestured towards it. 'May I?' he asked.

'Go ahead,' said Omar.

He sat down at it, fished inside his day sack and pulled out the map. He flipped open his notebook, selected a number from a list at the back.

We clustered around him, watching every move. He glanced up. 'Ops room', he murmured, as he punched out a little electronic tune on the keypad. His face set firm as he listened to the ring tone. Then his eyes gleamed and we heard him say, 'Who's that?' followed by 'Hallo Martin. Guess who?'

I imagined the explosion of disbelief and excitement from Martin O'Reilly, the adjutant at the other end. We were all grinning like idiots. My eyes were brimming. I had to struggle to stop myself from whimpering. It was the old Zac we were hearing again now. 'Yes, of course we're OK,' he said impatiently. 'Now stop flapping and listen.' He rapped out our coordinates. For a minute they batted information to and fro.

As they talked, my mind was working furiously through the logistics of a rescue. It was half past four now, an hour until the light started going and just over ninety minutes until darkness fell. Helicopter movements were more risky at night.

Martin O'Reilly had one big failing. He talked a lot. Zac's head bobbed up and down with frustration as he listened. 'Yes,' he was saying, then 'no' then 'I can't really answer that' and finally: 'Look, can you please listen? We haven't got the time for this. We need to get out of here. Now.'

This seemed to have had some effect, for a few minutes later he was nodding and studying the map and saying, 'There looks like a reasonable LZ just to the southwest at . . .' He gave the coordinates. Then: 'OK, 1800 hours. Don't worry. We'll be there.'

He pressed the off switch. Omar had been standing quietly by during the exchange. As soon as the call finished, he held out his hand for the phone.

'Thank you,' he said, as Zac passed it over. Omar stood back and looked us over affectionately, like a good host saying farewell to his guests.

'Well, I'm going to have to leave you now, so this is goodbye.' He waved a hand. 'I wish you a safe onward journey.' I wanted to laugh. The last time I had heard that phrase was on an easyJet flight.

We watched him walk away. 'Right then, boys and girls,' said Zac. 'Let's get going.' We stowed the bottles of water, picked up our kit, and descended the veranda stairs. As we crossed the compound, Ghazala walked beside me. She smelled of soap. She looked up at me and her eyes were smiling as if she was encouraging me to keep my spirits up.

The bodyguards stopped their chatter as we passed, staring at us blankly. At the gate a sentry slid back the bolt and pulled the door, which opened with a sinister screech. We stepped over the threshold and on to the path outside.

16

Zac had picked out a small field about two kilometres southwest of Mir Muhammad's house for the rendez-vous with the helicopter. It looked like a good choice when he showed it to me on the map. It had a row of trees running down one side, which would help the pilot to identify it from the air. It also appeared to be planted with low-lying crops, which ought to make the landing relatively risk-free. You could never completely trust the maps, though. The satellite imagery was always at least a few months out of date and we sometimes found that new crops had been planted and compounds had been built up or knocked down when we came to match the reality to the image. Another thing in the landing zone's favour was that it was nice and remote. There were no houses nearby and we could be in and out before anyone had time to raise the alarm.

We skirted the south wall of Mir Muhammad's compound and took off along a track that led through an orchard. The path stopped at the edge of a large ploughed field. When we started walking across it we found that the sunbaked furrows were as hard as concrete. Ghazala got into difficulties straight away. I saw her stop to retrieve a sandal. Twenty metres further on she lost another. Grant noticed that she was in trouble and turned back. He scooped her up and hoisted her on to his back. She clung on to him and her burqa rode up around her thighs, exposing her white leggings, grimy now with mud and dust.

In the west, the big orange disc of the sun was sinking fast. At last we reached the far side of the big field and arrived at a path that ran along a canal. We walked for ten minutes, through more orchards and vegetable patches, until the track turned sharply to the right. We turned the corner and there in front of us was our LZ. It was in the shape of a rough triangle. Stubble from a recent harvest poked through the dirt. It was a perfect spot for a chopper to put down on.

Half a dozen large eucalyptus trees ran across the far side, their dusty, grey-green branches glowing in the fading sunlight. There seemed to be a gap between the tree line and the field beyond – another path, probably. To the south of the trees stood a cluster of low, mud-brick buildings. They looked like storehouses. You saw them dotted all around the landscape: big sheds, basically, where farmers kept produce before taking it to market.

We reached the field. There was a sort of trench running around it, a dried-out drainage ditch I guessed. It was about three or four feet deep and quite wide and would easily conceal us from any passers-by. We climbed into it and sat down to wait. After a few minutes I asked Zac for the map and the binoculars and stood up cautiously to have a look around.

About two or three kilometres to the northwest I could see the low, grey line of a road standing out from the fields. It had to be the main highway. Nothing appeared to be moving along it. In fact, there was no sign of anyone anywhere. The landscape was dozing in the late afternoon heat. The smell of wild herbs mingled with the spicy scent of baked earth and the loudest sound I could hear was my own breathing.

I looked at my watch. It was 1740. Twenty minutes to go. As I registered the time, I felt a flutter of alarm. Suddenly, the peace and quiet seemed sinister. This was a fertile area. It was the busiest time of the farming year and there was still half an hour of daylight. The fields should have been full of men, women and children, cutting, digging and loading. Where the hell were they? Then, out of the silence, I heard the faint puttering of an engine. I listened hard. It seemed to be coming from the north.

'Someone's coming,' I said. Zac, Grant and Robbie got to their feet. So did Majid. He seemed excited and nervous at the same time. Maybe he was as anxious for this to be over as the rest of us.

'Not you,' said Zac, and pushed him down again.

We strained our eyes in the direction of the noise. It was coming from the northwest, from over towards the road. It wasn't a car and it wasn't a motorbike – it was something in between. Then I recognised it. It sounded like one of the quad bikes used by the richer farmers.

Sure enough, a few seconds later, not one but two quads came into view, bumping down the track that ran behind the line of trees at the far end of the field. We crouched down out of sight and peered over the top of the ditch. I could see them clearly. Each quad had a driver crouched over the handlebars and towed a trailer. The trailers were piled with sacks. There were men perched on top of the sacks, three on each trailer. They looked young and were dressed in the long khaki dishdashas that field labourers wore. They seemed in high spirits, chattering and laughing as they jolted and swayed along.

I relaxed again. It was just a bunch of farm boys finishing up for the day. The tension leaked away. From the cover of the ditch we watched them disappear behind the low mud storehouses to the south of the trees. The engines stopped. The noise of laughter carried over to our hiding place. I pictured them lugging the sacks off the trailers. If those guys are still there in ten minutes' time, I thought, they are in for a big surprise.

The quads started up again. We couldn't see them now but we heard the engines fading as they moved off down the track. We wouldn't have an audience after all. I looked at Zac and grinned. He smiled back and flashed a thumbs-up.

Seven minutes to go. I searched the sky to the south. The blue was deepening to violet as the sun touched the horizon. I couldn't see a thing. Then Grant tapped me on the shoulder and pointed.

'Where?'

It was no more than a black speck, suspended in the middle of the sky. As it got larger I saw two smaller dots hovering above and below. It was them, it had to be, a Chinook with an escort of two Apaches, arriving right on schedule.

Robbie started to get to his feet but Grant pulled him down.

'Relax everybody,' said Zac. Then I heard him say, half under his breath, 'Nearly there, nearly there.'

The dots in the sky were growing. I could make out the twin rotors of the Chinook and heard the faint throb of engines. The three shapes hung in the sky, slowly getting bigger and more real. Then, when they were a mile or so away, the Chinook suddenly plunged into a steep descent, only pulling out when it was less than a hundred feet from the ground and safely below the range at which the warhead of an RPG would detonate. The Apaches stayed high, darting to left and to right, ready to blast any threat with cannonfire and missiles.

Three minutes. I could picture the scene inside the Chinook – the door gunners swinging their Jimpys left and right, the pilot combing the landscape, trying to match the landmarks he had been given to the satellite coordinates.

The helicopter was racing towards us now, the downdraught kicking up a huge plume of dust. It was twisting, pitching and yawing as the pilot tried to reduce the size of the target he presented to the ground and give the gunners maximum arcs of fire. Then, abruptly, just as it was almost upon us, he lifted the nose so the Chinook was almost standing on its tail, using the belly as an air brake to slow the forward velocity. It hung there for a moment or two before sinking down, its rear wheels kissing the ground in a hurricane of dirt, grit and flying vegetation.

We climbed from the ditch and set off trotting towards it. Debris lashed my face and a whirlwind tore at my hair. Just in front of me, Ghazala was leaning into the dust storm, her burqa flattened against her thin limbs. The ramp at the back was fully lowered and the loadmaster stood outlined against the dim light of the interior, waving us forward. I caught Ghazala's arm and dragged her behind me. Grant was leading the way, one arm held up to shield himself from the blast of the rotors, the other clamped to his rifle, and behind him came Zac.

The loadmaster was squatting on the edge of the tailgate now, one hand outstretched, straining to haul Grant aboard. Grant's long arm reached forward. Their hands were almost touching. Then something happened. A look of surprise crossed the loadmaster's face. He raised himself upright and clutched his chest.

He stood there for a second immobile, then toppled backwards on to the ramp.

I didn't hear the shots. They were swamped by the din of the rotors. I saw them, though, stitching along the fuselage, sparking and fizzing. A stream of green tracer flowed around the helicopter, bouncing off at mad angles as it struck metal. I saw the ramp lifting and Grant falling from it. I threw myself down, pulling Ghazala with me. The engine roar rose sharply, climbing the scale until it was a continuous scream. Flattened against the stubble, I watched the wheels part from the ground, then a giant shadow blotted out the dying rays of the sun and when I lifted my head the helicopter was tilting and straining, upwards and away in a shower of tracer.

The first time I had ever come under fire I was pleased to find that after the initial surprise, the crack and buzz of incoming rounds had a strangely bracing effect. My mind cooled and focused. I found I was able to make a dispassionate assessment of the situation, to weigh options, to choose the best one and to act.

I had felt the same throughout every firefight I had experienced since. I did not feel that now. My head swam. My arms and legs ignored my orders. I didn't feel frightened, though. It was worse than that. Fear might have got me moving. Instead I was powerless and utterly resigned to whatever happened next.

It was Ghazala who snapped me out of it. I felt a tug at my arm and looked up to see her flimsy little body crouched next to me. I rolled over and together we scrambled along, bullets cracking and thumping above our heads, and flopped into the cover of the ditch.

The shooting slackened and then stopped. At last the drills kicked in. I pulled my rifle into my shoulder and popped my head up to look for something to shoot at. It was dusk now. The trees on the far side of the field stood out starkly against the pale mauve sky. That was where the fire seemed to have been coming from but there was nothing to see there now. Then, from the southern end of the tree line, I saw a flicker of yellow and half a dozen rounds flew overhead. I sighted down the SA80 and fired three rounds in return. A few seconds later there was another short burst. The shooting was definitely coming from just south of the trees.

The volley was answered by the flat crack of rifle fire off to my left. Someone else was shooting back. I searched the shadows on the eastern side of the field. After a few seconds there were some more single shots and small points of muzzle flash appeared in the gloom.

'Is that you, Zac?' I shouted.

'Yeah,' he yelled back. 'Where are you?'

'Over here. In the ditch. Back where we started.'

There was a pause, then another gust of automatic fire swept across the field.

'Wait there,' called Zac. 'We'll come and join you.'

A little later there was a scuffling to my left and Zac was crawling towards me. Grant was just behind. I felt pathetically relieved. There were only two of them, though.

'Where's Robbie?' I asked. 'And Majid?'

'We thought they must be with you,' said Zac. 'They were right behind you when I last saw them.'

'They can't be far,' said Grant. He cupped his hands and yelled Robbie's name. There was an immediate burst of automatic fire from the trees in response.

As the echo of the rounds faded, a familiar voice drifted over from the direction of the trees.

'Grant you useless twat! Where the fuck are you?'

'We're here,' shouted Grant. 'In the ditch, straight in front of you.' The yell was followed by another squall of fire, this time right over our heads.

'OK, that's enough,' said Zac testily.

A few seconds later, we heard Robbie's voice again. 'OK,' he called. 'Don't move. I'll come and find you.'

We peered over the top of the ditch towards the line of trees. There was another longer burst, and this time the stuttering yellow flashes from their Kalashnikovs gave away their position.

'They're in the storehouses,' I said.

'How did they get there?' asked Zac.

I remembered the jolly farm boys. 'On the quads,' I said. 'We *heard* the bikes leave. But we didn't see them. We just assumed those guys went with them. Quite clever really.' It was more than clever. The Talibs had suckered us brilliantly. They had moved into position right under our eyes, with their weapons, no doubt hidden underneath the sacks. The obvious question swam into my mind.

'How did they know we were there?' I knew the answer as soon as I said it.

'Fucking Mir Muhammad,' said Zac bitterly.

There was no time now to reflect on the treachery of our host. I was suddenly aware of a low buzzing overhead. I remembered the two Apaches which had escorted the Chinook in. I looked up but couldn't see anything. Even in daylight, attack helicopters often flew too high to be visible. It sounded, though, as if there was still at least one in the area.

'Hear that?' I pointed upwards.

Zac and Robbie nodded.

So they hadn't abandoned us completely. Somewhere above us a pilot was quartering the area, staring down at the screen on his console that picked up the heat signature from every living thing that moved on the ground below. The six of us would show up clearly, outlined in cathode rays like shimmering green amoebae. The Talib gunmen would show up just as clearly too. The pilot had only to roll a cursor on to the shapes wriggling on the screen, press the button and, seconds later, without any bang or comet streak of flame to announce the arrival of death, a Hellfire missile would explode among them.

The problem was, he had no idea which glowing cluster was which – which was us and which was the enemy. Unless he could positively identify his target, there was nothing he could do. Without a radio, there was nothing we could do to help him.

Suddenly there was another roll of fire, louder and uglier than before, and the dirt in front of our trench was whipped into a curtain of dust. I knew that sound. It was the industrial hammering noise made by a heavy-calibre Dushka, the machine gun they had used to try and bring down the Chinook. It was followed by the flat bang and whoosh of an RPG round, which streaked through the darkness and exploded some-where behind us.

They must have heard the Apache. But its presence obviously didn't bother them. That was unusual. Normally, the Taliban were shit scared of Apaches. Perhaps, I thought, Mir Muhammad had told them that we had no radio with us and that they had nothing to fear? How could we have been fooled by his greasy smile and phoney hospitality?

The flurry of fire was followed by a creepy silence. Apparently, they had decided to take their time. The quiet just made things worse.

Zac turned to me. He was breathing hard and his eyes were red-rimmed and desperate-looking. 'We'll have to make a break for it sooner or later,' he said. 'Where the hell's Robbie?'

It was my turn to yell his name. This time there was no reply, just another long volley from the Dushka directly towards us that sent us diving for the bottom of the ditch.

Then his voice carried plaintively across from the tree line.

'I'm still here,' he said. 'I'm not sure I can move right now. I've got a bit of a problem. Can someone come and give me a hand?'

'Are you hurt?' I shouted. Before he could answer there was another burst from the Dushka.

'Just get over to him, will you?' said Zac sharply. 'He seems to be in among the trees somewhere. You should be able to work your way round to him if you go along the ditch.'

I scuttled away, crawling on all fours. The ditch ran the length of the field towards the northern end of the tree line. After ten metres or so, I raised my head for a cautious look. I could see the nearest storehouse quite clearly. The buildings were less than a hundred metres away. There was no sound and no movement. For a foolish second I thought that the Talibs might have decided to pack it in for the night, then the quiet was ripped apart by a stuttering burst from the Dushka. The tracer seemed to be coming from the nearer storehouse.

Afghans tend to be pretty extravagant with their ammunition, blasting away until they run out. Whoever was on the Dushka, though, was a model of restraint. He fired short, economical bursts that would have earned him a clap on the back from our weapons instructors.

I pushed forward a bit further. I was now almost at the corner of the field. Ahead, the ditch took a left turn, running parallel to the tree line and the path the quads had taken to the storehouses. I turned into it. There, crouched in the darkness five metres away, was Robbie.

'Hallo mate,' I said. 'Are you all right?' My voice sounded horribly loud. He put a finger to his lips.

I drew closer. He raised his head a fraction above the parapet of the ditch. Slowly I followed suit.

'See that?'

A body lay stretched out on the field in front of us, immobile, about fifteen metres away.

'Majid?' I whispered

'Yeah. He made a run for it when the shooting started. I can't tell whether he's dead or just hurt.'

I remembered now how Majid had seemed excited by the arrival of the quad bikes. Had he known what was going to happen? It didn't really matter right now. Whether he had or hadn't, I felt no great urge to go to his rescue. The only thing that concerned me was our – and particularly my – survival.

'Looks like he's had it to me,' I said quickly. There was no way I was going to check. 'Let's get out of here.'

'We can't just leave him without making sure,' he said.

'Yes we can.'

'All right, then.' He sounded disapproving. That was a surprise. It hadn't occurred to me that Robbie would give a toss about Majid's fate.

I turned to crawl back in the direction I had come from. As I did, Majid's beseeching voice drifted over.

'Help me. Please, for God's sake, someobody help me.'

My heart sank. Why couldn't he have done me a favour for once and stayed looking dead enough, long enough, for me to get away?

Robbie had his hand on my arm. 'We've got to do something,' he said.

There was a warning as well as an appeal in his look. I could imagine how Zac would take the news that we had left his prize captive to die – not to mention how it might look at any inquiry.

'OK,' I sighed. 'You win.' We lifted our heads tentatively above the edge of the ditch again. Majid lay there as inert as a sack of rice. Right on cue, he let out a dramatic groan.

Fortunately I didn't have to order Robbie to do what he knew I was extremely unwilling to do myself.

'I'm going to get him,' he said. 'You cover me. But don't fire unless you have to. With any luck I can get to him before they see me.'

17

Robbie slipped out of the ditch and rolled into the field and began to drag himself on his elbows through the stubble. He was a few metres from Majid when the Dushka gunner spotted him. The first burst overshot by four or five metres. The next one fell short. Robbie knew very well where the next one would hit because he stopped crawling and jumped to his feet and sprinted like crazy over the last few metres.

I had my rifle at my shoulder and banged away in the direction of the muzzle flashes. I didn't have much hope of hitting anyone but it must have been close enough to force their heads down because the third burst never came. Robbie, meanwhile, was working frantically, hooking his hands under Majid's armpits and hauling him backwards, one agonising heave at a time.

I fired nine or ten rounds before the gunner started up again. The heavy bullets flailed the dirt a few feet away from Majid's trailing legs. In a few seconds they were sure to hit him. I steeled myself for the sight. Big calibre bullets had an extraordinary effect on human flesh. I had once seen a sniper take out a Talib with a fifty cal. A single round sent him cartwheeling ten feet in the air.

The Dushka's bullets, though, were falling short. I guessed the gunner's field of fire was blocked by the nearside storehouse. With every heave of his beefy shoulders, Robbie was dragging Majid a metre nearer to safety, while the rounds kicked the ground frighteningly but harmlessly in front of him. Then, with a last effort, he fell backwards into the ditch pulling Majid down on top of him.

He crouched beside me, panting. Majid rolled off him and lay on his back. I raised my head and searched for a wound. I couldn't see any blood anywhere. Robbie took over, crouching over him and running his hands expertly over his limbs.

'Nothing broken,' he said. He took Majid's wrist between finger and thumb.

'Pulse is OK too.'

His eyes were closed. As Robbie's hands began a careful exploration of his head, they opened. They were full of pain and fear.

'You're going to be OK mate,' said Robbie gently. 'Just take it easy. We're going to get you out of here.'

He turned Majid's head a little to the side, feeling the back of his skull. Majid winced. When Robbie withdrew his hand I could see the fingers were dark with blood.

I looked at him. 'Time to go.'

He nodded.

'I'll take his arms. You take his legs.'

I grabbed Majid under the armpits and Robbie picked up his ankles and we staggered to our feet. The ditch was filling with smoke. The tracer from the Dushka had set the stubble smouldering. That was good. It would be harder for the gunners to see us now.

We set off, half crouching, along the ditch, with Majid sagging between us. We tried to be careful but it didn't make much difference. His head kept banging against the sides of the ditch and every time it did he yelled in agony.

It took only a few minutes to reach the others. We laid him down. Robbie retrieved his medical pack from his day sack and resumed his examination. The hair on the back of Majid's head was matted and black with dried blood.

'What do you reckon?' I asked.

'Can't say for sure,' he said. 'All I can do is clean him up and stick a dressing on him. But it doesn't look to me like a bullet wound. More like a bash on the head.' He got busy and I crawled around him and over to Zac.

It was quiet again. I realised that I could no longer hear the drone of the helicopter. I looked upwards.

'He's gone,' said Zac. 'Must have been low on fuel.'

A few seconds later, the Dushka started up again. It was followed by a bang and whoosh and an RPG flew out of the dark. It hit the rear wall of the ditch six or seven metres away. The blast made the air wobble.

'Jesus that was close,' I said. 'It really is time to move,' As soon as we left the ditch, though we would be right in the arcs of their guns. Even if we managed to crawl out of the line of fire and make a run for it over the open ground to the east or the tree line to the west, the chances were that there would be more of them, waiting there to cut us off. We couldn't just lie here, though, until we ran out of ammunition. I started to consider what would happen if we surrendered.

It had never happened before. No British soldier had ever waved a white flag in Afghanistan. Mercifully things had never got that desperate. It didn't take much imagination to work out what would happen to anyone who did. The best outcome would be a quick, clean execution. That wasn't very likely though. They would want to keep us alive. We would come in very handy next time they tried to get some of their guys out of prison. We would also make brilliant propaganda.

I imagined myself in front of the video camera, denouncing the occupation and pleading for my life. I could see my mother and father and my friends and old girlfriends watching me with a mixture of pity and embarassment. I had never thought of myself as particularly brave but I was brave enough to think that death was preferable to that humiliation. I felt my courage swell inside me. Fuck them. I was going to go down fighting.

Zac's voice broke in. 'Get ready to move,' he said.

'Where are we going?'

He didn't reply but turned to the others, who were now both tending to Majid. 'You two. Stop that and get over here.' They shuffled closer. 'Here's what we're going to do,' he said.

He looked hard at each of us in turn. 'The one thing they won't be expecting is for us to come straight at them,' he said. 'So that's what we're going to do.' He turned to me. 'Miles. Take Robbie and move up on the right flank. I'll go with Grant on the left. Now Robbie.' He put a hand on his shoulder. 'A lot depends on you. I'm relying on you to start taking these bastards out from the rear. You're going to have to get behind their position. If you can knock enough of them down it will give us a chance to rush them from the front.'

He sounded reassuringly bold and confident. 'If this works, we're all in line for a gong. Fucking VCs if I have anything to do with it.'

Robbie nodded to himself, psyching himself up. All we had between us were our rifles and a few grenades. His sniper rifle was our only serious weapon. Stuck here in the ditch, though, he had no chance of using it. So far, the men who were firing at us had kept well inside the cover of the storehouses. To be effective he had to have a clear shot. If we could move beyond the arcs of their fire and manoeuvre beside or behind them, he might just get one.

Zac slapped the butt of his rifle.

'Let's go,' he said.

I squeezed past Majid and Ghazala. He was sitting up now, gulping water from one of the plastic bottles Omar had given us as a parting gift. He seemed OK to me.

Robbie was ahead of me as we crawled along the ditch and turned into the dogleg. The stubble fire had died out but a haze of smoke still clung to the field. It was quiet. The Talibs had seen the helicopter leave and were probably getting ready to close in and finish us off. Even so, they would be sensible to take their time. If I was their commander, I thought, I would order the guys I suspected were blocking our escape routes on either side and behind to come forward and close the net around us.

I poked my head above the edge of the ditch. The storehouses were only seventy or eighty metres ahead. Nothing was moving.

'See over there?' I said to Robbie, pointing off to the right.

'There's a path behind the trees. It runs past the storehouse. If we can get across it without being seen, we can take cover in the cornfield and move up on them from behind.'

'Sounds good.'

We slipped out of the ditch and between the trees. On the far side of the path was a field planted with waist-high crops. I glanced down the path. The trees obscured the view of the outhouses. The fact that we couldn't see them didn't necessarily mean they couldn't see us. It was too late to worry about that now.

'Three, two, one, go!'

We jumped up and darted across the road and into the bushes and lay there rigid for a few seconds, bracing for the zip of bullets and the patter of falling foliage. Nothing happened. We relaxed. The plants gave off a powerful, herby smell. The leaves were long and spiky. Marijuana. Every male around here smoked it. The Afghan guys we sometimes fought alongside liked to go into battle stoned.

We crawled ten metres further and reached the edge of the field. We lay half in and half out of the vegetation and studied the landscape. A stretch of open ground lay ahead. Across it and to the left, about forty metres away, were the storehouses. They were low and square with flat roofs. There had been eight men all together on the quads and trailers. It needed two men to drive the bikes away. That left six. I was pretty sure I could make out one of them now, stretched out on the roof of the nearest storehouse. The man on the Dushka, perhaps, though I couldn't see a machine gun.

I was about to point him out to Robbie but he was already shifting the long barrel of the rifle towards the shadowy outline. He glanced over and winked. It was an easy shot. That would take care of one of them. That still left five more to worry about.

He looked questioningly at me, asking for the OK to shoot. I was about to nod when I heard a grating noise. A door opened in the side of the nearest storehouse and a figure emerged. He walked round to the back and balanced on the balls of his feet facing the wall. He lifted up the front of his dishdasha, pulled down his pants and started to piss.

Robbie glanced at me again.

'OK, now,' I said, softly. 'Take the guy on the roof first.' There was no way he could miss. The shot sent him flying. He hung for a second, suspended in mid-air, his dishdasha puffed up like a parachute, as he flopped to earth. At the thump of the gun the man on the ground spun round to face us. The next shot slammed him against the wall as if he had been punched by a huge fist. I took a grenade from my webbing, gripped the lever and pulled the pin. We got to our feet and ran.

I could hear firing out on the far side of the outhouses but nothing was coming our way. My rifle was in my left hand and the grenade in the other. Pure rage flooded through me. For the first time in my life I was fighting mad. I screamed as I ran. I skimmed across the path, past the dead Talib, straight towards the open door. When I was a few metres away I bowled the grenade underarm into the dark interior and threw myself against the wall. Robbie cannoned past me and collapsed alongside. I heard panicky yelling. I imagined the desperate scrabble for the grenade. Then came a great thud and smoke and dust belched from the doorway.

I was shaking and soaked with sweat. I got up and ducked under the doorway. It stank of burnt powder. A body was flung out on the ground. Another was half lying against the wall facing me. His eyes were open. I put two rounds through his head and backed out.

Robbie was crouching at the corner of the outhouse, peering out. I stood behind him and caught my breath, then peered, cautiously, out. Automatic rifle fire was spurting from the second outhouse, northwards, across the field towards where Zac and Grant should now be. I couldn't see them – no silhouettes, no muzzle flashes. I imagined they must be lying flat out in the darkness. We were in no position to help them. The shooters were well protected inside the thick mud walls of the outhouse. There wasn't an opening on this side that I could chuck my remaining grenade through. There had to be an entrance somewhere – on the far side, maybe. I signalled to Robbie to follow me and walked round to the back. The ground was wet with blood.

We dashed across the short gap between the two buildings and into the cover of the back wall. There was no doorway. That meant it was either on the far side or round the front. I pulled the pin from the last grenade, gripped the lever, and launched out of cover. As soon as I turned the corner I saw that there was no entrance on this side either. That left only the front. I edged along the wall with Robbie behind me. The men inside were putting down a steady rate of rounds, methodically, in economic bursts of four and five shots. I reached the corner and peered round. The ground in front was flat and featureless, except for a dark shape in the middle distance. After a few seconds I realised what it was. It was some kind of old vehicle, a van or a pick-up, that had been left to rust in the fields.

I saw a flicker of yellow to one side of it and rounds smacked into the front of the storehouse. Zac and Grant were firing. They had taken cover behind the wreck. I heard excited voices coming from inside and tracer streamed out across the field. Several rounds clanged off the vehicle in a shower of sparks. Zac and Grant were pinned down. Unless I could take out the Talibs in the next few seconds, they were certain to be hit.

I could see the entrance to the storehouse now. It was square in the middle of the wall. There was a window on the far side. It was from there that they were shooting. I held up my free hand to Robbie, motioning to him to stay put. I dropped down and crawled along the front of the storehouse, past the doorway, with the grenade in my right hand. The opening was only a body's length away. My heart was thumping and I had to fight to control my breathing. I could see the cutaway tip of a Kalashnikov barrel poking from the window. As I watched, it jerked and flamed and spat a short burst. My fingers were clamped tightly round the grenade lever. My palms were slippery with sweat. I breathed in, pulled myself up and flipped the grenade through the opening. I heard it bounce, then, as I scrambled back, a shout of alarm and the sound of violent movement.

I looked round just in time to see a dark shape flying out of the opening – my grenade. It landed just in front of the outhouse and exploded in a sheet of flame. The blast sent me staggering back. Robbie grabbed my arm and together we scrambled away from the storehouse and into the shelter of a broken wall that lay ten metres to the right.

We raised our heads in time to see that Grant and Zac had left the cover of the vehicle. They were on their feet and racing forward towards the outhouse. Rounds bounced around them. I banged away at the muzzle flashes flickering in the opening, and Robbie joined in with his rifle, knocking great chunks from the wall.

Grant and Zac were still coming. Grant was in the lead, his rifle in one hand and a grenade in the other. Zac was right behind. I saw him stagger, right himself, and rush on. I was firing as fast as I could pull the trigger and Robbie's rifle was barking and big lumps of mud were flying from around the window.

Ten metres from the wall, Zac staggered again, and this time he fell. Grant galloped on, tracer slicing the air around him. His arm went back, whipped forward. The dark grenade flew, bounced on the sill and dropped through the window. There was a flash and a deep, sinister thud. Smoke gushed from the opening. Grant was at the wall now and threw a second grenade through the hole. There was another blast and the door flew open. A deep, obliterating silence rolled in. It was followed by a loud singing in my ears. I looked around. Grant was collapsed against the wall, his eyes blank and his chest heaving. Zac sat on the ground nearby. His helmet had gone and he was rubbing his eyes.

I went over. His face was twisted with pain. I crouched down next to him.

'Are you hit?'

He nodded and pointed to the wet patch, black in the darkness, glistening at the top of his thigh.

'Robbie!' I shouted. 'Get over here.'

We carried him into the lee of the wall. Robbie ripped open his trouser leg and began prodding and pushing.

'Jesus! Careful will you?' yelped Zac.

'Sorry boss,' mumbled Robbie. He turned away, rummaged in his day sack and produced a field dressing.

I looked into Zac's eyes. They were blurring in and out of focus. He tried to talk but all that emerged were a few disconnected words.

'Find his morphine,' ordered Robbie.

I tore open his shirt and pulled out one of the two auto-injector pens hanging round his neck. Robbie snapped off the shield and stuck the needle into his good leg.

Grant had joined us now. His face was blackened with smoke and his shirt was torn and sweat-soaked.

'You OK?' I asked.

He nodded. 'Glad that's over,' he said. He stared down at Zak's slack, unconscious body.

'Looks like you're in charge now.'

So I was. I moved away. I struggled to think straight. I was still breathing in panicky bursts. I tried to calm down. What were we going to do now? Every fucking insurgent in Helmand must be on his way here. We had to leave immediately – to where didn't matter, but we had to move fast. That was going to be bloody difficult, now we had Zac as a burden.

I turned back to the others. 'Time to move,' I said. 'We'll just have to swap around carrying him.' I pointed to Zac, who had a look of stoned contentment on his face. 'You two start, will you.'

'Sure,' said Grant. But as he bent over to pick him up he hesitated.

'What about the others?' he said.

'Who?' I had no idea what he was talking about.

'Majid and Ghazala.'

I had completely forgotten about them. We'd left them back in the ditch. They would have heard all the racket and were no doubt wondering whether we were dead or alive. There was no way I was going to waste time going back for them.

'Forget it,' I snapped. 'They'll just have to take their chance.'

Grant looked at me coldly. It reminded me of the expression I had seen not very long before on Robbie's face.

'You're the boss,' he said.

He bent down and hooked his hands under Zac's shoulders. Robbie grasped his ankles.

The fire in the storehouse had really taken hold now and burning straw was dancing crazily in the scorched air. I had a last glance back and started walking. I had only gone a few metres when Grant shouted at me to stop.

'What is it?' I spun round.

He was pointing back beyond the burning buildings. I couldn't see a thing through the smoke and the shadows thrown by the leaping flames.

'Just fucking move it, will you?' I yelled, and stomped on.

But now Robbie was shouting too. 'Look! There!' he said.

I turned again. Thirty metres away, two shapes were emerging from the ditch.

The taller of the two was waving his hands and was shouting something in Pashto.

I shouted to the others to get down. We dropped to the ground and I raised my rifle and sighted it on the lead figure. I was just about to pull the trigger when Grant put a restraining hand on my shoulder.

'It's Majid and Ghazala,' he said. 'It looks like they're coming with us after all.'

18

The funny thing was that I was quite relieved to see them. I'd known as soon as I said it that it was a mistake to leave them behind. As they stumbled towards us through the smoke and the flame, I finally grasped something that Zac, Grant and Robbie already understood. We had to bring them back alive. It was the only thing we would have to show for what we had been through. I could think of all sorts of justifications for abandoning them, that would sound plausible enough if we ever made it home. They wouldn't wash with the others and not even with myself. There was no way round it. It was a betrayal. The guilt would always be there, buried deep most of the time no doubt, but never quite dissolving.

The relief at seeing them again didn't last long. I felt now the full weight of the burden pressing down on me.

I was in charge. There was no Zac to blame if things went wrong.

I looked at them struggling frantically towards us. Majid was in front. He was hobbling and the bandage around his head was flapping loose. He was shouting something unintelligible.

He stopped ten metres away from me. I scrambled to my feet.

'Oh, it's you,' he said.

'Who did you expect it to be?' I asked.

He didn't reply and then it dawned on me. He wasn't sure. All he knew was that there had been a battle. Hiding back there in the safety of the ditch, he would have had no idea of who had won it. Maybe he was hoping we'd lost and he could hook up again with his Taliban comrades. I remembered how chummy he had been with Omar and the guards back at the compound. It struck me that he must have known something about the ambush. Well, he was stuck with us again now.

Grant went forward to meet him. 'How's your head?' he asked. He tucked away the flapping end of the bandage.

'All right, I suppose,' Majid replied. He sounded dazed.

Grant nodded towards the girl, standing a few paces away. 'Thanks for taking care of Ghazala.'

'She just tagged along,' said Majid. 'Nothing to do with me.'

'Well,' said Grant gently. 'No one got left behind, that's the main thing.'

The smoke from the burning buildings was stinging my eyes. I was desperate to get moving.

'Let's get the fuck out of here,' I shouted. Now Majid was with us again he could pull his weight. That would free up Grant to act as point man, ready to react when the Talibs attacked, which I was sure they would any minute. I would bring up the rear. 'You. Majid. Give Robbie a hand with him.' I pointed at Zac who lay stretched out unconscious on the ground. 'Grant. Lead on, will you?'

'Sure,' he said calmly. 'But which way are we heading?' His composure was starting to bug me. There was only one route out as far as I could see. I was still assuming the ambushers would have men behind and on either side of us to block off our retreat. We had no choice but to press on, straight ahead towards the highway and the river.

'Straight on,' I ordered.

We had to wait while Majid and Robbie struggled to lift Zac. As they took the first stumbling steps, he hung jack-knifed between them, his head rolling from side to side. I picked up his rifle and day sack and we left the burning storehouses behind us and crossed the path into an open field.

We moved extremely slowly. Zac was not that big but he was a dead weight. Robbie had his shoulders, Majid his feet. Majid was panting and swearing. He soon lost his grip and Zac's legs thudded on the ground.

'Sorry man, but he weighs a ton,' said Majid, looking at me. His nasal voice was almost apologetic.

'OK, step aside,' I said. 'I'll carry him.'

I handed the two rifles I was carrying to Grant and lifted Zac's legs. The field dressing seemed to have stemmed the bleeding. The wounded leg, though, was caked with drying blood.

We shuffled along a little faster. My only plan was to get as far away from the ambush scene as we could before our strength gave out. Then we would find somewhere to lie up and work out what to do next. I fought to damp down the dejection welling up inside me. We were on our own again. We had no food and most of our ammunition had gone in the fight. We were close to exhaustion and were carrying the burden of a badly wounded man. I had tested myself a few times in my life, but I'd never faced a major challenge that I hadn't planned for. Now I was looking at one that would have frightened anyone. I didn't want it. But there it loomed, huge and inescapable and, if I failed it, I would die and so would all the people I was now responsible for.

I glanced back over my shoulder at Zac. His head was lolling back and his eyes were closed. He looked childish and vulnerable. I had nursed some hard feelings towards him these last few days, and come close to hating him sometimes. Now all I felt was pity and a determination to get him home alive.

But Jesus, that was going to be difficult. Zac was not a big man, but it was like lugging a sack of stones. I had a stabbing pain in my back and the tendons in my arms burned with the strain. There was no way we would be able to carry him two kilometres, let alone the fifteen to twenty I reckoned we would probably have to cover before we reached Longdon. Robbie, one of the strongest and fittest guys I had come across, was already huffing and puffing.

'How's it going?' I asked.

'So so,' he said grimly.

I was about to say something encouraging but saved my breath.

We reached a broad track that ran between some fields and turned left, which put us on a heading due south. Over to the right I could see the dim line of the hills on the far side of the big river. We had only moved about three or four hundred metres from the storehouses. The light from the fires still danced against the sky behind us. I needed to stop, though. My back and arms were throbbing. I called a halt.

'Thank Christ for that,' said Robbie as we lowered Zac gently down.

'Two minutes, no more,' I said, and took the map and compass from Zac's day sack. The path ahead ran parallel to the highway on the eastern side. It led almost all the way to Longdon. The danger was that it passed through a string of villages that straggled along the roadside.

I glanced across to the hills and the river that flowed below them. The river was the only part of our world that ever felt any good to me. The desert was ugly and cruel. Only a liar could claim to see any beauty in it. The green zone was bursting with life. From a distance it looked benign; *bucolic* was the word that sometimes came to mind. But inside it was full of danger and deadly surprises. The river was clean and unthreatening. It felt somehow familiar. With its shoals and banks it looked a bit like the big French rivers, the Loire and the Dordogne, where I'd spent a few summer holidays with my parents when I was a kid. Standing there in the heat of the night, while the others stretched and drank, the river felt like deliverance. I felt a sure instinct that the closer we stuck to it, the better our chances would be.

I took a slurp from the bottled water I'd poured into my Camelbak at Mir Muhammad's. It tasted pure, sweet almost. It seemed like a good sign.

'Right,' I called. 'Let's be on our way.'

Robbie and I changed places. I slipped my hands under Zac's shoulders and felt the damp heat of his armpits. He groaned as we lifted him up. Grant led off, with Ghazala close behind. Majid was next in line but, as the others trudged away, he stayed where he was, looking into the fields.

I wasn't in the mood for any further bullshit. 'Oy, you,' I said. 'Get going.'

He didn't seem to hear me. I shouted at him again and he looked round.

He held up a hand. 'Wait a minute,' he said. 'I've just seen something.' He walked to the side of the path and scrambled over a low mud wall. I shouted at him again but he ignored me and set off jogging across the bare field on the other side.

We were all yelling at him now but he kept on running. He seemed to be heading towards a cluster of sheds and a jumble of what looked like farm machinery, tucked in the corner of the field about fifty metres away. I looked at Grant. He seemed as baffled as I was. There seemed to be no point in him making a run for it now. Anyway, we couldn't waste any time chasing after him.

'Fuck him,' I said. 'Let him go.' I felt sad when I said it. Half an hour ago I wouldn't have given a toss. It would have been one less thing to worry about. But things had changed since then. The job we had set ourselves would not be completed. Zac's prize was lost.

I took a last look at him trotting across the bumpy stubble. As he approached the sheds he speeded up. Then the shadows swallowed him and we lost him.

'Well, that's the last of Majid,' I said and turned away. I bent down and raised Zac's shoulders.

'Come on, Robbie,' I said. 'Give us a hand.'

But Robbie was still staring off into the fields.

'Come on,' I repeated. 'Grab his feet, for Christ's sake.'

Grant was staring too now.

'Put him down,' he said. He beckoned to me. 'Look over there. You're not going to believe this.'

I lowered Zac's feet and stood up.

Majid had reappeared. He was coming across the fields towards us and he was pushing something in front of him.

It took me a few seconds to see that it was a wheelbarrow.

'Brilliant,' shouted Robbie. 'What a fucking star!'

Majid was trotting now and the barrow was bouncing in front of him over the uneven ground. When he reached us he was grinning with delight.

'This should speed things up, eh?' he said. 'Stroke of luck. I saw something propped up against the wall over there. Thought it was worth a look.'

'Well done, mate,' said Robbie, and clapped Majid on the shoulder.

Majid shook his head modestly and stood back while we lifted Zac into the barrow. Thanks to the morphine he was as limp as wet spaghetti. We laid him down with his feet dangling over the front and his head hanging over the back. I draped his arms across his chest. I stuffed his day sack behind his shoulders and put mine under his knees as protection against the hard rim of the barrow. My spirits lifted. Thanks to Majid, our chances of survival had just got much better.

I had a quick look at the map. The others stood by expectantly. When I spoke I found I was including Majid in the brief.

'We're going to head along this path until we find a route that'll take us west towards the road and the river,' I said. 'Then we're going to stick as close to the river as we can while we head south. There are fewer people living along there and …' I couldn't think of another concrete reason for the decision. 'Well, it seems to me to be the best option,' I finished, lamely.

Grant and Robbie nodded.

'Let's get moving then,' said Grant. He picked up his rifle and day sack and took his place at the front. Robbie lifted the handles of the wheelbarrow and began trundling along the path behind him. Ghazala went next, then Majid, then me. I fell into step beside him.

I nodded at the wheelbarrow, bobbing along ahead of us. 'Thanks for that,' I said. 'It's going to make a real difference.'

'No problem,' he said.

I felt I couldn't leave it at that. I wanted to understand why he had done what he had. 'You could have got away if you'd wanted,' I said. 'No one was going to stop you.'

'Yeah,' he said. He laughed softly. 'I wouldn't have lasted long out there, though, would I?'

'Oh really?' I couldn't suppress a malicious thought. 'I thought these were your people. They're the ones you're supposed to be liberating, after all.'

'That's right,' he said sharply. I seemed to have

touched a nerve. 'They are. But it's not as simple as that. People are suspicious. They have to be. They need to know you in order to help you.'

'So you reckoned you were better off with us?'

He looked uncomfortable. 'I suppose so.'

I stopped walking and took his thin arm. 'So from now on we're all in this together, then. Right?'

He sighed. 'If you say so,' he said, glumly.

It didn't sound very convincing. I fell back and let him go ahead. I was the back marker. The moon was full and the night was light. The silhouettes of the others stood out clearly, strung out along the path in front of me. We were a procession of ghosts. Our moon shadows flickered alongside us, marching in step. The moon was huge tonight. It felt like a navigation light guiding us on, towards the river and home.

'Boss.' Grant's voice carried back to me. I hurried forward to the head of the column.

'See up ahead? There's a path off to the right. I reckon it must lead up to the highway.'

'Well take it then,' I said.

I stayed by his side. Fifty metres later we turned on to a muddy track skirting a ditch. The highway looked to be less than a kilometre away. We were moving at a good pace. The chances of our enemies catching up with us now were fading all the time. I could see compounds lining the road to the north. A few lights were burning. I turned back and warned the others to keep quiet. The wheel of the barrow had started to squeak. It sounded hideously loud in the deep silence of the fields.

We padded on. The crops on either side were thinning out. Even though there was no sign of life, we were more visible now and that made me feel vulnerable and nervous. I told Grant to speed up. In my mind the road had become a kind of frontier. It seemed, to me, for no logical reason, that once we were across it, we would be on safer ground. Then there it was, just ahead, bleached white in the moonlight. We moved to the side of the path as we drew up to it, making use of the cover provided by the sparse crops that ran alongside.

'Stay here,' I ordered. I crouched down and moved cautiously up to the edge of the road. The potholed surface stretched away on either side, littered with loose rocks. All was utterly still and unthreatening.

'OK everyone,' I called back. 'Over we go.' I stood back as they scuttled across, with the wheelbarrow squeaking manically, then followed them over. The path we had been following continued on the other side. We plunged down it, through a succession of shadowy orchards.

The path was wide and rutted with wheel tracks. I guessed it led to one of the chain ferries that connected the east and west banks of the river. As we emerged from the orchards, the landscape opened out, lit starkly by the flat light of the moon. To the south, the wall of hills curved away, marking a great bend in the river, which straightened out on to a long, straight reach that took it, eventually, past the walls of Longdon.

The sight of it filled me with hope. I clung to the thought that home was just around the corner.

19

Over to the north, a few kilometres away, a cluster of compounds stood out in the moonlight. I checked on the map. The place was called Jusay. I didn't need to go there to know what it was like. Life there would be stuck in the Dark Ages. I checked my watch. It was 1100 hours. Everyone would be asleep now, men and women, old and young stretched out on *charpoy*s and bedrolls, snoring and twitching, dreaming their unimaginable dreams.

On the last tour I had spent six months patrolling through villages like Jusay. I'd been feeling positive about the mission then. I'd ordered the guys to take off their sunglasses when we were going into populated areas, so the people could see our eyes. It would make us seem more human and less like invaders from space. So they looked into our eyes and we looked into theirs. It didn't make much difference. Try as I might, I never felt that I had the faintest idea of what anyone was really thinking.

The path plunged into a maize plantation and Jusay disappeared from sight. Robbie's heavy breathing carried back to me. He was starting to flag. I called a halt and volunteered myself for wheelbarrow duty. Before we started off again, Robbie checked Zac's pulse and examined the dressing, which was black with dried blood. Zac stirred and moaned.

'What do you think?' I asked.

'Those shots last about four hours,' he said. 'He should be coming round by now.'

'What does it mean then? The fact that he's not?'

'It's hard to say,' he replied. 'It may be the blood loss. I don't know. The trouble is that there's not a lot more that we can do for him, except change the dressing and control the pain if it gets too bad. We've still got seven more injector pens between us.'

What I really wanted to ask was what were the chances of him dying if we didn't get proper help soon. I couldn't quite bring myself to say it though.

'How much danger is he in, potentially?' I asked instead.

Robbie looked up. 'Quite a lot,' he said. 'All sorts of things could happen if the wound isn't seen to properly. Septicaemia. Gangrene. There's a good chance he could die if he doesn't get to a hospital soon.'

'OK,' I said wearily. 'Thanks for that.'

I lifted the wheelbarrow and started pushing. Zac's hanging legs bounced slightly with every bump and ridge. He looked pathetic, lolling there like a guy on bonfire night. A wave of affection broke inside me. I leant over and whispered into his ear. 'You're going to be all right,' I said. 'We're on our way home.'

We had been going for ten minutes or so when a sheet of lightning lit up the sky ahead. It flickered for a second and died.

'Electric storm,' I said.

' I don't think so,' said Grant. 'Look.'

The sky had turned red now and a banner of black smoke unfurled across it.

Suddenly the air shook and a deep thunderclap rolled past us.

We stopped and stood, gaping, with the noise eddying around us.

'Jesus,' said Robbie. 'What the fuck was that?'

'It was a Predator strike,' said Grant. He was staring ahead at the rosy glow, his face hard and blank. 'Had to be.'

Predators were UAVs – unmanned aerial vehicles. We used them all the time now to take out Taliban leaders or drop bombs on insurgent positions.

'I wonder who they were after,' said Robbie.

'Well, they must have got them,' I said. 'That was a big bomb. A thousand-pounder, I reckon.'

The air strike was going to complicate our situation. The attack would wake the whole district up. The survivors would soon be running around picking up the pieces. We had to get past the scene of the bombardment while they were still recovering.

I had been pushing the wheelbarrow at a fairly brisk pace but I knew that Grant could push it faster. 'Sorry mate,' I said. 'You're going to have to take over.'

He smiled at me. 'No worries,' he said, as if he meant it. He handed over his rifle and set off at a jog. The wheel squealed madly. I shouted at the others to follow and tucked in behind them. I had three rifles slung over my shoulders now and they rattled and clashed and messed up my stride. It was warm inside the green walls of maize and soon I was soaked in sweat. Ghazala was ahead of me. I kept having to slow down to avoid bashing into her.

We managed to keep this up for fifteen minutes or more. Stuck inside the foliage it was impossible to see the exact site of the attack. Now, though, the red glow in the sky was off to our right-hand side. That was good. We were moving away from it.

Then the maize stopped and the track broadened out into a wide path. We were passing between head-high mud walls enclosing fields and orchards. I was hot and thirsty and out of breath. It was time to ease off. I called a five-minute break.

We sank down by the side of the path. I sucked on the Camelbak and passed it to Ghazala, who took it gratefully and drank. Her eyes lit up in a smile as she passed it back. I looked at my watch. It was nearly midnight. A hell of a lot had happened in the last six hours.

I closed my eyes and immediately started to doze off. It took a great effort to force my eyelids open again.

A few seconds longer and I would have been fast asleep. We had to push on. There were only six more hours of darkness and we had to get as far as we could while the going was this good.

'On your feet everybody,' I called. There was a groan from Robbie.

'Are you alright to carry on with the wheelbarrow?' I asked Grant.

'Sure,' he said, amiably.

'Good,' I said. 'You can take it a bit slower this time.'

We hauled ourselves up and the procession reassembled.

Ahead, the path curved off to the right around a clump of tall trees. As we reached the bend I thought I saw lights flickering on the horizon. We turned the corner and on to a long, straight stretch, bounded on either side by high mud walls. There was no doubt about it now. Straight in front of us, bright points of light stood out of the darkness. I shouted to everyone to stop. A few seconds later a thin yellow beam slanted down the path towards us. Then there was another and another. Vehicles were approaching, how many or what they were it was impossible to say. We could hear the noise of their engines now and the headlight beams were bouncing and swinging left and right as the drivers negotiated boulders and potholes.

'Off the road,' I shouted. But the way to the fields was blocked by the high mud walls. I looked desperately for a gateway but there was none – not even a ditch that we could throw ourselves into. We stood there uselessly as the vehicles got closer and closer.

There was no way that we would not be seen now. The wall seemed a sort of refuge. We scuttled off to the right of the path and pressed ourselves against the crumbling mud. The rocks on the road threw long shadows as they caught the lights.

I could see three or four smallish-looking vehicles now. They were driving as fast as the road would allow, revving and swerving. Over the straining engines came human noises, people shouting, people crying. The headlights were sliding along the walls on either side, sweeping away the darkness. Then they were only twenty metres away. There were four pick-up trucks, their bodywork battered and spattered with mud. There was a collapsed culvert diagonally opposite where we stood. The lead truck had to slow to walking pace to get over it. I could see the driver clearly. He was shouting angrily to himself as he fought with the wheel. Women and children were huddled in the back. One of the women held a small bundle tightly to her chest. She turned towards us as she passed and our eyes met. We stared at each other as the truck bumped slowly past. There was nothing in her expression, not fear or anger or even curiosity. Her look felt like a curse – as if I would have to pay in some way for what had just happened and that one day the evil she had suffered would visit me and mine.

The trucks crawled past over the broken concrete of the culvert. With each jolt came ragged cries of pain. Then the last one jerked clear of the rubble and the convoy rumbled on its way. I was shamefully aware of the relief I felt as the engine noise faded.

I looked at the others. They were staring down the path at the dwindling lights.

'What do you reckon happened?' asked Robbie.

'The usual,' said Grant wearily. 'Just another fuck-up.' He gave a bitter laugh. 'Of course, you know what the irony is? They're probably taking the casualties to Longdon. We should have asked them for a lift.'

We turned away. Only Majid stood staring down the path where the only sign of the convoy now was the occasional red glow of brake lights. His thin body was shaking. Grant went over and put his hand awkwardly on Majid's arm. Majid shook it off and shuffled away.

Grant turned back. 'Best get moving, eh?'

We covered the next few kilometres in silence. The walls stopped and the fields opened up. Off to the right we had a clear view of Jusay, or where Jusay had been. A glowing red layer covered the ground, shot now and again with spurts of yellow flame. A thick pillar of smoke rose above it.

I knew by now how the story of Jusay would be presented to the outside world. It would start off with reports from the Afghan side that Allied aircraft had bombed a village killing lots of innocent people. The media would pick it up and ask NATO for explanations. The NATO spokesmen would stall, saying that the reports were being investigated, but adding that an operation against the Taliban had been mounted in the area, and hinting heavily that the dead were in fact all insurgents. Then, over the following days, the truth would emerge. NATO would apologise, an inquiry would be announced and an American general would give heartfelt assurances that it would never be allowed to happen again. Then, a month or two months later, there would be another Jusay.

These incidents used to make me feel – for a short time at least – angry and guilty. By now, though, a sort of numbness had set in. What was the point of thinking about such things? There was nothing I could do. I had given up asking myself what we were doing here and why we were doing it, probably because – although I did not want to admit it to myself – I already knew the answer. However good our intentions, however desirable the original aims, it just wasn't working. Keeping on trying was just going to make it worse. But I also knew that we would keep on trying. The politicians were never going to admit their mistake and we, the soldiers, were not going to force them. The truth was that fighting is what we do and – at the beginning at least – most of us were delighted to have the chance to do it. It was only now that we were getting sick of it. I looked down at Zac, lolling in the barrow. Would he still be up for all this if we ever got out of here?

I glanced around. The bluffs lining the far bank of the river stretched along the horizon, no more than three or four kilometres away. The path was leading straight to the river. At some point it should intersect with a track that led along the bank. The ground was turning to gravel the nearer we got to the water. The crops grew sparser and eventually gave way to coarse grass and scrub. Streams and ditches gurgled on other either side of us.

We crossed a wooden bridge. A track went off to the left. I called a halt and went to the front of the column to check it out. The river bank was a few hundred metres away on our right now. The water glistened in the moonlight as it slid between the shingle shoals. It was here that the river made its westward curve. Once we were round it, we were on the straight stretch home.

We turned on to the track. I took the lead, walking fast. I had a brief fantasy that there was a rope stretched between us and the fort and I was hauling us all to safety. If we kept up this pace we would be round the bend before daylight. There were no compounds showing on the map along the curved stretch. Beyond that, though, a string of small villages lined the bank almost continuously all the way to Longdon. Once dawn broke we would have to find a place to lie up until darkness. We dared not risk another clash. But by midnight tomorrow we could be walking through the big steel gates of the fort.

The path was rutted and bisected by waterways. The bridges across were narrow and rickety. As we were bumping over the broken planks of one of them, I heard a low groaning noise. I looked back. Zac's head lifted for a second then sank back.

A few minutes later he moaned again. I told Grant to stop and went over.

Robbie crouched down next to him and took his pulse. Slowly, Zac's eyes opened. I saw his pupils focus, and recognition dawn. 'Hallo Milo,' he said. 'Have I been asleep?'

'Yes,' I said. 'You did nod off for a while. How are you feeling?'

He gave a lazy smile. 'Bloody good, actually.' He paused. 'The morphine, I suppose.' He glanced down. 'Where was I hit?'

'Your left leg. The thigh. The bleeding's stopped now. You're going to be all right. We're nearly home. Just lie back now and we'll get on our way.'

'Wait a sec.' Robbie produced his Camelbak. He placed the nozzle betwen Zac's cracked lips. Zac sucked thankfully , then his head fell back. 'Thanks,' he said and closed his eyes again.

We padded along at a good, steady pace. By 0300 hours we were at the start of the loop in the river. Half an hour later we were at the shoulder, where the river turned to the right before shifting eastwards again then straightening out.

As we were negotiating a rutted stretch of the path, I heard a loud cry of pain. I looked back. Zac had propped himself upright in the wheelbarrow. I stopped. He looked over. 'Sorry about that,' he said. 'It's just that the feeling's coming back. Every bump is bloody agony. Can Robbie give me something?'

Robbie looked doubtful. 'Well, I could give you another shot,' he said. 'But I'd rather not. You're not supposed to have more than one every twenty-four hours.'

'I'm not sure I can keep going without one,' he said. 'What's the risk?'

Robbie smiled. 'Well, that when you nod off, you might not wake up again.'

'Ah,' said Zac. 'We don't want that. Better just crack on then. I'll try not to make too much noise.'

I looked at my watch. It would be dawn in an hour or two. We were coming to the end of the deserted stretch of the river bank, and the first houses lay only a few kilometres away. It was a good time to stop.

'Don't worry mate,' I said to Zac. 'I'm calling a halt as soon as we find somewhere to lay up.'

A little further on we came to a bridge that spanned a wide irrigation channel. It was a solid construction of wooden planks laid across thick steel beams. To the right, a metal sluice gate spanned the canal, controlling the flow of water to the fields.

Beside it, perched on the canal bank, stood a small, square building, built out of breeze blocks. I called a halt and walked along the bank to investigate. The wooden door stood open. I peered inside. It smelt musty and looked unused. It seemed a good place to wait out the coming day.

20

It was nice and cool inside. The space to the right of the doorway was taken up by a hunk of rusty machinery. It had cogs and wheels and was bolted to the floor. I had no idea what it was supposed to do. Whatever it was, though, it looked as if it hadn't done it for a long time. The space behind was littered with lengths of wide-gauge plastic pipe, coils of rope and empty sacks.

Grant offered to take the first turn on stag. I took off my helmet, day sack and Camelbak, unsnapped my webbing and stretched out on the cement floor. I enjoyed the feel of the cold cement underneath me. Then I plunged into a deep sleep.

When I woke it took me a few seconds to remember where I was. I opened my eyes to see the lights of reflected water dancing on the concrete above my head. My watch showed 0930. Zac was stretched out on a mound of sacking. Ghazala was curled up neatly on a wooden bench at the back. Robbie was on the floor underneath, snoring steadily. Majid was awake, though. He was kneeling with his arms outstretched, praying. After a few moments in this position he got to his feet and raised his hands to his head. I found myself wishing that I had some religious belief that I could hang on to now when I most had need of it.

Light was streaming through the door where Grant squatted with his rifle resting across his knees. I went over. The glare outside hurt my eyes. On the other side of the canal, the river bank ran straight. I could just make out some compounds in the haze, a few kilometres away. Tonight we would be creeping past them. Longdon was no more than ten kilometres away now and the river path ran straight. By midnight, I told myself, we would be safe.

'Hallo,' said Grant. 'Sleep well?'

'Like a baby.'

'You needed it.'

'You should get your head down now. I'll take over.'

'Sure,' he said. But he stayed where he was, scanning the landscape.

'Not much further now, mate. Soon be over.'

'You reckon?'

He glanced up at me. There was something in his eyes that disturbed me.

'Sure,' I said. 'We've done the hard bit.'

He looked away. 'I suppose so,' he said.

I didn't like that either. Grant was Mr Positive, the guy who always claimed that things weren't as bad as they seemed. I had never felt the need to gee Grant up before. I did now.

'It's only eight to ten kays to Longdon,' I said brightly. 'That means three hours max. We'll have to leave it quite late before we push on, though. I don't think we should start before 2100 hours. That way, by the time we reach the first houses, everyone should be in bed.'

'So all we do now is wait.'

I nodded. 'And hope no one finds us.'

'No reason why they should,' he said. 'No one's going to spot us here.'

'No, we're pretty safe here, I reckon. In the meantime I'm taking over and you're going to get some kip.'

'Sure.' He got to his feet and retreated to the back.

Behind us I heard Robbie stretch and yawn. I turned towards him.

'Have a look at Zac, will you?' I said.

'Right boss.' He moved over and crouched down next to him. He lifted Zac's arm, felt for the pulse and checked it against his watch.

'Seems OK,' he said. He placed a hand on his forehead. 'He's running a temperature though.' Gently, he began lifting the corners of the blood-blackened dressing. 'I'm going to change this. I've still got two more left. I'll try not to wake him.'

But as he gave a final tug at the bandage, Zac's eyes jerked open, bright with pain.

'Ouch,' he said.

'Sorry about that,' said Robbie. 'How are you feeling?'

'Weird. I had some very strange dreams. The

morphine, I suppose. Talking of which, any chance of another shot?'

'Are you hurting?'

'Frankly, yeah. It's not just my leg. My whole left side is throbbing.'

'All right then,' said Robbie. 'But wait till I finish this.' The wound lay exposed. The skin around the bullet hole was puckered and grey. I caught a whiff of decay. Robbie produced a bottle and dabbed some liquid on the wrinkled flesh. The liquid fizzed and turned bright yellow. He unwrapped a dressing and, quickly and deftly, bound it round his thigh.

'Boss?' Robbie was holding out his hand.

'Eh?'

'Morphine, please.'

'Oh, sure.' I unhooked the second auto-injector from Zac's neck and handed it over. He pulled off the cap and rolled Zac on his side. He pulled down his fatigues and shorts and jabbed the needle into a lean buttock.

Zac lay back. His forehead was blistered with sweat.

He smiled dopily. 'Thanks Robbie,' he said. 'It's good stuff this. You can see why it's so popular.' He giggled. A few seconds later he was asleep.

Robbie stowed his kit. His face was stern.

'Don't like the look of that,' he said. 'Did you smell it? The necrosis? It means it's starting to get infected. Without antibiotics it'll only get worse. The good news is that there's only one wound to worry about. The bullet's still in there somewhere. I can't see any damage to major blood vessels so, touch wood, he's not going to bleed to death. The main worry is the anaerobic bacteria.'

'What do they do?'

'They cause botulism or tetanus.'

'How bad is that?'

'Depends. Neither of them is immediately fatal. It's a question of how fast the infection develops.'

'I see.' All the grim possibilities raced through my head – delirium and death at worst, at best amputation. I looked at my watch again as if time might magically have accelerated, but the hands showed 1000 hours. Eleven hours until we could move in safety.

I heard someone stirring at the back. Ghazala slipped off the wooden bench and walked over to the entrance.

'Where are you going?' I asked.

She turned back. The outline of the blue burqa glowed against the hard white light beyond.

'Oh.' I understood now. 'Out you go then.' I mimed looking around nervously. 'But keep out of sight, won't you?'

She smiled as if she understood and stepped out into the sunlight.

A few minutes later she reappeared. As she was coming through the door she tripped over one of the wooden sleepers at the base of the machine at the entrance. She tipped forward. There was a nasty thud as her head hit the floor. We darted forward and rolled her over. Blood was seeping through the cloth of her headdress where it covered her forehead.

Robbie sighed. 'Can't see a thing,' he said. 'It's going to have to come off. Get some of them sacks will you, boss?' I collected some sacking and we laid it out in the light near the entrance. We lowered her on to it.

'You do it, will you?' said Robbie. I nodded.

It felt like an act of violation. I held my breath and lifted the thin blue cloth. There was the delicate throat I had glimpsed, and, above it, a neat, heart-shaped face. Her eyes were closed. Her full lips were half open showing small white teeth. High on her cheeks there was a dusting of pockmarks. It didn't alter anything. By anyone's definition, she was beautiful.

'Not what I was expecting,' said Robbie. It wasn't clear whether he was referring to her looks or her injury. He prodded delicately at the wound. It was shallow and oozing crimson.

'It isn't serious,' he said. 'A bit of Elastoplast will do it.' He unfolded his medical kit. As he was applying the plaster, she opened her eyes. They were swimming with pain.

'Don't worry, love,' Robbie said. 'It's nothing to worry about. You'll have a bit of a headache, that's all.' He pulled out a silver sachet of Nurofen. 'Take these.' The alarm in her eyes faded. She softened and smiled. 'Thank you,' she said.

'Hear that?' said Robbie, smiling. 'She's learnt some English.' I handed her my Camelbak and she swallowed the pills. I watched her drink. Then, she lifted the veil away from her face and shook her head. Her hair swung around, framing her oval face. It reached to her shoulders. She looked serious, intelligent. If you took away the tent you could easily imagine her in a barrister's gown or a surgeon's scrubs. She saw me watching her and her grave expression changed to a smile and in that moment she became an innocent girl again. She moved out of the sunlight and sat down by the side wall.

'Well done, Robbie,' I said. 'You're having a busy morning.' He repacked his medical kit and I moved back to the entrance. I settled down in the doorway and swept the binoculars over the landscape ahead. The only thing of any interest was a small boat that was making its way across the river from the far bank. It was carrying about half a dozen passengers, most of them men, and a flock of goats. It seemed dangerously low in the water. I had lost track of what day of the week it was but now I realised it must be Thursday. That was the day the local farmers took their goods to the market in a town on the river just south of Longdon. The operation had started on Sunday night when we had helicoptered in to the ambush site. We had been travelling for three days. It felt like three months. I knew then that one more day would finish me. I shoved the thought away and resumed watching the slow progress of the ferry.

The boat reached the bank and a handful of passengers got off, followed by the goats. The last to leave was a man pushing a small motorbike. I saw that he had his wife in tow, walking a few yards behind him, crushed and subservient looking.

The sight sent me back to London and an incident during the last few days of my leave. It had been dad's idea to go and have a lunchtime drink. It was something we hadn't done for a long while. He was in Cyprus most of the time and our paths seldom crossed. I couldn't help taking mum's side when they split up. Whenever we met thereafter I could feel myself radiating a little force field of resentment that pushed him away. It was fading now. I wanted things to get back to something like they had been. We'd never been intimate exactly but we had been been comfortable with each other.

He'd seemed very pleased when I said yes to the drink idea and we set off out of the flat and down the mews into a glorious early summer London day.

It was not too hot and there was a nice breeze rustling the trees as we turned up the path through Holland Park towards a pub off the Avenue which I quite liked. The streets were full of men in shorts and women in micro-mini and cropped T-shirt combos, the tops and bottoms separated by a strip of tanning salon-cured flesh, enhanced by the occasional belly-button ring. Dad smiled approvingly. He was not so happy about some of the other females we encountered. Even I was taken aback at the prevalence of women in veils. Some of them had gone further, and were smothered in full-on burqas the size of spinnakers that would have fitted in well on the streets of Musa Qala. After the third or fourth one sailed by dad couldn't contain himself any longer. 'It's like a bloody *contagion*,' he hissed 'What is *wrong* with these people?'

I sort of agreed with him. They didn't belong in London, any more than, as I now knew, we belonged here.

The man bumped off down the river path on his motorbike with his wife sitting sidesaddle on the pillion. For a moment they no longer looked like master and slave. They seemed almost romantic, a knight and his lady riding out. I wondered what they said to each other when they were alone and whether they shared private jokes that made them smile at the end of long day in the fields. The bike got smaller leaving only a thin trail of dust. A scuffle of boots brought me back to earth. Robbie squatted down beside me.

'Fancy a brew?' he asked.

I thought he was joking. 'Yeah,' I said. 'Lapsang Souchong would be super,' I added with a camp lisp.

'No I'm serious.' He waved a teabag. 'I found this in the bottom of my day sack.'

'Well what are you hanging about for?'

I felt ridiculously cheered by the prospect. Good old Robbie. He went back inside with one of the small disposable stoves that came in the ration packs. He sat down with me in the doorway and struck a match. The smoke from the Hexamine fuel block filled the air. It was one of the smells of army life, like aviation spirit and cheap male deodorant.

He squirted some water from his Camelbak into the metal mug from his water bottle and placed it on the stove. After a while, the water began to shimmer, then to bubble. He pulled the mug away. He dropped in the teabag, then a sachet of powdered milk and a packet of sugar and stirred.

We let it sit for a bit. Then he handed it to me. It was still too hot but I didn't mind. It tasted of home.

'Better let the others have some,' said Robbie. He took it from me and moved back inside.

The sun was beating down now. My skin felt raw and stretched. I retreated to the shade just inside the doorway and looked around. Grant was awake again and on his feet. He took the mug from Robbie and moved over to the wall where Majid was sitting with his head resting on his knees.

'Budge up,' he said. Majid obeyed without a word.

'Here,' said Grant. 'Have some of this.'

Majid looked up now. He looked exhausted and miserable. He took the mug and drank.

'What's up?' asked Grant, gently.

Majid didn't reply. Grant persisted. 'It was that business on the road last night, wasn't it?'

Majid nodded. 'That. And all the rest of the shit.'

'I know how you feel,' said Grant. 'Well, I don't really, not as much as you do anyway. After all, they are your people.' I'd said the same thing to Majid a few hours before. The difference was that Grant meant it nicely.

Majid gave a sad smile. 'Not really,' he said.

'What do you mean?' asked Grant warily.

'Just that. They're not really my people.'

'But I thought you said . . .'

'. . . that I was an Afghan?' Majid finished the sentence for him. ' I didn't actually. I said I was Pashtun. It's not the same thing. The fact is –' He hesitated. 'This is the first time I've ever been here. I only set foot in the place last week. You know more about Afghanistan than I do.'

Robbie was listening closely. He moved over quickly and squatted down opposite Majid.

'Here, give me that,' said Robbie. Majid handed over the brew and he took a sip.

'But you *are* from Birmingham?' he asked tentatively.

Majid laughed. 'Yeah. I'm a Brummie all right. My parents moved there from Pakistan – Peshawar up near the Afghan border – before I was born.'

'So how come you joined the Taliban?'

'It's a long story.'

'Go ahead. We've got plenty of time.'

'OK,' said Majid. He stretched out his legs and reached for the mug. Robbie passed it over and he drank.

He handed back the mug. 'I didn't expect it would turn out this way. Not much fun, is it?' A mischievous smile lit up his face. 'I don't suppose you guys did either.'

Robbie chuckled. 'You're right there,' he said.

Majid was serious again. 'Well, when I was younger

I just wanted a normal life. A decent job, a bit of money. A nice car and a girlfriend. No hassles.'

'So what went wrong?' said Robbie, good-naturedly.

'I dunno really. But I'm still glad it did.' He reached out for the tea again and Robbie handed it over. He took a sip and looked at him for a second or two.

'I bet I was just like you when you were a teenager. I wanted a bit of adventure. As soon as I could, I broke away from home. Started to hang out with some other Paki lads. Ran after girls, did a bit of drugs.'

Robbie frowned. 'Speak for yourself,' he said.

Majid ignored him.

'Anyway, I used to deal a bit. Ecstasy and whizz. Crack, now and again. I didn't use it myself. After a bit I started to make some real money. I bought a car. A Renault hatchback it was. I had gold chains and new trainers on my feet every week – a right flash twat.'

I had a brief vision of Majid in all his bling glory. He was smiling at the memory himself. Then his voice was serious again.

'Well, one day, I got nicked. I was done with a bag of skunk and half a dozen wraps. I went to the magistrates' court and got six months suspended. I tried to keep it quiet but someone told my dad. He went mental and kicked me out of the house.

'I didn't have anywhere to go. I was on the streets – literally – and completely skint. I suppose I could have got a job. I'd got used to the money, though. It was asking for it, going back to dealing. The police knew me now and if I got caught again I was pretty well certain to go down.'

He sighed. 'It didn't stop me though. Well, of course I got nicked again and this time I got six months. I started off in Winson Green then got moved to Swinfen – it's a young offenders' institution near Lichfield.'

He paused and looked around, fixing each of us with his sharp, black eyes. 'And that's when my life changed,' he said. 'That's when I met Ibrahim.'

2 I

Majid looked around as if he was waiting for a cue. No one spoke, so I supplied it.

'Who's Ibrahim?' I said.

'A very special man,' he said, reverently. 'He changed my life.'

Robbie held out his hand for the mug. 'So what was he in the nick for?' he asked inconveniently.

Majid looked irritated. 'Well, GBH actually. But that was in his old life. I was amazed when I heard that. He was the most gentle man I'd ever met.' His eyes lit up. 'It was Islam that turned him back to God.'

I could picture Ibrahim. I'd come across his type in London, pushing religious CDs and pamphlets in shopping centres on Saturday mornings. He would have a long beard, glasses and wear one of those white, little round hats on his close-cropped head.

'So how did Ibrahim get you to see the light?' I asked encouragingly. I didn't want him to clam up now. I needn't have worried. He seemed eager to keep going.

'It took time,' he said. 'My religion didn't mean anything to me any more. My dad took me to the mosque when I was a kid.' He looked at Robbie. 'The big one on Belgrave Middleway – you must know it. When I fell out with him, though, that went out the window too. But then I started thinking about it. It kept cropping up in my mind.'

He paused to get what he was going to say next straight in his mind. 'The thing about prison is that it's full of twats,' he said. 'It sounds obvious, doesn't it? But it doesn't really strike you till you're in one. You have to be a twat to end up there. You have to be a twat if you want to fit in. The lads I was hanging out with were stupid. All they talked about was what they were going to do when they got out – the drugs they were going to take and the girls they were going to shag. They acted like they were all mates – a band of brothers and all that. But I knew that, given half a chance, they would fuck each other over without thinking.

'I talked like them, acted like them. But I didn't feel like one of them. At night, when I was lying awake, I felt ashamed of the way I laughed at the jokes and went along with their bullshit fantasies. My mind kept going back to the mosque. I liked the way the men were all together – the Pakis and the Afghans and the Indians; the rich ones who owned the shops and restaurants and the businesses and the poor ones who worked in the kitchens and drove the vans. Inside the mosque they were all equal.' He smiled at the memory.

Robbie intervened to drag him back to the point.

'So he recruited you, did he?' I asked. 'This Ibrahim?'

'No,' said Majid emphatically. 'I approached him. I just asked him a bit about his beliefs. He was a good talker. He kept it simple. He didn't ask *me* anything. He just answered my questions. He was always reading – books and pamphlets. I asked if I could borrow them. They were comforting. They taught me that everything had a meaning – even the shitty things. Everything was God's will and that through his compassion and mercy, everything would be all right in the end.' He closed his eyes. '*Alhamdilallah* ...'

'So after that you decided to go off and join the Taliban,' I said. 'To spread some compassion and mercy about.'

Majid looked at me. 'You'll never be able to understand,' he said.

'Probably not,' I said. 'But try me anyway.'

'All right then,' said Majid. You could see he was enjoying himself now. When he spoke again it was with quiet pride. 'Before my release, Ibrahim told me about a mosque,' he said. 'It was in Small Heath, and when I went there I found it was full of foreign lads – Pakis, Afghans, one or two Egyptians. Some of them were real fighters. There was one guy, an Algerian, who'd fought the Russians in Afghanistan and Chechnya as well. I wasn't too interested in doing anything like that myself. But I loved hearing his tales. I loved the feeling of belonging too. There was real – what do you call it? *Camaraderie*. They were totally different to the phoney mates I had in the nick.'

He plucked at his dishdasha 'It was then I started wearing shalwar kameez,' he said. 'I became one of them. Moved in. Worked for the imam. I was the caretaker.'

Grant had been watching, saying nothing. Now he asked, 'When was this?'

Majid thought. 'About 2003,' he said.

'So after 9/11.'

'Yeah.

He grinned at the memory. 'I was pretty pleased when *that* happened. It just seemed like an amazing stunt. The guys who did it had real guts. They weren't losers. They were rich kids who could have been anything they wanted.' He scratched at the black down on his cheek. 'Well, after that, I decided *I* was going to do something.'

So had a lot of young men, I thought to myself. In America the services had been swamped with recruits.

Grant leant forward 'Those guys were suicide bombers, Majid,' he said. 'Is that what you had in mind?'

Majid shook his head. 'No.' He gave a rueful smile. 'I knew that wasn't for me. Most of the brothers at the mosque were from Pakistan. That's where they encouraged me to go. By the time I arrived, of course, everything was over. The Americans were in Afghanistan and the Taliban had been kicked out. I ended up on the border. It was full of fighters. They didn't need any more.'

'So what did you do?' prompted Grant.

'Hung around. Got depressed.'

'And then?'

'And then you lot turned up,' said Majid brightly. 'So there was a job for me.'

'I see.' Grant nodded. 'What kind of a job?'

'Intelligence gathering.' Majid said it with a touch of pride. 'Once the Brits showed up in Helmand they wanted me to find out everything I could about them – who they were and what they were up to.'

'And how did you do that?' coaxed Grant.

'Well, it was off the Internet mostly. You'd be amazed at how much stuff you can pick up. I went through all the papers, read them online. Made lists of all the units involved, all the names mentioned, the equipment and the tactics. It was good stuff. I got a lot of credit.'

'So you never got out on the ground then?'

'No,' he said, carefully. 'Not until last week. I'm not a fighter really. They didn't want me to be. They think I'm more use doing what I'm doing now. Information work. Propaganda. They're probably right.'

He sat back complacently. So Majid wasn't a jihadi at all. He was a Taliban spin doctor. In his dealings with us he'd certainly shown aptitude for the work. Almost everything he'd done and said until now had been designed to deceive.

What exactly had he got up to after we had been separated at Mir Muhammad's house? There was no point in beating about the bush.

'You knew about the ambush, didn't you?' I asked suddenly.

'What are you talking about?' He managed to sound mystified.

'Don't lie. We saw you talking with Mir Muhammad's men. What did you tell them? That we were on our own? With no radio or backup?' He lowered his eyes. There was a guilty silence.

'Yeah,' he said, finally. 'I did. I had to. They didn't trust me. They knew I wasn't one of them. They would have killed me if I didn't tell them what I knew.'

That was true. It would have been stupid to assume that he would do otherwise.

He grabbed my arm. 'But I swear I didn't know about the ambush.' He seemed desperate to make me believe him.

'Really?' I said. I remembered his disappearing act at the landing zone. 'Well, why did you make a run for it when the shooting started?'

He looked at me as if I was very stupid. 'Because I panicked.' His voice rose. 'Because I didn't want to die.'

Maybe that was true too. He had no way of knowing how it was going to pan out. Maybe he had done what any panicky civilian would have done and legged it as fast as he could.

It had been foolish to expect satisfactory answers. I said no more.

When he spoke again there was concern in his voice. 'What do you think they'll do with me?'

'I don't know. You're a bit of a unique case, aren't you? A British Talib. You are a British citizen, aren't you?'

He nodded. 'Yeah. But I ought to be treated as a prisoner of war. After all, I'm a soldier.'

'Really?' I said. 'I thought you were a PR man.'

That seemed to strike home. He got up carefully and, without a word, moved to the back.

The others had stayed out of the exchange. I suspected Grant felt some sympathy for Majid. He felt sympathy for everyone. Maybe, as another Birmingham boy, Robbie felt some too. Perhaps he saw in Majid something that he recognised in himself. They were both lads from the bottom of the pile. They had both had the guts to leave behind their preordained lives and gone in search of adventure. I didn't feel anything much towards him except a conviction that he wasn't to be trusted.

I looked at my watch. It was past noon. Someone else could take a turn on stag. I told Robbie to take over and moved towards the back, stopping to check on Zac as I passed.

His forehead was bubbled with sweat and his breathing was slow and shallow. I went outside and slid down the bank into the canal. I unwound the grimy *shemagh* from my neck and soaked it in the water. The surface glittered in the sunlight. There were fish in the canals. Sometimes the boys caught them with hooks baited with processed cheese and gave them to the Afghan army and police guys to barbecue. The thought triggered hunger pangs. Well, I told myself, with any luck we would be eating properly tonight.

I scrambled up the bank and back inside. I lay the damp cloth on Zac's forehead. He sighed and opened his eyes. They burned in the dim light. His lips were cracked and dry. I reached for my Camelbak and fed him some water. He opened his mouth and gulped it gratefully. His breath was sour. The smell mingled with the stink rising from the bandage on his thigh. He sniffed the air.

'Oof,' he said. 'Not nice, that.'

I wasn't going to lie to him. 'Robbie's worried that it's infected.'

'Robbie should know,' he said. 'He's wasted being a soldier. He should have been a doctor. A nurse at least.'

'Well, you'll be seeing a proper one soon. A doctor, I mean. We'll be in Longdon by midnight. You'll get treated there and be on the way to the base hospital in the morning.'

He smiled at me. 'Sure,' he said. 'Thanks, Milo.'

I got up. 'I'll leave you to rest,' I said.

'Don't go,' he said. He grabbed my hand. 'Stay here. Talk to me for a bit.'

I sat down beside him. He kept hold of my hand. His palm was slippery with sweat. He looked up at me. 'I've let myself down, haven't I?' he said.

'I don't know what you mean,' I said firmly. I didn't like where this was going. There was a time and a place for the post-mortem, and this wasn't it.

'Yes you do. Don't turn nice on me, Milo. I'll start to think I'm dying.'

'You're not, believe me.'

He smiled. 'Not just yet, maybe. Anyway, I've had plenty of time to think these last few hours. I'm not a complete arse. I know that I made some bad decisions and I know I behaved like a twat sometimes.'

He squeezed my hand. 'I'm sorry for that. The fact is I've fucked everything up. This was the big test. I thought I'd come through it OK. Maybe even salvage a bit of glory from it. But I haven't, have I?'

'You've done fine,' I said. 'We all have.'

He smiled. 'OK, if you say so. But whatever happens, my dancing days are over. Not going to be much of a soldier with one leg. That's what this means, doesn't it?' He glanced down at the black, crusted bandage.

'Too soon to say that,' I said soothingly.

'Please, Milo. I said no bullshit.' He closed his eyes. 'Anyway, it's done me a favour in a way.'

'What do you mean?'

He didn't answer. 'Can I have some more water?' he said. He took the nozzle himself this time. He lifted his head and drained off the last of the clean water.

'What do you mean?' I repeated.

He thought for a minute. 'Well, it's made things clearer. It's made me understand what I have to do next.' He struggled half upright again from the pile of sacks. I tried to push him back down again gently, but his fingers dug into my arm. 'You've got to get me back, Milo,' he whispered. 'Do you promise me? You see, there's something I have to put right.'

'I promise,' I said.

He seemed satisfied. 'Thanks,' he said, and sank back down.

I thought he had fallen asleep but then his eyes flickered open again.

'You remember how we felt when they told us we were going to Afghanistan? Back in 2005?'

I nodded. 'We were over the moon,' I said.

'Yes,' he said. 'Our main worry was that there wouldn't be any fighting.'

We both laughed.

'Well, everyone's had their fair share now,' he said.

He coughed. His brow furrowed in pain. He started to speak again.

'Save it, Zac,' I said. 'You'd better rest now.'

He nodded and shut his eyes. I watched him for a while. He was sweating badly and his breathing was shallow and irregular. The smell from the wound was sickening.

I went to the back, cleared a space among the litter of ropes and plastic pipes and stretched out along the wall. I felt desperately tired. The next thing I knew was

that Grant was crouching over me, shaking me awake.
'What is it?' I asked.

'Sorry boss,' he said. 'It's Zac. You'd better take a look.'

22

Zac looked terrible. His tan seemed to have faded away and his skin was the colour of putty. He lay there, rigid, staring at the ceiling. I leaned over and spoke to him but he didn't seem to hear me. His mouth was clamped shut. His lips were flecked with spittle and the muscles in his cheeks were working away as if he was trying to grind his teeth to powder.

Robbie knelt by his side, holding his wrist in one hand and checking the pulse against his watch.

'What's happening?' I asked.

'The infection has really set in now,' he said. He touched. 'See that?' He pointed at the dreadful grimace on Zac's face. 'That's lockjaw, that is. It's a sure indication of tetanus.'

'Shit.'

'You said it. If we don't get some antibiotics into him soon, he's fucked.'

'You mean you haven't got any?'

'No,' he replied fiercely. 'I took the minimum. It was meant to be only a twelve-hour op, remember?'

'Yeah.' I nodded stupidly. 'Right.'

The hut was silent except for the sound of Zac's laboured breathing. I could feel Robbie and Grant's eyes on me, waiting for me to do my job and come up with a plan to deal with the emergency. The more they stared at me, the blanker my mind became. I tried to sift through the alternatives, the way I'd been trained. It didn't take long to realise that we only had two choices. We could stick to the original plan and wait until darkness. I glanced at my watch. It was 1600 hours. That meant another four hours sitting here, watching Zac slowly die. Or we could leave, right there and then, knowing that we were virtually certain to run into another ambush.

I looked at Zac's stiff, sweat-soaked body. I looked at Grant and Robbie standing over him. I knew what they would do if they were in my place. I knew that I was going to do the same, even though it might well mean I was condemning us all to death. Our code was that you didn't think twice about trying to save a mate's life, even if by doing so you were likely to lose your own. It was a matter of honour. It meant that you knew that – no matter how bad things were – you weren't going to be left to die alone.

'OK,' I said. 'Get your kit together. We're out of here.'

The pair of them snapped into action as if they couldn't wait to get going. Grant gathered up the weapons and day sacks while Robbie fetched the wheelbarrow from the corner.

It was Majid who raised an objection. 'Are you sure?' he said anxiously. 'If we head off now, the roads will still be full of people. We won't get a mile before we run into trouble.' He turned to Robbie. 'How much difference is a few more hours going to make?'

'You heard him,' said Robbie harshly. 'So stop dicking about and give me a hand.' He slipped his hands under Zac's feet. Majid tugged half-heartedly at his shoulders. I pushed him aside, hooked my hands under Zac's armpits and heaved. I could feel his heart thumping inside his ribcage. We laid him down awkwardly in the trough of the barrow. As I stood back, Majid put his hand on my arm.

'This is mad,' he said. 'We won't stand a chance out there.'

He was tugging at my shirt. 'Don't do it,' he pleaded. I pulled my sleeve away. I almost felt sorry for him. Until this point he had managed to hang on to his dignity. Now it looked as if his bravado was all used up.

'Stop arguing,' I told him. 'You heard what I said.'

His shoulders sagged and he stood back. I knew what he was feeling. He'd convinced himself that once he left this place he was setting off to his death. He hadn't been able to stop himself making a last effort to avoid his fate, and in the attempt he'd let himself down badly. We'd all seen his desperation. We'd all probably felt something similar at some time. The difference was, with us the fear of showing ourselves up in front of our mates was stronger than the terror bubbling away inside. Poor old Majid was on his own, with no one to bolster his courage.

But fear was contagious and I would have much preferred if he had kept it to himself. The trouble was he was right. Once we left our refuge we were totally exposed. Our little column would be spotted immediately. In no time, a dicker would send word to the Taliban and sooner or later they would come for us.

I hung back in the doorway, putting off the moment when we stepped out into the white glare. I lifted the handles of the wheelbarrow and looked around. Robbie was bending over Zac, giving him another shot of morphine for the journey. I waited for him to finish. 'Ready?' I asked.

Robbie stood up. 'Sure,' he said. Ghazala was standing behind him. The headdress was back in place, I noticed. She seemed to understand what was going on because she gave a firm nod as if she was psyching herself up for what happened next.

'OK,' I said. 'Off we go.' I pushed the barrow out on to the stony path that led to a wooden bridge running parallel to the sluice gate.

We'd gone a few metres when Robbie called out, 'Hold on a minute, boss.'

I lowered the wheelbarrow. 'What is it?'

'I'm just going back to get some of that sacking,' he said. 'It'll make it a bit more comfortable for him.' He gestured at Zac, crunched up painfully in the barrow.

'Get a move on, then,' I said. He disappeared back through the doorway.

I looked out over the flat landscape. In the distance a few figures stood out in the heat haze shimmering on the path that led along the river. I could hear odd scraping sounds coming from inside the hut.

'Come on Robbie,' I shouted impatiently. 'What are you doing in there?'

There was no answer. Then he appeared in the doorway. He looked hesitant.

'Just come in here for a minute, will you?' he said. 'You too, Grant.'

I groaned, but I lowered the wheelbarrow.

'OK,' I said. 'This had better be good.'

We ducked through the doorway and into the musty coolness. Robbie was in the back, crouched down among the detritus of rope and plastic pipes.

'What is it then?' I asked.

Robbie looked up. 'Just listen to me for a minute,' he said. 'If you think it's bollocks just say so and we can get on our way again.'

I nodded. 'Hurry up then.'

He talked fast. 'The safest way to get to Longdon would be on the river, right? There are no people to bump into and no checkpoints. Also it would be much faster. We wouldn't have to worry about Zac.'

'Sounds great,' said Grant, drily. 'All we need is a boat.'

'I know that, dickhead.' Robbie pointed to the junk around his feet. 'That's where all this stuff comes in.'

I hadn't really taken any notice of the rubbish in the hut. I did now. I counted four lengths of plastic. They were made out of blue PVC and were each about three feet in diameter andtwo metres long. You often saw them dotted around the fields. The locals used them as irrigation pipes.

Robbie stood up and rolled one out for inspection. 'This should float OK I reckon,' he said. It didn't look like that to me, but what did I know?

Grant was rummaging about on the floor now. He held up a coil of nylon rope.

'Let's get this lot outside and see what we can do with it,' he said. He looked at me for approval.

I thought of the dangers on the road ahead. 'Why not?' I said.

We rolled the pipes across the floor and out the door into the sunlight. That was the extent of my contribution. I was useless at this kind of thing. I stood back and let them get on with it.

They rolled the pipes back and forth experimentally, trying to find the best fit. Soon they had arranged them in an oblong, about six foot by twelve foot. Grant fussed about with the rope, passing it back and forth through the pipes. Eventually he pulled it tight and the plastic cylinders drew snugly together.

'There you go,' said Robbie triumphantly. 'Win a raft race in that, easy.'

It looked quite impressive sitting there gleaming dully in the sunshine. 'Right,' I said. 'Now let's see if it floats.'

'Course it will,' said Robbie. 'But before we do that . . .' He went back into the hut. We heard some wrenching and splintering noises and he came out again waving a length of wood. 'We're up shit creek but at least we've got a paddle,' he said.

We each took a corner of the raft and lifted. It weighed much more than I thought it would. It didn't seem very seaworthy – or riverworthy, or whatever the word was. We struggled over to the bank. Below, the canal gurgled through the open sluice gate, on its way to meet the river.

Robbie took charge. 'I'm going to get into the water to stop it drifting off,' he said. 'When I tell you to, shove it down the bank.'

He slid down the gravel and sank into the water.

'OK, here we go. When I say so, give it a good shove.'

He waded through the fudge-coloured water to the middle of the canal and turned round.

'Right, let it go.'

We gave the raft a hefty push. It slithered a few feet then stuck fast. I scrambled down with Grant and Majid to investigate. It was wedged against a lump of rock. We braced our feet against the side and pushed again. I felt it break free and it scraped down the rest of the bank in a shower of stones and ploughed into the water. I saw it settle for a moment.

'Brilliant,' said Majid. As he said it, there was a loud gulping noise and the raft slid out of sight. No one spoke. We stood staring hopelessly at the giant bubbles breaking on the water. And then, something stirred. A flash of blue showed through the murk. A moment later, like a surfacing whale, the raft broke free and sat bobbing in the current.

Robbie pulled himself on board. He got to his feet and the raft rocked drunkenly. He waved us towards him. 'Come on then!' he yelled. 'Get on.'

Grant and I climbed back up the bank. The wheelbarrow was sitting where I'd left it on the path. Ghazala was stooped over it, trying to force some water between Zac's cracked lips. She looked up questioningly. Grant said something and she nodded in agreement. She gathered up the hem of her burqa and picked her way carefully down the bank. She stood there uncertainly for a moment then stepped delicately into the water. As she sank, the cloth spread out around her, like a bright blue lily pad.

I took Zac's shoulders and Grant picked up his legs. He cried out as we lifted him.

'Easy, mate,' I said. 'It's nearly over, I promise you.'

We laid him down on the bank. Then, as gently as we could, we edged him down the crumbling slope and into the water. Robbie dragged the raft over to the bank and together the three of us pushed and pulled Zac aboard. Ghazala was clinging to the side of the raft. I lifted her up and she scrambled alongside Zac. I could feel her bones, as light as wicker, under the sodden cloth.

I grabbed a rope, and held on, anchoring the raft against the tug of the current while Grant went back for our kit. He passed the rifles down to Majid, who handed them to me. I lay them along the grooves between the pipes. Then came the body armour and helmets which I put in a pile. Finally he passed down the day sacks, which I stacked on top.

We were ready. Majid and Grant slipped down the bank and into the water. We each took one side of the raft and pushed it out into the middle of the channel. I felt the current take hold and we waded through the chest-deep water, holding on to the ropes, steering it downstream towards the river.

The place where the canal joined the river was only fifty metres away. As we approached it, the water level dropped. The bottom of the raft scraped and snagged on stones and gravel. We had to push and pull it the last ten metres. Then we were through the shoals and up to our waists again in a stretch of open water. The river slipped smoothly southwards, glittering in the late afternoon light. We waded out towards the middle. The water reached my chin. Then I lifted my feet and felt the current carry us away.

23

The river was wide and fast. It shouldered its way between shoals and sandbanks and tumbled over shallows and rapids. The deepest and swiftest channel lay in the middle. Grant had moved to the front edge of the raft. From there he was able to manoeuvre us round the boulders and humps of gravel until we reached midstream. The current picked us up and whisked us along and it only needed a touch of Robbie's paddle now and then to keep us on course.

There was nothing for me to do then but enjoy the ride. I clung to the rope, letting my legs drift behind me, loving the caress of the cool, clean water running over my body. Over to the west the sky was turning violet as the sun dimmed, tinging the bluffs candy-floss pink. On the eastern bank I could see a few tiny figures dotting the fields in the distance. Somewhere between the fields and the river bank lay the path that led south, through a string of villages, towards the fort.

The putter of engines drifted over. A pick-up truck was approaching from the south, followed by a couple of motorbikes – farmers, on their way back from the market, I guessed. They disappeared behind a compound wall and we swept past them unseen.

We moved along at a brisk marching pace, much faster than we would have managed on land. My mind was starting to wander when I heard a shout of warning from Grant. I looked ahead. The river was changing colour, turning from grey-blue to brown. The surface ahead was choppy and streaked with foam.

I shouted to everyone to hang on. As we got nearer, waves thudded against the front of the raft. The leading edge dipped suddenly and brown water surged around Zac's shoulders. Ghazala gave a panicky cry and lifted Zac's head clear. He coughed and blinked. He looked at her then at me. His eyes were flat and confused. At least he was conscious again. I worked my way round to his side.

He smiled at me, the way a child does, trusting and looking for reassurance. I took his hand and squeezed. The raft bucked and started to spin slowly in the boiling foam. It shuddered as a corner struck a rock. Then it flicked round and I was facing backwards. Zac's grip tightened. His eyes were wide open now and bright with fear. There was another shock and the raft turned again. My feet were bumping the bottom and I felt a jarring pain in my left knee as it hit something. We were spinning. The landscape revolved around me. The raft dipped, wallowed, reared up again. Then we were facing forwards again and the spinning slowed and the foam subsided and we were being swept along smoothly once more.

Zac's fingers relaxed. The look of panic faded. He lay back and turned his head towards me.

'Where are we going?' he said.

'To Longdon.'

'Really?'

'Yes, really.'

He closed his eyes. 'Milo,' he whispered.

'Yes?'

'It's going to be over soon, isn't it?'

'Very soon. I promise you.' I squeezed his shoulder and he turned his head away.

I was starting to believe it myself. Surely there wasn't far to go now? I gripped the side and worked my way round to the front for a better look. Grant turned to greet me. The water was breaking over his broad shoulders. He grinned and his teeth showed white against his tanned face and blond stubble. 'Fun eh?' he said. 'People in the real world would pay a lot of money to do this.'

Ahead, the river ran straight. The fading light threw the compounds on the left bank into sharp relief. A row of timber shacks stood out above the shore. It looked like one of the ramshackle bazaars that cropped up along the roadsides. The channel shifted to the left now. The raft moved with it, taking us towards the line of stalls. Here and there, a strip of neon lighting glowed.

In a gap between the stalls a group of men sat at a table, smoking. A shout of laughter carried across the water. It was strange, gliding silently along, seeing for once the people that we moved amongst as they really were, not as they showed themselves to us when we loomed up among them, Teletubbies in body armour. The laugh rang out again. It sounded innocent and normal – a little burst of spontaneous happiness that you might expect to hear anywhere – except here.

The bank was getting closer. The shapes on the shore grew larger. The smokers were only fifty metres or so away. They were at ease, relaxing after a long day. One of them got to his feet. He stretched his arms above his head, working the stiffness out of his muscles. He turned and flicked his cigarette butt towards the river. I saw it arc and fall, imagined the hiss as it died in the water. He stood looking out across the river.

I saw him stiffen as he saw us and heard his grunt of surprise. He turned and shouted something. There was a scrape of chairs and the sound of raised voices. His mates hurried down to the water's edge to join him.

They stood there, peering into the dusk towards us, pointing and shouting. They sounded angry – as if they had caught us sneaking up on them. One of them turned and ran. A two-stroke engine started up and a motorbike wobbled away and up the river path ahead.

The current pulled us on. The figures on the shore dwindled into the twilight and their voices faded and died. The channel shifted course. Soon we were back in middle of the flow, and the only noise was the rushing water.

The water suddenly felt chilly. We had been seen now and the news would be rippling down the valley at the speed of the man on the moped. We could only hope that by the time anyone had time to do anything about us, we would be safely downstream at Longdon.

'We've been dicked,' I said to Grant and Robbie. As if they didn't know.

Robbie stopped paddling. 'It doesn't matter now, does it?' he said. 'We must be almost there.'

'I don't know,' I said. 'There could be another five kays to go. Anyway, for Christ's sake keep your eyes open.'

I worked my way back to the stern of the raft. The river glowed molten red in the rays of the dying sun. It was sweeping us on to safety. The bluffs on the western bank came right down to the water. We had nothing to fear from there. The straggle of compounds on the eastern side thinned, and gave way to empty fields.

A line of poetry floated into my head.

Oh, hark to the big drum calling. Follow me, follow me home ...

It was Kipling. My grandpa liked to recite it when we were returning from family outings.

The sun collapsed behind the bluffs. The river turned grey, then black. Above it, the violet sky surrendered to the darkness. At Longdon about now the boys would be lining up for evening scoff. The beat of the rhyme was stuck in my head. I couldn't shake it free.

Hark to the big drum calling.

In the ops room, they would be finalising the helicopter movements for the following day.

Follow me, follow me home . . .

I reached out and squeezed Zac's hand again. He was turned away from me, awake or asleep I did not know. I leaned forward, put my mouth close to his ear. 'Deliverance,' I whispered. 'Deliverance is at hand.'

My voice sounded strange. It was as if someone else was speaking. Fucking hell. Where had that come from? I looked up to see if anyone had heard me. Robbie's paddle rose and fell. He didn't seem to have noticed. Grant and Majid were hidden in the gloom.

I raised myself up on my elbows on the edge of the raft for another look ahead. The course of the river was shifting slightly to the left. If I remembered the map correctly, this marked the beginning of the reach that flowed below the walls of Longdon.

I searched the darkness. About two or three hundred metres in front a short jetty stuck out from the shoreline. There was still just enough light to see its reflection on the surface.

It was the sort of place where noisy little boys played in the summer, diving and jumping into the water. I glimpsed some movement on the bank. A figure flickered, darted, disappeared. My first thought was that it was children, getting in a last swim before bedtime.

I looked harder. A shape appeared, then another. They moved stealthily along the length of the jetty then flattened out. They were too big to be little boys, and there was nothing moving in the water.

'Look Robbie,' I called to the others. 'Over there, on the left.'

I could sense their sharp eyes sweeping the bank.

'Got it.' Grant's quiet voice carried back.

'Me too,' said Robbie. 'Three of them, I reckon.'

'Four,' said Grant. 'There's another one just inside the bushes.'

I told Robbie to stop paddling and take aim with the sniper rifle. As he raised the barrel, Grant and I tried to steer the raft to the far side of the stream, to put some distance between us and the men on the shore. It was no good. The current was too strong, and we gave up and reached for our guns.

I put the rifle to my shoulder and propped it against the corner of the raft. I could see nothing at all on the jetty. Then a stream of green lights flowed out over the water. The tracer seemed to move slowly at first, then it accelerated, flicking past with a buzz and crack.

I sighted on the shore and pressed the trigger. There was a flat click. I pressed again. The same thing happened. I re-cocked, pulled, and heard another useless click. I could hear Grant banging away, then a huge boom as Robbie got off his first shot. I could see Grant's rounds striking the shore and the jetty. They were followed by a curtain of spray, racing towards us across the water as the attackers returned fire.

There was another thunderclap from Robbie's sniper rifle. I saw a dark shape lift from the jetty, turn a somersault and flop to earth. There was a second or two of silence, broken by the sound of someone sobbing. Ghazala was flattened on the floor of the raft, trying to make herself smaller. I lunged forward, grabbed her arm, pulled her down into the water next to me. I placed her hands firmly on the ropes and told her to hang on tight.

Another line of bullets stitched the water ahead. It swept past, missing by a few feet. Robbie and Grant were laying down rounds as fast as they could but they didn't have the firepower to force the attackers' heads down. They were shooting ahead of us now. The current was pulling the raft straight into their arcs. A gust of tracer swept towards us. There was a flurry of sparks and Robbie screamed and fell backwards. He lay there, sprawled on his back, cursing and clutching his arm. Blood was welling through his fingers.

We were parallel with the jetty now. Muzzle flashes flickered in the darkness. The next volley came square at us. I braced myself for the sound of splintering plastic but instead the rounds snapped harmlessly over our heads. The shooters kept on firing but their aim seemed wild now. They were losing us in the darkness. I looked back as they shipped behind us. The jetty was disappearing into the murk. The muzzle flashes faltered. After a minute they stopped.

Robbie had stopped swearing. His face was turned

towards me and his eyes were closed. I shouted to Grant to climb on to the raft and help him.

There was no reply.

I yelled again. 'Grant! Answer me, for Christ's sake.'

This time the silence felt bad.

Now Majid was speaking. 'I'm going round to the front,' he said. I heard him grunting and splashing as he worked his way to the leading edge.

Then his voice came back, sharp and urgent. 'He's been hit,' he shouted. 'He's caught underneath.'

'Hold him up,' I shouted. 'I'm coming.'

Hand over hand, I pulled myself to the front. Majid's arm was wedged under Grant's shoulder, trying to keep his lolling head above the bow wave, but the big man's weight was pressing him down. Just as I reached him, Majid slid under the water. Moments later, he struggled to the surface, gasping and spitting. 'I can't hold him,' he said. He broke away and Grant slumped back into the water.

I lunged forward in time to get a hand on him, but could not stop him slipping under the front of the raft.

Majid sucked in deep lungfuls of air. He looked at me.

'Ready?' he shouted.

'Ready,' I said.

We plunged in together. Grant had already slid halfway along the underside. I managed to grab his belt and a few seconds later felt Majid's hand scrabbling for a hold. We struggled to pull him forward but it was no good. The force of the water was too powerful and it swept us back with him. As the raft's rear edge passed over us, I flung out my arm and just managed to get my free hand on a trailing rope. I thought the river would drag us away. Then Ghazala was leaning over us, holding on to Grant's shoulder long enough for Majid to grab hold of the side.

The three of us shoved and hauled and levered. Twice we had him wedged on the edge and twice he fell back. My muscles were melting, flooded with the sick feeling that precedes total uselessness. I was limp with fatigue and ready to give up and to let the river have Grant. It was Majid who wouldn't let me.

'Come on you useless bastard!' he shouted. 'You're not trying.' Numbly, I obeyed. We shoved and pushed and tugged until he was over the edge and lying half in and half out of the water in between Zac and Robbie.

It was a while before I could think properly. I was too busy trying to breathe.

Then I heard Majid calling for help. He was trying to haul himself up. I did the best I could, bracing his back with my hand so he was able to get one knee aboard, and then another, and with a final effort he pitched forward on to the raft.

He turned round and pulled Grant on board next to Zac. Grant lay face down. His eyes were closed and he wasn't moving. He seemed dead to me. On the other side, Robbie was lying on his back and Ghazala was bending over him. She had ripped open his sleeve and was prodding at his upper arm. Two red lips of exposed flesh gaped on his bicep. She raised the hem of her burqa and tore off a strip of cloth. She lifted his arm carefully, and began to wind it tightly around the split flesh.

'Out the way,' ordered Majid.

She squeezed closer to Robbie, making a little space. Majid gently turned Grant's head to one side and crouched over him. He flattened his palms against Grant's long back and pushed, steady and methodical, upwards along his ribcage. After a few repetitions, water gushed from Grant's mouth. Majid kneaded harder. There was another flux of brown water. Majid quickened the rhythm and a steady trickle started to flow from Grant's lips, flattened grotesquely against the blue plastic.

Ghazala stopped tending to Robbie for a moment and the pair of them turned to watch. 'Keep going, mate,' Robbie croaked. 'Keep going. You're winning.'

I don't know how long Majid kept at it. He seemed to feel there was a spark of life left to tend and he was nurturing it, feeding it, coaxing it, willing it to burst into flame. For a second I thought I saw Grant's eyelids flicker; but it was just wishful thinking. Majid pushed and pulled, with a sort of frantic energy. It was as if his own life was at stake here as well as Grant's. But the flow of water from Grant's lungs was turning to a trickle. Then it stopped completely.

Robbie laid a hand on Majid's forearm.

'Stop,' he said gently. 'It won't do any good now. He's dead.'

Slowly, Majid moved away. He squatted down. His face was blank.

'Thank you for what you did,' I said.

He looked at me and nodded and turned away.

We floated along in silence. From the water, the silhouetted figures above me looked as if they were cast in metal, figures on a monument. And then, beyond the grey outlines, I saw an artificial yellow glow in the sky ahead. I worked my way, hand over hand, round to the front of the raft.

There, on the left bank, no more than a kilometre away, a squat mass loomed up from the bank. It was crowned with a chain of glittering lights that burned coldly out of the darkness.

'Do you see that?' I shouted. 'It's Longdon. We made it! We're home.'

But no one answered me. I was celebrating alone.

As we neared the fort I tried to steer the raft towards the bank, but I was too weak to do it on my own. I called up to Majid and he slipped down into the water next to me. Holding on to the side and kicking our legs behind us, we managed to propel it out of the main stream and into the slacker water near the bank. Eventually our feet touched the bottom; then the water was waist deep and we could push the raft along.

The walls of the fort grew taller as we approached. I

could see the sandbagged sangars on the corners. There was no movement and no sign of life. I knew, though, that scores of eyes were watching every movement, and dozens of guns were trained on us, ready to rip us to pieces at the first sign of danger.

When we were a hundred metres away, the raft began to scrape against the gravelly bottom. It slowed and snagged and then stuck fast. Majid and I waded the last few steps. As we climbed on to the bank I turned to him and held out my hand. 'Thanks for everything,' I said.

He took my hand and our eyes locked. He looked pathetically thin and vulnerable standing there in his sodden dishdasha, with his wispy beard stuck to his hollow cheeks. God knows what they were going to make of him. The simple truth could be taken any number of ways. I had a sudden, depressing vision of the endless debriefings that lay ahead. The story that emerged would shape the rest of all our lives. I decided that, initially at least, there should be only one version of the truth.

'From now on, you say nothing,' I told him. 'You don't speak English, OK? You act dumb, like the first time you met us.' I looked back towards the raft, at Ghazala sitting on the bank. I groped for a story that might stand up for a few hours. 'And tell her that if anyone asks. She's your sister. Got it?' He smiled and nodded.

I turned away and lifted my hands above my head.

'Come on!' I shouted up at the walls. 'Give us a hand, for Christ's sake. We've got wounded men here.'

A disembodied voice told me to wait where I was. A few minutes later there was a squeal of metal and a door opened at the foot of the wall. A six-man patrol in full kit moved warily towards us, pointing their rifles. The lead soldier's face was all but hidden behind night-vision goggles. He stopped a few metres away.

'Sorry about that,' he said. 'Can't take any chances.' He peered over at the raft and the two men stretched out there. 'Get them to the aid post,' he shouted, and his men ran forward. He looked again, at the slumped figures of Majid and Ghazala.

'Who are they, then?' he asked sharply.

'Never mind,' I said wearily. I felt my knees buckle and I started to sway.

His hand went out to steady me.

'Are you alright?' he asked earnestly.

I looked up at the high walls and the clouds of insects battering themselves to death against the harsh white lights and the guns poking comfortingly from the mounds of sandbags around the sangars.

'I'm fine,' I said, and I meant it.

24

For the next day or two I was the centre of a lot of attention. It was the sort of fame that I could have done without. I was more of a curiosity than a celebrity – one of the guys who had come back from the dead. It turned out that, after the initial inspection of the ambush site, everyone had soon assumed the worst. The pick-up helicopter had landed, conducted a ground search and recovered the bodies. They had also discovered our shot-up radio and worked out that – with no way to call in a chopper – our likeliest course of action would have been to try and make it home on foot.

Three search-and-rescue missions had been flown in the first two days. After that, the pressure on helicopter hours meant they had to stop. A couple of foot patrols went up the highway from Longdon but they had picked up no hard information, just some confused stories from the locals. By the time we reappeared, it had been assumed that the Taliban had got us. The expectation was that our bodies would show up in a day or two, brought in to the fort by farmers hoping for a reward.

After my wobble on the river bank they helped me in and put me to bed. I woke up ten hours later, ravenously hungry but otherwise OK. The others had gone, flown out at dawn. I could have gone too, but someone thought it would kinder to let me sleep. From what I learned from the base commander, a twitchy-looking major, Zac and Robbie were treated at the main base before being sent straight back to the UK. As far as he knew, Majid and Ghazala were still there.

I was due to fly out myself at noon. I washed under a solar-heated shower bag and had my first shave for nearly a week. I expected that the experience would have left some physical traces, but the face staring back at me in the small, cracked square of mirror looked remarkably sane and healthy.

A quick medical revealed nothing wrong other than a sore knee from the knock I took from a boulder in the river. I thanked the doc and went over to the cookhouse. I sat down and ate a huge breakfast – cornflakes, reconstituted scrambled eggs, sausages, beans. It tasted great. I washed it down with mugs of sweet, milky tea.

There was a constant flow of people coming and going. The FOB was manned by a battalion on its first tour and there were no familiar faces. They all seemed to know me though. There were a lot of whispers and surreptitious looks. Most of them left me alone. A few came over to say 'cheers, mate' or 'well done', though what it was I had done well I had no idea. After twenty minutes I went back to my cot, feeling completely stuffed. I lay there for a while looking at the rubbery pinups in *Nuts* and *FHM*, which are the only kind of magazines you ever find in Afghanistan. Then I went to sleep. A few hours later I was woken and told the helicopter was on its way.

The journey to the main base took twenty minutes. We followed the river south, whop-whop-whopping over the green zone. It seemed weird flying above it, safe from all the dangers lurking inside.

When we landed, I was met by a cheerful young staff officer, who drove me straight to the Brigadier's Portakabin.

I had met the Brigadier once or twice before. He had spent his career in the fast track and was smart and clued-up politically. He was also quite good-looking and was often on the telly, putting the Allied case.

I stepped into the air-conditioned chill of his office. He was leaning over a map table conferring with one of his officers. He looked up as the door slammed shut. 'Miles,' he said, holding out his hands in greeting. He looked me over wonderingly for a moment. It was the back-from-the-dead treatment again.

He advanced and put a hand on my shoulder. 'Come with me,' he said, and led me into a cubicle in the corner. As we entered he turned to one of the staff. 'I'm not to be interrupted for the next half an hour,' he said. He paused. 'Unless it's *really* urgent, of course.'

He motioned to a chair. 'Fancy a brew?' I nodded. He busied himself with the kettle. I had noticed before that some senior officers liked to make a point of putting on the tea themselves. It was in order to demonstrate their democratic credentials, I suppose. In the Brigadier's case I was prepared to believe that the hospitality was genuine.

'You've had a hell of an ordeal, I know,' he said. 'I don't want to add to it by asking you to go through it all again in fine detail. The priority is for you to get your strength back.' He looked at me meaningfully. 'Physical *and* mental. You'll get all the help you need to recover, I can promise you that.' He paused to pour the water. He placed the mugs on the table and sat down opposite.

'I do need to know the basics of what happened out there, though.' He sipped, winced at the hotness, and sat back. 'But take your time. No rush.'

I had of course worked out by now what I was – and, more importantly what I wasn't – going to say. Before I started, though, I wanted to know about Zac and Robbie. The answer he gave was pretty much what I had expected. Zac was out of danger but would probably lose his leg. Robbie would be OK in a week or two.

Then I started my story. On the whole it was a tailored account rather than an embroidered one. I cut things out rather than added untruthful adornments. My one aim was to avoid trouble for any one of us. There was no mention of the rows, no mention of Zac's bad decisions or the concerns Grant and I had over his capabilities. We all came out of it pretty well. No one was going to contradict my version of events. Zac was hardly likely to argue with a tale that gave him a starring role. I couldn't imagine that Robbie would want to rock the boat – and Grant was dead.

The Brigadier listened without interruption, making notes in a little black Moleskine notebook. Sometimes I thought I saw scepticism, even disbelief in his expression, but it was probably my imagination. He was much too shrewd an operator to let his feelings show.

When I finished he went over my account again, asking questions here and there. Mostly they were points of detail – about a time or a location.

But he did press me on two matters. One was the role of Mir Muhammad in the helicopter ambush. I didn't have much compunction about dropping him in the shit. In retrospect, everything he had done appeared dubious and I spelled out my suspicions, admittedly unsupported by any hard facts. The Brigadier seemed unsurprised.

'We know quite a lot about him,' he said, neutrally. 'In fact, we've had a few dealings with him ourselves.' That figured. Of course Mir Muhammad would keep his options open, taking tea with the occupiers in the morning and tipping off the insurgents in the afternoon. It was what you did to stay alive in Afghanistan. I realised, even as I was denouncing him, that my indignation was half-hearted and I couldn't really be surprised by what he might have done.

The other area of the Brigadier's interest was Majid. And here I began to feel – and, I was sure, *look* – shifty, as I parted company with the truth.

'Now this Majid,' he said, leaning forward in his chair. 'You say he's the girl's –' he consulted his notes '– *Ghazala*'s . . . brother?'

'That's right.'

'How did you establish that?'

'With difficulty. It took a bit of time.'

'So when you first saw him you thought he was an insurgent?'

'That's right. We took him prisoner, and it was only when Grant – Corporal Gibbs, that is – interrogated him, that we discovered the relationship and that he was picked up at the same time as they captured her.'

'Did she confirm that?' His tone was definitely sceptical now.

'Yes.'

'Well I suppose she would, wouldn't she?' said the Brigadier lightly. There were no further questions. The subject appeared to be closed – at least for the time being.

I relaxed but not for long. The story would not hold up under another interrogation. I had to get to Majid and brief him on the line to take – better still, to find some way of shielding him from difficult questions altogether.

'Would it be OK to see Majid?' I asked. ' I wanted to thank him . . . for the efforts he made to help Grant.'

'Sure,' said the brigadier. He looked at me shrewdly. 'Why not? I hadn't forgotten that part of your adventures. It might come in useful – media-wise, I mean.'

'How so sir?'

He smiled. 'Well, it's a feel-good story, and we could do with one of those. The rest of the narrative –' he emphasised the word as if he liked the sound of it '– is pretty much one catastrophe after another. Let's see . . .' He ticked off the disasters, one by one. 'Special operation launched to grab high-value target. High-value target escapes. Six soldiers killed. Failure of rescue missions. And then there's Gibbs's death. Normally we would try to keep it all in the family. Learn some lessons, move on. Unfortunately some of the story has already leaked out.'

'Via who?' I asked. There was no one to tell the tale, apart from the participants – and they were all dead or accounted for.

'Remember the news team? The ones who arrived with Zaifullah?'

I had forgotten them.

'Oh, yes sir.'

'Well, they've already put out a report on the ambush. The package includes an interview with Zaifullah, boasting about how we will never nail him, and so forth.'

He looked thoughtful for a moment. Then he brightened up. 'Anyway, what you've told me may give us something to spin the thing our way.' He stood up, indicating the meeting was over.

I wasn't finished yet. 'And what's going to happen with Ghazala?' I asked.

'Ah . . .' The brigadier's eyebrows rose. 'You've posed us a few problems there,' he said.

He leaned back and linked his hands behind his head. 'We don't have much experience with dealing with a case like this. The trouble is, her life in Afghanistan – or in her home village anyway – is finished. Her honour's been destroyed by her association with you. If we send her back there's a strong chance she'd be killed. So we're still thinking about that.' He smiled. 'You can see her too, if you want. She's being looked after by our female translators.'

He was looking at his watch now. 'Anyway, Hugo will take care of you.' He beckoned through the window to the adjutant who had met me off the helicopter. He stuck his head in, wearing an eager grin.

'Just give him whatever he wants, will you?' said the Brigadier. He turned to me and gripped my shoulder. 'The sooner you get home the better. We've put you on the flight to Brize tonight. There's a plane leaving for Kandahar at 1800.' He held open the door. 'Is that all right with you?'

'Brilliant sir,' I said as he shook my hand with an iron grip. 'Thanks.'

More than anything now I wanted to be home. But before I could go there, there was urgent business to clear up. We stepped out of the antiseptic chill of the Portakabin and into the hairdryer heat of an Afghan afternoon.

'Where to now then?' asked Hugo brightly.

'I need to see Majid. The Afghan who was with us.'

He nodded. 'Come with me,' he said. He led me to the car park and we climbed into a Land Rover. As we drove slowly along the dust-choked roads of the base, sticking religiously to the five-miles-an-hour limit, a plan formed in my head. My aim was to prise Majid out of the machinery of the military investigative process before it swallowed him up, and to release him somewhere where he could take charge of his own destiny. As long as the cover story stood up, that shouldn't be too difficult to pull off. Hugo had been told to do whatever I wanted and he didn't seem the type to ask questions.

'While I'm talking to him I need you to sort a few things out,' I said in my most authoritative manner.

'Right-oh,' he replied. 'Fire away.' Thank God for the army can-do spirit, I thought to myself.

'Majid needs to get to Kandahar as soon as possible. He has to make some family arrangements. Sort out what to do with his sister, etcetera. I'd appreciate it – and I'm sure the Brigadier would too – if you can arrange transport for him immediately.' I watched him closely as I spoke. He didn't seem to find anything unusual in the request.

'No problemo,' he said cheerfully. 'In fact there's a convoy leaving this afternoon. A bunch of local staff are going on leave. There's no space on the flights and they don't want to wait so they're having to go by road.' He looked at me. 'Of course, if he wanted to hang on a day or two, I'm sure a seat would be available on an aircraft.'

'No,' I said forcefully. 'That will suit him fine. They can drop him off in Kandahar City. He can make his own way from there.'

'Sure thing,' he said, and drove on.

I felt a twinge of guilt at exploiting his good nature. It soon passed. I was pretty sure that I was doing the right thing. Majid had done his best to betray us at the beginning. But he had earned a reprieve by the end. I doubted very much that he would return to the ranks of the Taliban and he would find some other path to lead him through life. If I failed to get him away, though, he was ruined. He would be a media ogre for five minutes. There would be charges, a trial, a return to prison. No good would come of it.

There was another consideration at the back of my mind. No outsider had the right to make judgement about what had happened out there. It was between us – and by the end the 'us' included Majid. I wasn't completely sure that Zac or Robbie – or Ghazala, for that matter – would approve of my decision. But I knew that if Grant were still alive he would be with me all the way.

Hugo swung the Land Rover into a parking bay by a row of prefabs.

'Here we are,' he said. 'He's through that door over there. I'm going to leave you here while I sort out his transport.'

I pushed open the door and stepped into a long corridor with rooms either side. The first door on the left was open. I peered in. Majid was lying on a bunk bed studying a copy of *Nuts*.

He looked up and saw me and immediately tossed it aside. 'What a load of crap,' he said.

'Dreadful,' I agreed. 'Presumably you were checking that the others were all just as bad.' I pointed to a pile of similar mags on the chair next to the bed.

'Nothing to do with me.' His face took on that familiar sulky pout. Then he grinned. 'OK. You got me,' he said.

There was no time to waste. Hugo would be back soon. I got down to business.

'You haven't said anything to anyone, have you?' I asked.

'No one's asked me anything. They treat me like a dumb Afghan.'

'Well, that's good. Keep it that way.'

I pulled up the chair and sat next to him. 'Now here's what's going to happen,' I said. 'I've told them that you're Ghazala's brother – you've got to go back home to link up with the family. I'm arranging for you to go to Kandahar with some workers from the base. They'll be leaving very soon. You're to keep your mouth shut. If you start talking, they'll spot your accent straight away. It's unlikely that they'll drop you in it but you never know. I imagine you'll be put down somewhere in the city. After that you're on your own.'

He swung his feet down on the floor and sat up. 'Why are you doing this?' he asked.

'Never mind about that. I just am.'

He looked indignant. 'No,' he said. 'Come on. I want to know.'

I hesitated. 'All right then,' I said eventually. 'It's hard to explain. But I kind of think we're part of a team now. What happened out there brought us together. And if you're in a team you look after one another. That's what I'm doing now.'

He smiled and nodded. 'Yeah,' he said. 'I can see that. The weird thing is that I think I feel the same way.' He held out his hand. I took it and gripped it. The bones felt delicate and fragile, just as I remembered they had when I'd pulled him out of the ditch at the start of our journey. Then there was the sound of the outside door opening and we jumped apart guiltily.

Hugo hovered in the doorway. 'Right, that's all

sorted,' he said to Majid. 'Time to move. The bus is waiting. Oh . . .' He turned to me. 'I don't suppose he understands me, does he?'

I smiled. 'I think he gets the general drift,' I said.

25

We walked out into car park. Majid climbed into the middle of the Land Rover's bench seat and we set off. A bus was waiting by the main gate, curtains drawn across the windows in a vain effort to keep out the heat of the sun. I slid off the seat to let him out. He walked over to join the line of small, brown men boarding the bus. He was the last in the queue. Just before he climbed on he turned back. He smiled and waved and I waved back. Then, with a pneumatic hiss, the door swung shut behind him and he disappeared.

That was one duty discharged. Now it was time for the next one.

'Thanks for sorting that out,' I said to Hugo. 'Now could you take me to the girl, please?'

'No problemo,' he replied chirpily. It seemed to be his motto. As we crawled along the base roads he chatted away. I didn't listen very carefully but I got the gist. He loved his job with the Brigadier who was a terrific boss, but he'd much rather be out on the ground doing proper soldiering. 'Like you,' he added shyly. I realised that the silly bastard actually envied me. He yearned to have an adventure like ours. It would answer the doubts and questions he had about his own courage and abilities. It would mean he could hold his head up in the company of real soldiers. Oh well. I didn't want to dent his illusions. The one sure thing about this war was that sooner or later he would get all the action he could handle.

We stopped by another cluster of anonymous-looking Portakabins.

'I'll wait for you here,' he said.

The sign by the door told me I was at the headquarters of the provincial reconstruction team. Inside there was an office with several desks. Posters on the wall advertised the benefits of the occupation. A pale soldier with scraped-back blonde hair sat tapping at a laptop. I told her who I was and what I wanted. She looked at me with interest.

'She's down there,' she said, pointing along the corridor. 'Third door on the left. Corporal Kapoor is with her.'

'Thanks,' I said.

'Don't mention it.' She gave a shy smile. 'Welcome back,' she said.

I paused at the door. I could hear women's voices talking Pashto. I knocked and a voice told me to come in.

Corporal Kapoor was a slight woman with dark skin and black frizzy hair scraped back in the same style as the soldier in the front office. She was sitting on a cheap-looking blue sofa alongside Ghazala.

'You must be the captain,' she said in a strong northern accent. 'I've just been hearing about you from Ghazala.'

'Really?' I suddenly realised how much I wanted Ghazala to think well of me.

'All good, I suppose.'

'Not bad.' She chuckled. 'The one she really liked, though, was Corporal Gibbs.' At the mention of Grant's name, Ghazala's face clouded over. She was wearing a headscarf and a yellow burqa and looked tired and worn and yet very young.

'What did she say about him?'

'That he was kind. That he really seemed to care about her. She's very sad that he's dead.'

'Yes.' I nodded. It was always Grant who had showed her kindness and sensitivity, treated her like a human being rather than a burden. Christ knows she can't have had much of that in her life. It was typical of him. I'd avoided brooding on his death so far. I needed calm and distance to mourn him properly.

Corporal Kapoor looked at me expectantly, waiting to hear the purpose of the visit. I hesitated. Why *had* I come? To try and convince myself that we had achieved something, I suppose, and that she was going to be all right.

'How is she?' I said brightly, like a doctor at a patient's bedside.

'Why don't I ask her?' Corporal Kapoor said something in Pashto and Ghazala replied.

'She says she's very well and that she wants to thank you and the others for all you did for her.'

She paused. 'She's just being polite. The fact is that she's pretty confused.' She gestured round the room. 'All this is completely alien to her. She's only known village life until now and she knows if she goes back there she'll probably be killed.'

'I see.' If I'd been hoping for a bit of uplift, I wasn't going to get it. 'So what will happen to her?' I asked.

'We're trying to sort something out now. There are places in Pakistan for women who have run away from their husbands. They work as midwifes and nurses. Maybe we can find a place for her.'

It sounded pretty grim, but I made positive noises as if this might be an excellent solution.

Ghazala wasn't fooled. She looked at me searchingly with her serious brown eyes and I sensed her intelligence and spirit. What a waste of a life. Then she smiled and she was an innocent little girl again. I was thankful for that. I wished her luck and told her I would stay in touch. As Corporal Kapoor translated I headed for the door.

Hugo was waiting in the Land Rover. I told him I didn't need him any more. There was an hour until the helicopter left for Kandahar, plenty of time to pick up my kit. He offered to hang on and take me down to the landing site but I insisted. I watched him drive off, full of optimism and illusions, and felt rather sorry for him.

Almost everyone from our battalion was out on the ground. The stores were manned by a few grizzled rear-echelon veterans, who gave me a subdued welcome and commiserated about Grant, Zac and Robbie.

I still had a bit of time to kill before the aircraft was due to leave for Kandahar. I bought a phone card at the NAAFI and headed over to the communications cabins.

I had meant to call my mother but when I was halfway through dialling her number I stopped. I had been told at Longdon that they had delayed letting next of kin know we were missing until our deaths had been confirmed. Breaking the news that I was coming home early would only unleash a flood of questions. I would be in London tomorrow. I could tell her the whole story face to face. I checked my emails. Amid the usual junk there was one that made my heart lift. It was from my former girlfriend, Alix. I clicked it open and read.

Miles. I don't know how to explain this but I had a strange feeling last night that you needed me. Maybe I'm being ridiculous but please would you humour me and let me know that you're safe and well?

There were lots of xxxs after her name.

I was about to reply immediately when some shabby instinct whispered that it might be good to let her go on worrying a bit longer. I ignored it and wrote, breezily:

I'm fine, but I am on my way home. It's a long story. You could hear it if you had dinner with me next week.

I attached the same number of xxxs as she had – plus one.

Then I headed off to movement control to wait for the flight to Kandahar Air Field. Inevitably the plane was delayed. After a time I started to worry. I had a persistent unpleasant premonition that Hugo was about to appear and haul me back to the Brigadier to explain Majid's unauthorised departure. But eventually the flight was called and I climbed aboard the C130 and we lumbered into the darkening sky for KAF.

An hour later I was in the big departure tent with a couple of hundred others, waiting for the RAF Tristar to carry us home. A lot of them were going back after six months in some frontline FOB. You might expect there to have been a party atmosphere. There wasn't. I saw a lot of gaunt faces and vacant eyes, and those who weren't trying to sleep were mostly sitting in silence.

We boarded just before midnight. The drill was you had to wear your body armour and helmet for takeoff, in case of a missile attack. Half an hour later there was an announcement from the flight deck that we were out of the danger zone and we could take them off. I had the feeling as I unzipped the Velcro flaps on my vest and unhooked the helmet chinstrap that I had been wearing them for the last time.

26

I spent the first two days after I got back in London on my own. I couldn't face seeing anyone and those who mattered to me like my mother understood and left me to acclimatise in my own time. I stayed at the mews, watching DVDs and trying to read. Then, gradually, I resurfaced. I saw mum and made dates with a few non-army friends. The dinner with Alix did take place. It was not a success. We met in a gastropub in Shepherd's Bush. The noise the other diners made had me wondering seriously whether they were all mad and I was the only sane person in the place. I got that feeling quite a lot at the beginning.

I'd thought I'd be able to pour my heart out to Alix, but when it came to it I couldn't. It was the same, too, with my mother. I realised that the only people I would be able to talk to about it all would be Zac and Robbie and it would be a while before I saw them again. So that night in the pub I dodged Alix's questions and let her dominate the conversation. She seemed to be comfortable with that. She spent most of the time talking about her new boyfriend. It didn't sound as if it was going very well. I pretended to listen but I can't have been very convincing. It was clear by the time we said goodbye that if her relationship did go to rat shit, it would not be my shoulder she would be crying on.

In between the lunches and dinners and drinks I tried to reach a decision. In the end it was not that much of a struggle. I made up my mind that I was not going back to Afghanistan. If I wasn't going back to Afghanistan, there was little point in being in the army. The war was all that mattered at the moment. If you weren't in it, you weren't really being a soldier. I knew now, though, that Afghanistan had used me up. Someone had once said that courage was a finite resource and mine was pretty much finished. If I stayed on, the choice was between returning to operations and living in a state of constant, furtive anxiety or finding a cushy job on the sidelines and feeling guilty all the time. I found it surprisingly easy to write out my resignation. There was no one in my family I had to explain myself to. Dad was back in Cyprus and mum would be delighted when I told her. Eight days after I arrived back in the UK, I drove up to the battalion's headquarters in East Anglia to complete the formalities.

The procedure was pretty smooth by now. It would still have been an emotional business if there had been anyone there to share it with, but they were all away in Afghanistan. I collected my kit and signed some papers. We had shifted out of our old headquarters and were now housed in a big complex that looked like a gigantic Travelodge. I drove back to London without a twinge of nostalgia. When I got to the flat there was an email from PJHQ, the military joint head-quarters, waiting for me. They wanted me to come in for a debrief. Two days later I drove to Northwood. I was met by a brisk bureaucratic officer, in his late forties I guessed. He belonged to the tail end of the previous generation whose exploits in Ulster hardly counted as war stories now.

He took me through the narrative once again, reading off a list of questions pinned to a clipboard. I stuck to the script I had given the Brigadier. At the end he said he wanted to 'go back over a few specifics – or at least one in particular.' I knew what that would be. Sure enough it was Majid.

He came straight to the point. 'Who gave you the authority to go over the head of the Brigadier and organise his release from the base?' he asked sharply.

I'd already worked out my answer to that one.

'No one,' I said. 'It was my own initiative. A spur-of-the-moment thing. There was transport available and he had to make arrangements for his sister with the family so it seemed like a sensible thing to do.' I paused and smiled ruefully, hoping for the sympathy vote. 'As you can imagine, I was a bit confused.'

It didn't wash. 'Well, it's just as well you're leaving because otherwise you would be looking at discipli-nary proceedings,' he said grimly.

He laid the clipboard on the desk with an air of

finality. 'Though, as you know, there's nothing we can
do about him now.'

What did that mean?

'What's happened to him, then?' I asked cautiously.

'Surely you've heard?' He looked surprised. 'Don't
you follow the news?'

No I didn't. I hadn't wanted to see or hear or read
anything about Afghanistan since I got back. I shook
my head.

'Oh dear. Well, the bus he was travelling in was
stopped by the Taliban on the Gereshk–Kandahar
road. They shot everyone on board.'

'I see.' He was looking at me closely, curious to see
the effect of the bombshell he had dropped. 'There
were no survivors then?' I asked, as calmly as I could.

'None.'

He allowed me a minute to let the information sink
in. I had a terrible vision of the checkpoint, the workers
being hustled off the bus and lined up by the roadside,
Majid's desperate pleading that he was on their side,
the shots cracking out.

'I see,' I said eventually. 'Well if that's all . . .'

'Yes,' he said. 'I think that's it. There may be some
other points that come up but perhaps we can deal
with those by email.'

'By email, yes,' I said. He was holding the door open
for me. I walked through it in a daze.

In the days that followed I went over and over the
events of the last afternoon at the base. If I hadn't

concocted the cover story, Majid might be on his way to prison but he would still be alive. Yet I managed to persuade myself, at least some of the time, that I had done what I thought was right. How often had that been said in justification of some human disaster? The only consolation I could hold on to was that it was what Majid had wanted too. I remembered the hand-shake, his slight figure turning and waving before the doors of the bus closed behind him. I knew that he had been travelling hopefully, on his way to a new life, but the old one had reached out to claim him. It was what came of messing with Afghanistan. In some form or another it was what had happened or would happen to the rest of us too.

It was a month before Zac called to let me know that he was ready to see me. By then he had started at the rehab unit. I told him I would be coming on a Friday afternoon.

'Sure,' he said. 'If Robbie wants to come, bring him along too.' He sounded cheerful.

Robbie was back at battalion headquarters deciding his future. I picked him up at Liverpool Street and we drove down together in the morning. It was a hot, dry summer and the leaves on the trees along the drive that led to the centre were already turning brown from the drought. The unit was housed in an old-fashioned mansion. It was smothered in ivy and sprinklers were spinning on the billiard-table lawns when we drove up.

We presented ourselves to an Asian guy at reception and were told to wait. A few minutes later a young RAF nurse came out and led us along a series of passages.

'He's just down here,' she said, pointing to a big set of double doors at the end of the corridor. The noise got louder as we approached. I could hear shouts of encouragement, the slap of a ball bouncing on a wooden floor. She opened the door. About a dozen guys were playing basketball, overseen by a stocky instructor with a crew cut. He was the only man in the room with two arms and two legs. We watched for a few minutes. The players were completely absorbed in the game. Their sweaty faces shone with determination. After a while you stopped noticing the hydraulic cylinders and plastic flesh.

The ref called a break. Zac walked straight over, swivelling purposefully on his prosthetic leg. The top was hidden beneath his shorts. I could not help wondering how far up it went. The old ease had gone. He was brisk and upbeat.

'Fancy a drink?' he said. 'We've got everything here. Even a bar. Not bad eh?' He sounded heartbreakingly unsophisticated, like a teenager. It was as if his suffering had restored his innocence. He led us into a large loggia that looked out over the lawn to green hills beyond.

'What do you want?' he asked as we entered.

'No, let us get them,' countered Robbie.

But Zac was adamant. He stumped off up to the bar and returned with a tray loaded with beers. I could see that this is how it would be from now on. We sat down around a table by the window.

'We've got a little while before Rachel joins us,' he said. 'So . . .' He raised his glass. 'Here's to Grant.' We sipped our lager. 'And to Majid.'

And for the next half-hour we talked in a way that would never have been possible a few months before. There seemed to be little of the old Zac left now. The arrogance and certainty had been wiped away. It was almost as if he wanted to receive our absolution, though by then I had long ago stopped thinking that there was anything for us to absolve. I had my own guilt over Majid's death to carry and I found myself talking about it with a freedom I could never have imagined at the start of our adventure. They both told me I had nothing to blame myself for. We knew each other too well to pretend that I would not be marked by it – as we all would be by our journey.

And then the conversation stopped. A woman was approaching our table. She was slight and dark and a small hump showed sweetly under her T-shirt.

Zac stood up and kissed her. 'Hallo darling,' he said. He put a protective hand on her belly. I remembered what he had said to me in the shed by the canal. *There's something I have to put right . . .*

He turned back to us. 'This is Miles and this is Robbie. You can put faces to the names now.' He smiled at us. 'I've been boring her rigid, as you can imagine.'

She shook hands, gravely, but made no move to sit down. I got the message.

'Think it's time we were off,' I said, getting to my feet.

'No. Stay. Have some lunch,' said Zac. But his heart wasn't in it. He seemed relieved when we declined again. We said goodbye to Rachel. I gave her a hug this time, gently so as not to squash her bump. 'It's OK,' she said. 'You're not going to hurt her.'

'Oh, it's a her, is it?' said Robbie.

'Yes,' she said. 'I thought Zac would want a boy, but he's over the moon, aren't you darling?' Zac grinned and nodded.

He insisted on walking us to the door. 'She's a great woman,' he said. 'She's going to be a great mother.' The trainer on his prosthetic leg squeaked on the parquet as he stomped along.

We stood awkwardly on the steps for a few moments, thinking of something to say. There was a nice breeze blowing in from the Downs. 'So long, Zac,' I said eventually. 'I'll be back to see you very soon.'

He shook his head. 'The chances are I won't be here. I'm going back to the base. To work at brigade. They've asked me to take over a new welfare unit. Looking after people like me.'

I looked at him standing there, proud and yet humble, and I had to close my eyes to stem the tears.

We got into the car and drove down the drive and through the gates and along the winding lane to the main road. I switched off the air con and wound down the window. The trees made a tunnel and a sudden scent of roses swirled through the car. I remembered Zac's question when this story started – 'What's your idea of heaven?' he had asked me.

I didn't know then and I wasn't sure now, but it seemed to me that it must be the feeling that you were home, at last. I turned up the music and swung the car on to the big road that led to the M25.

Acknowledgements

This novel has its origins in a six week trip to southern Afghanistan in the summer of 2008. I went there with the Third Battalion, The Parachute Regiment to write a sequel to *3 Para*, which told the story of the British Army's arrival in Helmand in 2006. The result was *Ground Truth*, which picked up the narrative and described the difficulties facing British troops enmeshed in a harsh and bewildering conflict where satisfactions were limited and danger was everywhere.

Before I set off I had been halfway through writing another novel, set like my previous foray into fiction *A Good War*, in the Second World War. After I finished *Ground Truth* I returned to it. I did so with a slightly heavy heart. My attempts to recreate the past seemed rather laboured and artificial. I hadn't flown in a Lancaster bomber to Berlin or got drunk in a blacked out Lincolnshire pub. I had, however, flown in Chinook helicopters. I'd been on a patrol in the green zone and spent time in front line FOBs. That only qualified me as a war tourist. More importantly, during the trip and back home in the UK, I'd had many conversations with many soldiers, serving at all levels and carrying out a wide variety of the roles the military performs in Afghanistan. I could fit what they told me into a context, having, as a journalist, followed British forces in action in virtually every theatre they have been engaged in since I sailed with them when they went to recapture the Falkands in 1982.

All this persuaded me that I was writing the wrong book. I junked the World War Two novel with suprisingly few regrets and settled down to write this one. It is of course a work of fiction and at times the necessities of invention have caused me to stray slightly from the path of strict accuracy. On the whole though, I have tried to keep as close as possible to the facts in describing the reality of the conflict. If I have had any success in doing so, it is because I have seen a little of it myself, and heard a great deal more from those who have lived it day in day out for months on end.

My profound thanks are due therefore to the following men and women who took care of me in Afghanistan and who have shared their thoughts and experiences with me over the past few years. They are, in alphabetical order and shorn of rank: Craig Allen, Eoghan Barry, Stu Bell, Paul Blair, Steve Boardman, John Boyd, Maurice 'Moggy' Bridge, Matt Cansdale, Mark Carleton-Smith, Jim Castle, Bev Cornell, Jon Cox, Hugo Farmer, Adam Freedman, Peter Franks, Mike French, Nick French, Danny Groves, Stu Hale, John Harding, Ben Harrop, Chris Hasler, Ben Howell, Brett Jackson, Dan Jarvie, Brian Johnston, Adam Jowett, Mark Kennedy, Freddie

Kruyer, Zac Leong, Jamie Loden, Scott MacLachlan, Tam McDermott, Stuart McDonald, Ian McLeish, Wally Mahaffy, Andy Mallet, Andy Newsham, John O'Rourke, Phil Owen, Will Pike, Chris Prosser, Harvey Pynn, Ananda Rai, Nabil Rai, Dave Reynolds, Dan Rex, 'Rocky', Guy Roberts, Paul Rogers, Neil Sant, Graham Shannon, Mike Shervington, Wes Smart, Louis Smit, Frazer Smith, Marc Stott, Tosh Suzuki, Mark Swann, Martin Taylor, Matt Taylor, James Thompson, Mike Thwaite, Steve Tidmarsh, Chris Tilley, Giles Timms, Stuart Tootal, Michelle Warden, Dave White, Mark Willets, Huw Williams and Sean Williams.

I am particularly indebted to Perran Berry and Nick Wight-Boycott for the technical advice they generously gave on the text and to Roya Hayat for help on Pashtun matters. Thanks are also due to Nick Sayers for his perceptive editing, Tim Binding for his invaluable comments on content and structure and to my friend and agent Annabel Merullo for doing everything right with grace and good humour.

The convention, at this stage, is to pay tribute to one's spouse for transcribing the manuscript or looking after the children and enduring the writer's moods during the agony of creation. In this case, my gratitude goes way beyond mere formality. I am boundlessly thankful to my darling Henrietta for her wisdom, knowledge and infallible critical eye when reading and rereading the work during its protracted journey into print.

If you were gripped by FOLLOW ME HOME, don't miss Patrick Bishop's

A GOOD WAR

available in Hodder paperback

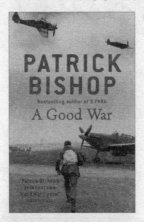

WAR MADE THEM FRIENDS.

Maverick Irish soldier and quiet Polish pilot, Gerry Cunningham and Adam Tomaszewski make an unlikely pair. But this is 1940, and nothing is ordinary.

LOVE MADE THEM ENEMIES.

As the Battle of Britain rages, days of brutal action in the skies are in sharp contrast to nights of drinking and dancing with the local girls. Until, in one act of betrayal, all is lost.

FATE HAS ONE MORE TWIST IN STORE FOR THEM BOTH.

But the two men will meet again, in combat behind enemy lines in war-torn France. And once again they will be tested to the limits of loyalty, love and courage.

'An enthralling tale'
Spectator

'Beautifully written . . . Bishop's gift in this book is to unoock the inner life of the hero'
Sunday Telegraph

'The perfect holiday book . . . a Polish airman's four-year struggle for love, redemption and ultimately survival. A compelling read'
Saul David, *Independent on Sunday*